WHAT THE FANS SAY . . .

✪ ✪ ✪

"Today's headlines have been ripped right from the pages of
Thoene's book!"

"I'm a former FBI special agent, now with the Department of Homeland Security. I love action novels but am a stickler for details,
particularly when it comes to firearms passages (I'm a firearms
instructor). I've read a few suspense/action novels written by Christian authors, and while some have been very worthwhile, your
series is the first to really give me everything I look for in a book.
My wife, who is a federal agent, read both books when I finished
them, and she enjoyed them almost as much as I did. Thank you for
putting out such quality writing and creating a central character who
shows that being a child of God does not preclude being a 'man of
action' who fights evil here in the mortal realm."

R.A.

"*SHAITON'S FIRE* IS GRIPPING. COULDN'T PUT IT DOWN. WELL DONE!"

KEN DONAGHY, ENGLAND

"For many years I have looked for Christian counterparts to novelists
such as Tom Clancy, Stephen Coonts, Michael Crichton, William
Gibson, and Neal Stephenson. I enjoyed Clancy's novels, but not his
characters' lack of a decent vocabulary. I thought I was going to have
to write the novels myself! Thank you for your thorough research,
careful plotting, and command of the written word. I may buy more
Christian novels instead of secular ones now!"

JAN T., ATLANTA

"This is my first response to a book I've read. I couldn't put *Shaiton's Fire* down. I read it in three days! Thank God for Christian writers."

N.H. YOUNG, MISSOURI

"I've really enjoyed your Chapter 16 series. I'm sharing these books with my husband and the squadron."

RUTH BABEL

"I LOVE YOUR BOOKS. I send them to my 96-year-old dad when I finish reading them. Hopefully many will read your latest series and realize they had better trust in the Lord Jesus Christ if they have not accepted Him as Lord and Savior."

ANNE MITCHELL

"I am the owner of Crimezone.nl, the number 1 Crime books Web site in the Netherlands (Crimson Zone). Recently *Shaiton's Fire* came out in our country, titled *Vuurproef*. I just read it and enjoyed it and ranked it with a 4**** review."

SANDER VERHEIJEN

"I LOVED *Shaiton's Fire* and look forward to the series! This is one I will definitely collect and spread to all my friends."

C. HARDIN, IDAHO

"I am buying every book you have ever written! My wife is a Ph.D. student in history, and I am a mechanical engineer. We look forward to your future projects!"

ERIK KIENTZ

"I just purchased *Firefly Blue* yesterday and couldn't put it down! I was very impressed with your message. It was so nice to read a good 'Christian' action novel. I love this type of story, and the positive Christian influence was great. God bless ya."

JEREMY

"An interesting coincidence . . . while reading the part in your book about Angel's bomb, CNN *Headline News* was on the break-room monitor showing the latest bus bombing in Israel."

MARK

"My sons (ages 18 and 21) both read *Shaiton's Fire* on our vacation last week and loved it. We went to three different bookstores to see if you had another one out! Can't wait to read your next endeavor. It thrills me that 3 generations in my family are enjoying your anointed works."

JAYNE WEIR

"You kept me guessing to the very end of *Firefly Blue.* Also thanks for explaining some very technical stuff in a way that I could understand. I have passed your books on to people here at my workplace, and they are enjoying them as well. Keep the books coming."

A BIG THOENE FAN, JIM KADLE

"ALL THE EVENTS IN *FIREFLY BLUE* COULD BE RELEVANT TO NOW. And it was great to read a techno-thriller with no swearing, immorality, or inappropriate situations. I am a Christian, and I believe reading material for Christians should be just like yours. Thank you for putting this book and books like this one out on the market."

STEVEN SUMNER

"I have long been a huge fan of your mother's writing and your father's research—in fact, they are my favorite novelists, and I recommend their writings to everyone. And now another Thoene has captivated me not only by the story of *Shaiton's Fire* but by your inspiration and research."

SUE KAITUKOFF

"I've read many intrigue novels and rate the tension in your books up there with the very best. I hope this series is a wake-up call to our nation's security for the future of all of us, especially the children."

BRUCE M.

"I started *Firefly Blue* about a week ago! **IT'S AWESOME!!** I take it with me about everywhere I go so if I get free time I can read it. I have to say this book is one of my top favorites. (Better than *Mission Compromised* by far!) Second only to *The Lord of The Rings*."

KEVIN, 14

"Just finished *Firefly Blue* . . . hard to put down. My spouse will read it next. You have a great ability to keep my attention."

SHIRLEY ATKINSON

"I loved *Shaiton's Fire*. You have a great talent. Enjoyed reading a thriller that has such a positive Christian message."

K.R. FOUNTAIN, PROFESSOR OF CHEMISTRY, TRUMAN STATE UNIVERSITY

"I'm intrigued by your character development and situational analysis—you obviously did a lot of background study to arrive at such convincing detail. I laughed out loud when the security guy calmly kicked his five-horse engine off the mounts. That was inspired humor. I predict great success for this one."

DR. T.

FUEL Th

JAKE
THOENE

THE FIRE

TYNDALE HOUSE
PUBLISHERS, INC.
CAROL STREAM, ILLINOIS

Visit Tyndale's exciting Web site at www.tyndale.com

TYNDALE and Tyndale's quill logo are registered trademarks of Tyndale House Publishers, Inc.

Fuel the Fire

Designed by Joseph Sapulich

Edited by Ramona Cramer Tucker

Published in association with the literary agency of Alive Communications, Inc., 7680 Goddard Street, Suite 200, Colorado Springs, CO 80920.

ISBN-13: 978-1-4143-0892-0
ISBN-10: 1-4143-0892-2
Printed in the United States of America

11 10 09 08 07 06
7   6   5   4   3   2   1

To the sons and daughters of fallen fathers
and the rest left behind. . . .
Your cross is far heavier
than the heroes you've lost.
Thank you for paying
the ultimate cost.

ACKNOWLEDGMENTS

*I thank God for his protection and inspiration, granting me the
knowledge and strength to fill in the blanks.*

Wendi, Chance, Titan, and Connor,
thank you all for being there, even when I wasn't.

Thanks, Mom and Dad, for giving me all that I needed
to come along for the ride.

Special thanks to the personnel of the Kern County Sheriff's
Department for their help in quenching my thirst for knowledge and
satisfying my hunger to serve. I'm proud to be one of you.

Thanks, Don and friends at martialarms.com.
Your training has been invaluable.

To *all* those individuals in law-enforcement agencies and branches of
the military who offer their lives—and especially to those whose
lives have been taken during the endless task of making America
and its allies the safest and greatest free society the world has ever
seen. Only God fully realizes your worth.

And to those who seek and speak the truth, thank you.
Our future depends on your bold and brave persistence.

Freedom is a fragile thing and is never more than one generation from extinction.
It is not ours by inheritance; it must be fought for and defended constantly by each
generation, for it comes only once to a people. Those who have known freedom,
and then lost it, have never known it again.

Ronald Reagan

This is not a battle between the United States of America and terrorism.
It is a battle between the free and democratic world and terrorism.

Tony Blair, British prime minister

To those who scare peace-loving people with phantoms of lost liberty, my message is this:
Your tactics aid terrorists, for they erode our national unity and diminish our resolve.
They give ammunition to America's enemies and pause to America's friends.

John Ashcroft

Terrorist attacks can shake the foundations of our biggest buildings, but they cannot
touch the foundation of America. These acts shatter steel, but they cannot
dent the steel of American resolve.

George W. Bush

Dear Mr. President,

The purpose of this letter is to personally inform you of another outstanding achievement by the domestic counterterrorism unit, designated Chapter 16, after its creation by the unifying Homeland Security Act of 2001.

Rooting out and eliminating terrorist organizations while preventing attacks aimed at our citizens are of paramount importance. Since its inception Chapter 16 has been able to fulfill that very demand, meeting the needs of Homeland Security in the twenty-first century by its ability to:

- quickly and accurately draw on all law-enforcement and intelligence community resources without being hindered by traditional bureaucratic protocol.
- process and use valuable information to anticipate, prevent, and neutralize terrorist acts once a threat has been detected.

As you have envisioned, the destructive and deadly plots that threaten law-enforcement personnel around the world are not single events but decisive battles in an ongoing war for the very lives and souls of every man, woman, and child who believes in freedom, truth, and democracy.

On July fourth of this year, terrorists plotting to kill thousands and destroy one of America's greatest icons with chemical weapons were defeated by the selfless, heroic acts of the men and women of Chapter 16, the FBI, and other Homeland Security agencies. Casualties and economic losses were minimized, while the entire action managed to remain beneath the headlines, thereby avoiding mass panic. And though the action was critical down to mere seconds, Operation Firefly Blue was a total success.

Without the sacrifices of many, and your vision and follow-through to construct a fast-response, streamlined, domestic counterterrorism unit, battles like these would surely be lost.

So it is with great appreciation that I thank you once again. The war may not be over, but battles are definitely being won!

Sincerely yours,

James A. Morrison
Executive Director, Chapter 16

PROLOGUE

HANGIN' ON

It was five in the morning when Marcos Caracas found himself dangling from a rocky cliff several hundred feet above a slag pile in a rocky gorge. The sun was beginning to peek around the earth again. In the distance the sky changed from electric blue to a delicate peach.

But not for Marcos.

Rain poured down around him as he clung to life like a hunting spider suspended from the edge of a flooding rain gutter.

Only now Marcos was the hunted.

A hundred feet above, many armed men searched for him, scouring the mountain near the patchy snow-covered edge.

Till just moments before he'd gone over the brink in an escape attempt, Marcos had been the stalker, watching those same men evacuate a camp. He was still uncertain who they were. Camels and horses were hidden beneath camouflage ghillie tarps near a cave.

To climb a gorge up the backside of an encampment—alone—how could he have risked his life so foolishly?

Marcos had known what he was up against in the rugged, lawless, no-man's region between Pakistan and Afghanistan. A single image had driven him to the border between risk and foolishness. It was an image that had been burned into his mind a thousand times: a wandering path through a lush, green, rocky valley where a tall, bearded man in robes and a long-tailed head scarf hiked using a walking stick.

It was as if a camera shutter had snapped. Even by moonlight Marcos had recognized the place. He'd felt the evil that surrounded it through his inner spiritual sense.

He'd dreamed about the valley a thousand times as well. And though Marcos had never been there before, he had known it completely . . . and been completely determined to press on.

"I wonder if the tape is even real," Marco whispered to himself while clutching a small package through the ripstop nylon of his pocket. He thought about the informant who had brought further proof. The mole had offered a pair of names: two men, already in America, who had recently trained for an operation. A *big* operation.

No more than ten minutes earlier Marcos had scanned the encampment, his excitement mounting. He remembered it all now. . . .

✪　✪　✪

His sixth sense warned him. Fear overtook him; the icy claw of evil gripped his neck.

Marcos dove for cover. Staying low, he collected himself. First he listened. The world grew loud . . . the sound of water trickling. Then the clink of broken rocks, clattering underfoot.

His heart throbbed in his ears, but he had to look up. He had to see what or who was out there, possibly waiting for him.

Marcos gently pulled a hood over his head.

A wandering figure traversed the shale hillside, rifle in hand, about 150 meters upslope.

Had the informant been followed?

Or had it all been a trap?

Illuminating the dark as seen through his rifle scope's night vision, Marcos made a slow scan for other guards. He neither saw nor heard anyone else. Tracks in the snow had revealed the fresh prints of a dozen men and several horses.

Marcos was overwhelmed by the potential of his find. Could this be the hiding place of Usama bin Laden and his men? He had to move farther, had to find out for sure.

All that was logical and scientific about Marcos Caracas quickly morphed into a bloodthirsty predator. Clutching his sound-suppressed AR-15, Marcos crawled on his belly. Inch by inch he scaled the path, scanning with ever-roaming eyes. Every few feet he carefully lifted his rifle scope toward the lone lookout.

An hour—maybe two—passed. He was unsure. An eternity seemed to pass between each heartbeat. Marcos had watched the figure move from position to position down the path.

Could be a forward scout. A point man. They must be moving.

When the scout turned directly toward him, Marcos's heart leaped. Should he shoot now? Should he run?

Then his instant of panic was replaced by total self-control. Marcos would lie in wait, and soon the guard would pass right by him. He visualized himself overtaking the man silently and undetected.

Marcos slithered off the path under some brush, where he played the scene over and over in his mind.

Steadily and cautiously the scout worked his way down the slope.

When the guard was but mere feet from him, Marcos slowly leveled his rifle on the man's head. He was careful to bury the scope to his eye, under his hood, fearing the green glow of the night vision would betray his position.

The advance scout fanned his right hand, signaling someone else onward.

Horses' hooves clattered against the loose rocks. Then gunfire echoed, distant but distinct. Marcos recognized the rattling three-round bursts of the American M-16 rifles, swallowed up by the clatter of fire from numerous AK-47s.

His squad was caught in a firefight.

Marcos needed to go help them at once, but he did not dare. The point man was barely a foot from him. Marcos held his breath as the closest adversary shouted an inquiry in an Afghani tribal dialect, asking others still unseen about the uproar.

Then it happened.

The guard slipped on the muddy earth, flailing his arms for anything that might stop his fall. Not a rock or a stick did he find, but a barrel.

The barrel of Marcos's gun.

It took the single greatest instant of self-control in Marcos's life not to pull the trigger prematurely, but hope that his presence would go undetected fled.

The sentry knew a deserted mountainside was no place for a stray piece of cold hard steel. The guard twisted his head. His eyes grew wide as he stared at the figure of a man in the bush. The scout opened his mouth, sucking in a full breath to scream a warning.

Marcos knew this had to be the moment. Twisting his rifle free from the guard's grip, he thrust it against the man's head and pulled the trigger.

Rushing air mimicked the sound of a pellet gun, followed by splatters and the tiny *tink, tink* of a single shell casing.

The guard fell over backward. His last breath, resonating a sickly moan, wheezed from his lungs.

Panic filled Marcos once again. Had the others heard? Where had the hooves gone?

Marcos listened a long while before he rose to see.

The voice of a second sentry called to the guard in their tribal language. "What has happened?"

Marcos knew the language and could decipher it, but he dared not imitate the voice of a man he had never heard. Besides, his eye was drawn to a tall figure on a white horse 30 meters away. Marcos stared at the mounted man, who seemed to stare back.

When a cold chill ran down Marcos's spine, he knew he was in the presence of pure evil. He could feel it all around him. "Usama," Marcos whispered.

Then there was frantic shouting. "An intruder! Intruder!" the second sentry yelled.

Marcos knew it was time to flee. He broke the gaze connecting him with the man on horseback and turned to run.

Shots rang out in the dark.

Let them shoot, he thought. *It will ruin their night vision.*

Marcos turned back, expecting to see the horseman riding away, but the man hadn't moved. Another shudder ran through Marcos.

Down, down the mountain Marcos ran, to the edge of the gorge. With a quick clip of his safety harness to the top rope he'd left, Marcos plunged over the side. It was dark, and Marcos was confident none of the men had seen where he'd gone.

✪ ✪ ✪

Now an icy breeze began to howl. Marcos swayed and flapped like a forgotten shirt on a one-ended clothesline.

Blinding rains pounded his body. If he should fall like a windblown shirt, the earth would surely be soiled with his crushed carcass.

How could he have been so stupid? Marcos challenged himself again. To climb alone? Leave his team below? But he knew the answer. Had known it ever since his briefing.

The entire mountain was guarded. The Pakistani authorities were unwilling to allow a large American force to invade the region. On a roll of the dice his highly trained team of seven men, AIF 17 of Task Force 121, had been inserted deep into Pakistan to meet the informant.

The only safe way to the rendezvous was for one man to climb the gorge alone. Marcos *had* had no choice but to go it alone.

So now he hung here.

Waiting for what?

He didn't know.

Cool and calm, Marcos was a warrior in many fields—an expert observer and a trained killer, cloaked by his government's desire to discover the truth covertly, to avoid adverse political consequences.

All that had ceased to matter several minutes ago.

How long would the enemy continue searching for him?

A microburst dumped upon Marcos, and a massive rush of wind slammed him into the rock face.

Marcos's head collided with the granite surface with a blinding *smack.* His body careened off into a spin. He lost his grip on the cord. If not for the safety harness and a well-made rope, he surely would have met his doom.

Marcos felt himself slipping into unconsciousness. His back was arched. His feet and head hung at the same elevation. He tried to fight the limpness that came over him. Almost came out of it.

Then another collision! Marcos's head was bloodied by the rock face, and all went dark. . . .

✪ ✪ ✪

Marcos dreamed . . . disjointed images at first. He recalled training for this mission, but there was something else.

The CIA. Yes, I remember. He mentally directed his dream.

What was I looking for? His subconscious sent out a command, and he waited for his memory to query the distant file. *Oh, yes. A black-op recon.* Task Force 121, the team of special forces dedicated to finding Usama bin Laden and Saddam Hussein and ending their reign of terror.

The American Central Intelligence Agency had been notified of suspicious movements in the region six weeks prior, when a bird did a flyover.

The high-orbit satellite was not scheduled for military intelligence purposes during that slot. A private investor had paid pennies on the dollar during the downtime for a look at the melting snow, for the purpose of measuring global warming.

As always, when a business hired an American bird for a flyover, the National Security Agency got first look at the photos. Usually only a cursory glance delayed the process before the purchaser received the

images. But on this occasion, what they found seemed more significant, much more disconcerting than melting snow.

The 43 seconds of digital photographs contained images of pack animals and at least a dozen men. There might have been more, though
the image resolution was spotty due to heavy cloud cover. Several
more flyovers of the same location and other places on the mountain
revealed nothing. This piqued the NSA's interest. They informed the
private investor that the images were destroyed and instead contacted
the CIA.

That's when Marcos and his team came into play.

Their mission: Scout the area. Search for individuals. And bring
back intel and any evidence that would reveal what the American
moles in the Pakistani government could not.

✪ ✪ ✪

Marcos opened his eyes to clearer skies and full daylight. He was still
hanging upside down. Blinking in the light, he wondered how long it
had been. Marcos lifted his limp arm to his bloodied face to study his
watch: 0623 local time.

Dread filled him. No more cover of night. Despite his best hopes, he
knew the enemy would continue looking for him.

At least the rest of his team would be looking for him too, if they
were alive. Apprehension washed over him, but the adrenaline rush
was not enough for him to straighten up. His back had molded into the
reverse fold that he had hung in for over two hours. He was stiff and
weak.

Marcos reached his fingers up to his waist, where the shiny metal
stitch plate held his safety rope securely to the harness. His fingers
crawled up the rope, using every ounce of strength they had to gain
upward distance. Marcos pulled slowly and steadily, rocking himself
forward. He shifted the weight of his legs down and his torso up, the
way a child would pump on the backstroke on a playground swing.

Steadying his feet against the rock face, Marcos looked down . . .

down . . . down . . . 150 feet to where his luggage hung. In the long white dangling sack were other ropes, climbing equipment, and his secure satellite phone.

He needed to make a call, let the Agency know things had gone downhill . . . like an avalanche.

As Marcos heaved the 40-pound sack upward, his belaying rope slipped.

An inch.

Then two.

Marcos swung his frantic gaze upward to where his highest safety cam wiggled in its crack, about seven feet above his head. *The rains!* Moss and debris had been forced out of crevasses during the flood, loosening the cam.

As the morning wind moaned around the edge of the cliff, Marcos held his breath, silently willing the cam to stay in place.

I've got to shore up here. He gently loosened the grip on the luggage rope, easing it back to the end of its tether. Marcos dug into the tangle of gear in his cargo pocket. The tiny package from the informant was in his way. As he tugged the gear loose he felt the cassette tape come with it.

Fearful the valuable contents might fall and be irretrievably lost, Marcos carefully removed the small package. But where to put it? He spotted a cleft, an indentation like a bird's nest, in front of him. *That should hold it,* Marcos decided, sticking the package deep into the hole, where it would be safe while he adjusted his gear.

Marcos removed a one-foot quick-draw, a length of nylon ribbon with a snap link at each end. He planned to hook one end to his harness before securing the other end to the stopper cable he had placed in the stone surface.

But something caught Marcos's eye. In the distance, across the wide crevasse of the gorge, lay the shadow of a man. Marcos was startled to see the shape staring back, leaning over what looked like a . . .

A rifle!

The opponent took aim.

Marcos scrambled to pull himself up the rock, while searching for his own gun. He had two choices: climb to remove the cam so he could go down, or climb past that point and continue upward. But as Marcos increased his weight on the rope, the cam popped.

And the decision about what to do next was no longer his call.

In slow motion Marcos saw the small blue hunk of metal fly out of the rock face. The rope went limp, and his body was momentarily suspended in zero gravity. Marcos had fallen before but never under these circumstances. His training took over, and he yelled to a partner who wasn't there: "Falling!"

The cam spun around the rope as he fell. Marcos watched with hawklike eyes as the rope looped near the next piece, which, an instant before, had been right in front of his face.

The rope snapped taut. Marcos bounced for a fraction of a second before that piece was torn from the rock face as well.

Down . . . down he fell.

His mind flicked through the science of gravity: *Force=Mass x Acceleration. The force of a body falling applies greater and greater force to the rope.*

And he was right.

The next nut slowed him only an instant before it also sprang. Down . . . down Marcos fell, losing all sense of balance. The zipper effect had taken him. A slew of now useless gear piled up on his rope as each piece was ripped free.

Marcos accelerated toward the ground. His downward force was too great for even the strongest cams to slow. Like buttons on a shirt, they popped freely as he fell until . . .

Snap!!!

Every bone in his body seemed to crack at once. His left leg slammed against the wall. Marcos felt nothing for a moment, as there was too much pain for his body to register all at once.

Then he screamed.

Finally a hex rock nut had held. And once again, Marcos found himself dangling from the rock face—though this time, a mere 10 feet above the boulders.

Despite the fact that his leg had found a new place to bend—in the middle of his thigh—he began to unfasten his harness. There was no time to stop and wait for help, no time to recover from the pain.

Someone wanted him dead.

Was it one of Usama's bodyguards or a local tribal terrorist? It didn't matter, nor could Marcos wait to find out.

For a few seconds he struggled with his harness, purposely designed to be impossible to remove while one was suspended in it. Then he whipped out his knife and began to saw at the rope. The strands encased in the thin nylon skin ripped in opposite directions. As the threads from within snapped one by one, Marcos sagged lower. Every muscle in his body tensed as he prepared for the fall.

Bang! With the force of a shotgun, the safety cord exploded.

Marcos readied himself for a collision course with the rock pile.

He knew it was going to be bad.

His good leg hit the ground first. Then the broken one. An instant later Marcos saw his thigh bone punch through his pant leg before his body flattened out on the ground. He cried out like a child, staring at the flesh-covered bone fragment that protruded from his clothing. His hands moved toward the wound, though he didn't even touch it before the pain worsened.

Pain!!!

Agony shot through his whole body! But he felt something warm. Something on his hand. Marcos looked to his side, where he had landed on his arm. The razor-sharp knife he'd used to saw the rope was buried in his rib cage.

The warmth was his own blood.

After several shallow breaths, Marcos yanked the knife out of his side. Moaning and grunting as the swelling and internal bleeding took hold of his senses, Marcos feebly reeled in his luggage bag.

There wasn't time or energy to waste untieing it. Marcos cut open the bag with the blood-covered knife and took out the soft black case containing his secure satellite phone. He opened the unit and powered it on.

Would it work down here in the gorge? Was there a bird that could connect him with the office?

The unit beeped every two seconds, signaling it was searching for a lock. Marcos looked up and spotted the rifleman again, hurriedly making his way down the slope on the opposite side of the gorge.

There would never be time to wade through the maze of secretaries in order to reach his boss. So as soon as the connection was made, he punched in the only extension he could think of—his own.

"Hello, this is Marcos Caracas at extension 2349. I'm currently on vacation until—"

"I know, I know. Hurry up!" Marcos urged the recording of his own voice as he witnessed the rifleman taking position again.

At last the beep.

His speech was disjointed. "This is Marcos." He winced in agony. Every breath seemed more painful than the last. "This is Marcos! AIF 17. In Quetta region . . . in gorge . . . ohhhh!" He moaned. "I met . . . informant . . . gave me proof—audio tape of UBL . . . al Qaeda." Marcos panted. His breathing sped up as the rifleman took aim. "Stuffed in . . . cleft before I fell. Someone . . . trying to kill me!"

A single shot rang out through the countryside, echoing and reechoing across the cliffs.

Releasing his grip on the phone, Marcos slumped over. Blood trickled from a single hole in his forehead.

ONE

LA County Tactical Operations Command Center
Los Angeles, California
Friday, 4 September
2223 hours, Pacific Time

BIG BAIT

The room was the size and style of an elementary school cafeteria. In it 60 to 70 FBI, SWAT, and other law-enforcement personnel scrambled about, making last-minute adjustments, tweaking and fine-tuning.

Computers, maps, and light tables displaying sketches of buildings and aerial photos showed every aspect of the plan that had been in the works for the last three weeks.

Four separate organizations—the FBI, LA Sheriff's Office, the Glendale PD, and Chapter 16, the FBI's elite counterterrorism unit—had converged with nine teams to conduct the early morning raid. Inner- and outer-perimeter positions had been determined over the last 48 hours.

A life-size mock-up of the floor plan of the house used by the Glendale 5 terrorists had been taped on the linoleum of the sheriff's activity center. The five entry teams, comprised of five men each, practiced the scenario numerous times, minding their fields of fire. Old walls were thin. Every inch of floor space had to be so familiar that each member of the entry team could perform the operation blind.

Hospitals and emergency medical technicians were on standby. Evacuation plans were created for getting neighbors out safely.

This was the ultimate, the climax, the pinnacle of all Homeland Security operations—hundreds of man-hours, constant 24-hour physical and electronic surveillance. Gathering every fiber of evidence before a puff of wind might blow it away. Stopping a runaway freight train headed for a crowd. This was what it was about: busting a terror cell in its early operational stages.

But even against terrorism there were rules, guidelines. Law enforcement in the twenty-first century was no longer about good and bad guys the way kids played cops and robbers. Counterterrorism operations were no longer merely against the bad guys themselves but against diplomatic considerations and political correctness. Lifesaving investigations were sometimes impeded by the very laws created by the people the operations were striving to protect.

One toe over the line, and America could lose the successful prosecution of a suspect . . . or even lose thousands of lives. This was the reason the best of the best had to be so good. The prowess of the FBI's HRT—Hostage Rescue Team—and other elite SWAT organizations extended well beyond marksmanship. Each member of the team had to know the tools on his belt like the fingers on his hand, had to instinctively understand the use of force continuum as automatically as breathing.

It was almost easier to be a bad guy, Steve Alstead mused as he lifted a stack of photographs. As Assault Team Echo 1 leader of Chapter 16, Steve burned the images of the Glendale 5 in his mind.

Members of a radical al Qaeda splinter cell called Allah's Will, the Southern California–based men were involved in a reported plot fast approaching completion. All of them were young Middle Eastern men between 24 and 33. And all of them were willing to die for their cause. Two had been linked to a terrorist training camp in Afghanistan.

Steve considered the limitations—all the hoops his team had to jump through to get the bust. It wasn't simply about going in with guns blazing and taking names anymore. Until the Patriot Act, without exigent circumstances, one almost had to ask the suspect's attorney for permission to investigate. Furthermore, gleaning intelligence, pulling off a successful investigation, and then making the case stick flat out took a miracle these days.

In spite of everything, Steve felt lucky. He had a solid team and a great support system. Steve glanced over at Special Agent Anton Brown, Chapter 16's Echo 2 leader and Steve's closest friend.

Anton gave him a confident nod, suggesting, *These guys are nothing. Piece of cake.*

Steve knew there was more to the big man's look than arrogance. By this point in their relationship, Steve and Anton had driven a lot of miles together. It had been Anton who had helped Steve hold it together when his son had been kidnapped by a terrorist. And Steve had been the one who had sat by Anton's side in the hospital while they waited for news about his baby girl. Now the time Anton had waited for was fast approaching, and this reality gave him an extra edge of confidence. When this operation was finished, Anton would be returning to Bethesda, Maryland, after more than two years of living apart from his son and estranged wife. Steve was glad for Anton, even though he'd miss him. The two shared an undying devotion to their faith and their families, even when times were tough.

After all the years of working together, Steve could read Anton's thoughts as clearly as road signs. Paralleling their mutual bold sense of duty were their strong feelings of caution, a high respect for justice, and a real understanding that things could go badly at any time. Living in the twenty-first century meant that the good guys didn't always win.

Carter Thomas, a short and squatty, muscle-bound, bald-headed humorist, tapped a mug shot with his middle finger. "That's the one I want, right there."

Steve's trance was broken. "Mabrouk?"

"Raggedy punk ringleader," Carter replied, an edge of barely controlled tension marked by his nervous humor. "Just look at his wannabe tough-guy sneer. I'd love to play dentist with that smile."

Steve chuckled softly at Carter's hard-nosed approach to life. His constant wisecracks were entertaining, if unconvincing. "You may get your chance tonight," Steve threw in.

Arms crossed, Carter leaned on the table. "Why're you so calm? What're you on? Sleeping pills? How can you be so cool right now? We're gonna crack some nuts tonight!"

Steve yawned as his body settled into complete peace—the sinking swell before the crashing wave. He and Carter had had this conversation before, but Steve said it again. "Prayer, man."

Carter shook his head in denial. "You know I don't believe in that stuff."

"What stuff? God?"

"What needs of mine has God ever met? And if there was a God, why would he allow trash like these fellas—" Carter smacked the photos with the back of his hand—"to threaten my life and the lives of innocent people?"

Steve considered the question objectively. "Maybe he's waiting for the free will of people like you and me."

"Say what?"

"Maybe if we all listened—I mean *really* listened—to what he had to say, the world would be different."

Carter sighed, then grinned since he'd been outsmarted. "Well, maybe someday I'll have to try that."

"Sooner is better than later," Steve claimed.

Carter simply rolled his eyes. "Preach it, brother."

"I'm serious, man. Could be life or death for all of us in a matter of seconds. You need more than body armor in this job—you need God on your side." Steve's hazel eyes intensified. "What if tonight's your night to go? What happens then?"

Carter's expression tightened and suddenly turned as serious as Steve's.

Just then the group was called to attention by the LA FBI's Joint Terrorism Task Force Special Operations Director (SOD), Carl Davis. With a wide head like a bulldog's and his hairline receding just enough to make his thoughts that much more aerodynamic, Davis's physical presence commanded attention. "Before we load up and gear up, I want to say, Great job. All of you." Steve knew that Davis was well aware of the dangers the entry teams and all involved in the operation faced. "From our investigators to our assault teams, you guys have thought of everything. Covered every aspect of the plan in exhaustive practice. You painted a picture of the future good enough to rival a psychic hotline."

The packed-out audience laughed in chorus. Steve grinned. SOD Davis had the men pegged psychologically. He knew that when men are close to the edge, sometimes a little humor is the only rope to keep them from going over.

Then Davis's tone changed. "You are here and you are prepared, and you are the best at what you do."

Steve scanned the room. Hang Fire, Mooney, Snake, Chapter 16's Executive Director Morrison, and Anton were a few of the familiar faces. All the others Steve didn't know personally, but they had proven their quality of character over the preceding days of training.

"We're up against it . . . ," Davis continued, though Steve's thoughts drowned out his remaining words.

It was a fine line they'd been casting: letting the Glendale 5 terrorists feed freely in the ponds of LA, while risking one getting off the hook and swimming away. Steve hoped they wouldn't miss a single critical piece of intel that might blow the whole operation; he prayed the five would lead them to even bigger fish.

It reminded him of fishing with his Uncle Earle when he was 12, on the big lakes in Oklahoma. "Why not just eat the minnows?" Steve had asked, referring to the six inches of live, wiggling bait.

Clean-shaven with messy hair, a big belly, and overalls, Uncle Earle had threaded a giant hook through the perfectly edible fish. Then he had said wisely, as he worked his tobacco chew, "Ya gotta use big bait if ya wanna catch big fish."

Steve remembered disbelieving that the minnow would bring in a real trophy, so he had prayed silently to at least bring in something.

Five minutes later both he and Uncle Earle had been astounded when little Steven pulled in a 27-inch bass.

"I told you 'bout havin' faith in that big bait!" Uncle Earle had said, shaking his head and chuckling.

Steve smiled at the memory. Then his attention returned to Davis's words. "You men have been hired to save this country one action at a time. So believe in your cause and your mission . . . believe in yourselves."

When the applause subsided, Davis brought the men back on point. "Almost time to roll out. Time to find a quiet place."

✪ ✪ ✪

Palmdale Warehouse
Palmdale, California
2238 hours, Pacific Time

MOVING IN

The warehouse location was satisfactory for his purpose—a mile from the interstate and in a vacant industrial park. Its windows and doors were intact. The building was not an abandoned, rusted-out derelict but the victim of a recent economic downturn. There was even a gate to the yard at the rear of the property, hidden by the structure from the frontage road.

Patrick Dennison wheeled his faded tan '85 Chevy pickup out of sight and turned off the ignition. He surveyed the premises. For a time only his brown eyes were in motion. His skinny, motionless body appeared much less animated than the jovial Social Distortion skeleton decals in his rear window.

Patrick waited a considerable length of time. No guard dogs emerged from the shadows to bark at him. No elderly, emphysemic, chain-smoking, minimum-wage, rent-a-cop stumbled out to demand his business. The place was really vacant. For protection the landlord apparently depended more on the lack of anything worth stealing than on the razor wire topping the mesh fence.

Despite Patrick's thin arms and 130-pound frame, six feet of rusty chain dropped away from the gate with one snap of the bolt cutters he produced from his trunk. He laughed at the padlock on the warehouse's rear roll-up entry door before dismissing it with the same tool.

Inside the building the power was off, but that was to be expected. Patrick's flashlight showed him all he needed to know. Stray beams bouncing back from the bare metal walls illuminated his pale skin and freckles, revealing the red tones in his otherwise mousy brown hair.

A quick survey was sufficient for now. Patrick returned the bolt cutters and flashlight to his trunk, shutting the lid above fading bumper stickers from the old rock bands Nine Inch Nails and Sex Pistols. He snorted at the memories the bumper stickers evoked. Where were the rest of his loser friends now, a dozen years after high school? Dead of ODs or HIV mostly, or stuck in dead-end jobs.

But Patrick was about to make a name for himself. He would make his mark at last.

Lee Harvey Oswald . . . John Hinckley Jr. . . . . Mohammad Atta . . . who had ever heard of them before critical moments when their plans unfolded? But who could ever forget their names now?

On his way past the front gate Patrick stopped once more to hang a fictitious street-number sign from the chain-link.

Driving off, he raised his fist in salute—the new owner had just taken possession.

Lasting fame was only hours away.

Suspect House
Glendale, California
Saturday, 5 September
0317 hours, Pacific Time

BIG BANG

The quiet residential street in an older part of Glendale had been deserted most of the night, except for the cast of cops and FBI agents disguised as joggers, walkers, drunks, and moonlighters who kept continuous surveillance on the house while remaining in a constant state of motion.

Twenty-two more worked fixed positions of containment and outer perimeter, acting as lookouts who could also fence in any perps who attempted to flee. As for the rest, all were either part of the five Echo Teams or part of the Command and Control structure.

Clothed Tijuana-style, Anthony Sanchez, one of the LA JTTF guys, leaned under the open hood of a green '80s Ford van, similar to Scooby's Mystery Machine. With flashlight in hand, he'd spent the night pretending to be working on the carburetor, the ignition, the starter, the windshield wipers. . . .

Two hours prior he had nearly awakened the entire neighborhood with a backfire after cutting the engine to coast in. An authentic touch if ever a cop on a stakeout had seen one. Every officer on the beat hopped out of his skin. Half pulled their weapons, thinking the sound had been gunfire.

Even Steve almost cleared the vehicle to leap for cover. Command and Control had to issue roll call to get everyone quiet again. With a total of 57 officers and agents in the field, it took five minutes to complete the list.

Sanchez wrenched and fiddled away, swaying the van ever so slightly. His efforts helped to disguise Steve's assault team, wiggling for every ounce of comfort they could find in the back of the cramped cargo space. Summer heat, along with 20 pounds of body armor and gear, added to the high price of leg room in the back of the beater van. It made for a long 2 hours, 14 minutes, and 43 seconds.

Twice Surveillance had informed Command and Control, aka Charlie, that a suspect had peeked through the blinds for a look at the van. The extra attention and fear of aroused suspicion prompted planners to adjust the Gas Company evacuation plan. The suspect house would not be getting the "dangerous gas leak" warning tonight.

Often in a dangerous bust, just prior to making entry, law enforcement evacuated neighbors to safety by sending men in gas-company uniforms to knock on doors. Residents were informed about a serious leak in a nearby gas main. They were told to evacuate or face a high risk of death or serious injury in the event of an explosion.

Residents actually faced a higher risk of immediate death by a stray bullet if a firefight broke out. Yet if an officer came through the neighborhood to tell the truth, many residents refused to leave. Many would watch from their windows, like targets in a shooting gallery, rather than find safety somewhere else.

Steve leaned from his confined position to spy Agent Sanchez's face under the hood. With all the time Sanchez spent banging and wrenching, Steve wondered if the agent wished he had a genuinely broken a part to fix.

"Charlie to all personnel," a female voice quietly squawked on the security-encrypted radio. "Neighborhood is clear. Suspect residence is dark. Prepare for entry."

Sanchez closed the hood in pretend defeat and started hiking to a position around the corner to the perimeter, where he'd help prevent any pedestrian traffic in or out of the area.

Steve tightened his tactical sling, making eye contact with each individual on his team.

The dark-skinned, tall, and lanky Special Agent Mooneyham nodded semivacantly. "I'm ready."

Special Agent Anton Brown, Steve's brawny HRT partner, winked and clicked his mouth.

Snake, the small and wiry West Coast HRT's covert entry man, nodded with the speed of a shivering Polar Bear Club swimmer after a January dip in San Francisco Bay.

Beads of sweat rolled down Carter's smooth head as he bit the candy off a Tootsie Pop. He yanked the stick from his mouth to point it at Steve. "Ready as a cat in a mouse maze."

Clicking into the net, Steve announced, "Echo 1 to Charlie, Echo 1 is ready for green."

"Copy that, Echo 1. Stand by for green."

Steve could hear the other four entry teams reply the same.

There was static on the radio. Then, "Charlie to Echo all, we have a final count of three Tangos in the residence."

Steve pressed the button on his left shoulder. "Echo 1 Actual, 10-4."

"Charlie to all perimeter positions. Be prepared to stop any approaching foot traffic. Also be advised that one suspect did not return to the residence."

A possible surprise element, Steve figured. Every operation's got one. His mind flickered through the images of the floor plan. Exits and nooks that might make for possible hiding spots. He visualized himself breaking the door and clearing the slice of the room in front of him.

Then, "Charlie to Echo all. Green in five, four, three, two . . ."

A moment later Echo 1 burst from the van's squeaky back door, shuttling across the street in a tight stream like a subway train, all of the men moving in fluid unison.

Across the lawn.

Up the front steps.

Crash! Anton shouldered his way through the door like an NFL offensive guard over a JV high school linebacker. "FBI, FBI! Drop your weapons!"

Echo 2 merged briefly with Echo 1 during entry before streaming off to the left to clear the living room.

"Clear!" shouted Steve as he led his team onward.

Crashing could be heard from the second-story sliding-glass doors. "FBI! Drop your weapon!" Echo 5 had made their presence known.

Echo 1 moved into the next room . . . the sitting room.

"Clear!"

Next room . . .

Steve led Echo 1 right through the dining room. SureFire lights mounted on the .40-caliber, sound-suppressed MP-5s lit up the room like searchlights in a Fourth of July sky.

No Tangos in the dining room. "Clear!"

Sounds in the kitchen.

"FBI! Drop your weapons!" Steve flagged his men to either side of the kitchen door, signaling Anton to ready the 12-gauge shotgun. On his mark they charged the room, packed in a tight formation like a flock of black crows.

Tango at 2 o'clock high, Steve's slice of the room. "FBI, FBI, FBI! Drop your weapon!" Steve's finger covered the trigger.

The suspect showed no sign of giving up. A split second more and the man had chosen his fate. The Tango attempted to swing his pistol round.

Training took over. Thousands of rounds fired in practice had cut a groove in Steve's decision-making process, forming an automatic response.

Front sight. Press!

Recoil.

Assess.

One round in the control box. Forget center mass. The decision had been made in planning that since these guys might be wearing body armor, Echo should go for the circuit board.

The man fell, knocking a door open.

"Suspect down!"

Moving on . . . wait!

Out of the side door charged a screaming man, upraised hammer in hand. This time Anton made the split-second decision. Leveling his Mossburg 590 on the attacker's chest, Anton loosed a round of double-ought buckshot with a monstrous sound.

The 12-gauge lit up the room. The tightly packed projectiles collided with the suspect's chest, flinging him to the floor as if he'd played tag with a truck. No blood, no holes . . . the guy was still breathing.

"Body armor!" shouted Anton as he ripped the hammer from the attacker's hand.

"Cover him!" Steve ordered.

Mooneyham and Snake pointed in on the suspect.

Steve clicked left from his slice to view the open door to the pantry.

Carter's voice was frantic. "Bomb! Bomb! Bomb! Kitchen pantry!"

Steve caught sight of an IED, an Improvised Explosive Device, and quickly realized why the suspect had run toward them despite their firepower: A jar of Green Dot pistol powder was wired to an egg timer and a tank of gasoline.

"Charlie to One. Evacuate immediately!"

Steve spotted stacks of documents and a laptop computer beside the IED. "They've booby-trapped the evidence!"

What Carter did next could only be described as reckless, foolish, and heroic—he dove for the computer.

Steve and the others from Echo 1 faced away to hold the perimeter around the pantry door.

"Got it!" Carter sprinted out of the room like a running back headed for the goal line. A small slip of paper fluttered out of the closed laptop he hugged.

Steve dropped his MP-5 to its sling in order to help Anton, who struggled to drag the unconscious suspect by the back of his shirt.

"I've got him. Go!" Anton waved Steve on.

The fallen paper slid across the floor. A whispered thought told Steve to grab it, so he swept it up as he ran by. In a full run, Steve rounded the corner into the dining room. He had nearly made the entryway when the bomb went off.

Air sucked past him for a split instant, popping his ears and stealing his breath. Then out of the silence came the concussion and the fiery blast. The suspect, who was mostly shielded from the blast by Anton's bulky form, was slammed against Steve.

Steve's legs buckled and gave way, as if the weight of an elephant was on his back. He was knocked forward, out the front door, where he rolled down the stairs as bits of glass and wood fell around him. He patted his head and face, checking himself for injuries. In the midst of the chaos, it hit him: Where was Anton?

The revived suspect scrambled to his feet. Steve charged back up the steps.

Anton, barely standing, wavered at the door. Steve instinctively reached for the drag handle on Anton's vest. It wasn't there; it had melted right off. Anton lurched forward and fell. Steve saw that the back of his friend's tac vest, his pants, and the back of his head had been burned up, blown off, or incinerated at the moment of the blast.

"Medic!" Steve screamed frantically. "Stay with me, Anton! Help is on the way!"

Anton hardly made a sound. His eyes rolled around in slow circles.

Steve tried to move him but was unable to find a way to grab hold without risking further injury. "Medic!"

A pair of LAC SWAT guys charged the now-revived suspect as he scurried to his feet again. They tackled him on the lawn. Once in control of the suspect, they dragged him toward a car.

Two EMTs rushed to Anton's aid with a portable gurney. They slid to the ground beside Steve.

"He's burned up pretty bad," Steve found himself saying as he realized Anton had shielded him and the second suspect from the brunt of the explosion.

Even the EMTs cringed at the sight of Anton's back, which looked as though it had been skinned and barbequed.

"Keep him facedown. Grab his other arm. You grab his legs," the EMT instructed Steve. "One, two, three."

The three quickly slid Anton onto the gurney. Bits of melted nylon stuck to their hands. They heaved the gurney into a run just before what must have been a propane tank ignited in a massive fireball. A shower of wood fragments chased the men across the lawn. Near the safety of the street, Steve tripped and fell. Two other agents sprinted in to take over, running Anton to the ambulance.

Steve was disoriented. In shock.

All sounds, all sights seemed to run together. The flashing lights ahead of him . . . the raging fire behind him. He was lost.

Someone helped him to his feet. The faceless voice was muffled and nonsensical as hands tugged at his arm.

Stand up? Okay. I can stand up.

There was something strange in his hand, Steve realized. What did he hold so tightly? He opened his blackened, bloody fingers.

The slip of paper, a cashier's check for $2300 made out to Mabrouk, had been salvaged in his grip. Perhaps it was the lead they all needed. Steve closed his hand once more so he wouldn't lose the paper and made his way to the medic.

Steve looked on as the ambulance moaned away up the street with his best friend, Anton, inside. And then he cried out, "God, help him. God, hold on to him!"

TWO

Suspect House
Glendale, California
Saturday, 5 September
0434 hours, Pacific Time

IN THE AFTERMATH

"Deputy Director Castillo, you have to see my point." Steve held a mobile phone to his ear while leaning, eyes closed, with his forehead against the Explosive Ordnance Disposal trailer.

Castillo's voice in Steve's ear was irritated, almost petulant. "I don't want to hear it. You were given an order. You risked your life and your men's lives."

"Special Agent Carter made a judgment call. His insistence is a good thing, because the evidence we recovered may save *thousands* of lives," Steve argued.

"Killed one of your colleagues in the process."

Steve was enraged that Castillo would speak of Anton so callously.

As if Anton were already dead.

As if it were Steve's fault.

"We've got the Glendale cell. One of them, anyway! You shot one of the others!" Castillo rambled on, overstating blame. "And another is missing! Hardly what I call—"

Steve made the command decision to hang up on Deputy Director Castillo of the LA Joint Terrorism Task Force. He tossed the phone back to Special Operations Director Davis. "What a donkey! This guy has totally lost perspective." Steve began to walk off.

"Alstead," Davis called after him. "Hey, man. You made a split-second decision that just may work out."

Steve eyed the burned-out house as he tried to swallow the lump in his throat. "Don't think Anton was worth the price."

"I'd have done the same thing," Davis argued. *"Anton* would have done the same thing. We're here to risk our lives so that others might be saved." He placed a hand on Steve's shoulder.

Steve fought back the emotion. "I realize that. I just never saw it comin'."

"Castillo's just torqued because he's lost the opportunity to be promoted off the convictions of these dead punks. He's torqued because they blew up the house and ruined his plans to pull this thing off covertly. It isn't about what you or anyone else on the team did."

"Thanks." Steve paused to face Davis. "You're a true brother. And if I know anything about Anton, he'll be back in action by next week."

"I'm serious. That's where it's at," Davis consoled. "Bottom line: You gave it your best shot. Now listen; forget about Castillo. Right now giving it your best means helping me guide Benny the Bomb-bot into the pantry."

Steve turned back to look across the street at what appeared to be a chrome trash can on gray rubber tracks, crossing the lawn toward the steps. Various mechanical arms with cameras and clamps were attached at different points. The machine paused at the base of the stairs to square up and lean forward.

Steve walked toward the entry to the white EOD fifth-wheel trailer. "You got it."

Steve and Carter entered the mobile EOD Command Center via the tailgate ramp. Several video monitors lined a wall above two keyboards and four complex control sticks. On one monitor Steve saw the suspect-house steps—cluttered with debris—as the robot climbed them. Another monitor displayed a higher image of the same scene.

Director Davis rested his hand on the shoulder of a small dark-haired man with a thick but well-trimmed mustache. "This is Senior Deputy Tommy Chavez of LAC EOD. He's driving the machine."

Steve shook hands with the deputy. "Good to meet you."

"Hey, likewise." Tommy spun back toward the control pod. "And this is Benny, our metal bomb dog. He's got a nose 10 times stronger than any canine." Tommy manipulated the main control stick, guiding the robot through the shattered front door. He pointed to a diagram of the house. "You say it's here?"

Steve traced the path of travel with his finger. "Yes, sir. Depending on the debris, you should be able to clear the dining-room table about there without a problem." He hesitated. "Kitchen door is pretty narrow."

"Not anymore." Senior Deputy Chavez motioned to the center screen. "Coming up now." He leaned his head from side to side, panning the camera left to right with the joystick. "Should clear the opening with about two feet to spare."

Steve spotted a gap, visible near the left edge of the monitor. "The pantry is—was—here."

Tommy rotated the control stick. The image swung left. "And there it is. Getting all kinds of spikes in the residue readings." Blue lines bounced up and down on a projected graph of the chemical environment, though the peaks remained proportionally high wherever the robot moved. "This middle section of the graph charts the nitrate levels."

Trying to make sense of what he saw on the video display, Steve realized that the tiny crawl space beneath a flight of steps that once backed up to a fireplace had been blown wide open. The walls and studs within had been shattered and bricks from the fireplace toppled. The staircase was now nonexistent.

"Oh, man!" exclaimed Chavez. "What a backstop. The majority of the explosion's force was directed right out the pantry door. Looks like second to go would have been this wall here, next to the laundry room."

Steve examined the holes in the staircase. "That's where all the shrapnel on the lawn came from."

Chavez nodded in agreement as he typed a command on the keyboard. The center image zoomed in. "This bomb was low-tech. There's a piece of egg timer. Wires are still glued on for contacts."

It was amazing, Steve thought, that after all the force and heat, there would be anything left.

Carter pointed to the left side of the image with another Tootsie Pop. "Round this side was where we grabbed the computer. Stacks of papers were over there."

By manipulating the controls Chavez craned the camera in the pantry, shifting the image up and around. "Can of gasoline for accelerant. And looks like some charred plastic."

"Would have been the jar of Green Dot," Carter interjected.

Chavez agreed. "Pistol powder for the primary charge. Definitely sophomoric, but it did the job." He swiveled around. "Director Davis, my spectrometer tells me the scene is clear."

Davis lifted the radio handset. "Director Davis to Command. Send in the K-9 to complete the sweep."

"10-4."

"Dogs are quite a bit more mobile and cheaper," Chavez added.

Carter motioned to the screen. "How much was that little trash can on wheels?"

"Over a million, easy."

Carter blew out a puff of air before a laugh. "Ain't from RadioShack, is it?"

"You can say that twice," Steve agreed. "But I'd rather see a million-dollar hunk of metal blow up before a dog any day."

Just then his B-com rang, and Steve's thoughts leaped to Anton. Caller ID indicated Chapter 16's founder and director, former senator James Morrison. Steve pressed his fingers into the print-recognition indentions on the back of the blue phone. "Senator Morrison. What's the news on Anton?"

Morrison was calm and solemn. "Not much—just that he's conscious. In a lot of pain but conscious. Doctors are trying to peel what bits of nylon tac vest they can out of his skin. Melted in there pretty badly. They say he'll have a tough few days ahead as he fights off the dehydration, but Anton's a strong boy. He'll make it."

Cringing at the details, Steve could hardly speak, but he remained optimistic. "I know he will. Thanks for the report."

"Secondly," Morrison resumed, "I think congratulations are in order for you and the team. Heard you boys managed to get a computer and one of the suspects out."

"Oh, yeah." Steve suddenly remembered the check. "In all the confusion I forgot to let someone know." He dug the wadded scrap out of his pocket and held it up. "Cashier's check for $2300, made out to Mabrouk Ziad."

Morrison cheered. "Good work! I doubt Mabrouk made the check out to himself. Need to get that one in for Ninhydrin lab work STAT. See who else's prints we can get."

"I'm on it."

Ninhydrin was a chemical dying process whereby paper and other soft porous evidence were soaked for hours. The purple chemical reacted with the oil imprints left by hands. Once dried, the evidence was placed under an intense light where the fingerprints could easily be seen and photographed.

Davis removed something from a box in the corner of the trailer. "Here you go," he said, handing Steve a Ziploc baggie.

Steve passed the check over to Davis. "See if the mobile crime lab can get a print test started."

Director Davis nodded with satisfaction. "Perfect. We can run the prints through the NCIC and Interpol."

"Good work," Morrison repeated.

Frowning, Steve warned, "Not everyone is happy with us."

"Talking about Castillo?" Morrison laughed.

"How'd you know?"

"Guess he called the wrong guy with a complaint. Director of Homeland Security is pretty pleased with you, Special Agent Thomas, and especially Anton. The director thought it pretty heroic. Ought to be ringing you soon."

"I'll look forward to it." Steve gave Davis the thumbs-up. "And what about jurisdiction on the evidence?"

"Looks like we'll be working together on this one. LAC District Attorney technical investigators will make a mirror copy of the hard drive. They've agreed to pool resources for investigations in that neck of the woods."

Good and bad, Steve knew. He'd have extra help, but with the added benefit of extra delays as well. He and Carter moved outside the trailer. "Sounds good, Senator Morrison. I'll speak with you soon."

"One more thing," Morrison said. "Abdel, the guy Anton saved, is in custody at the LA county jail. Kristi Kross is in the air, on her way to do the arson investigation. Teresa Bouche should be arriving any minute. She'd like you and Carter to go with her to interrogate Abdel. Up for it?"

What an opportunity that would be, Steve realized. "I think I can break every bone in his body without killing him, if that's what you're asking."

"Maybe you better wait outside and let Ms. Bouche do the talking then. But she'd like to have you there."

"Sure thing, Senator." Steve ended the call about the time a white, unmarked Crown Vic rolled in, lights ablaze. A thin, balding, older man in a suit hopped out, breaking into a brisk walk.

Davis came up beside Steve and nudged him. "That's Deputy Director Castillo."

"Perfect," mumbled Steve. "Situation handled, and this guy is still on a witch hunt."

"Special Agent Alstead?" Castillo called as he approached.

"Here it comes . . ." Steve rolled his eyes at Carter, then said to Castillo, "Yes, sir. That's me."

"Sir, I just want to congratulate you." Castillo extended a hand to Steve.

Steve didn't return the gesture.

Recovering from the shun, Castillo continued, ". . . for making a good call. I hear we've got a treasure trove of information in this little operation."

"Thank Special Agent Carter Thomas over there. He pulled it off."

Castillo glanced at Carter, then turned his attention back to Steve. "I hear you'll be working with us on the investigation."

"That's what I know." Steve's attention was drawn to a figure in a dark green hooded sweatshirt way down the street. A quick backward look and the man hurried suspiciously away. Steve couldn't help but think of the missing suspect. But there was no way a suspect would be caught around here right now.

Steve's thoughts were drawn away as he saw Teresa roll up in a second white Crown Vic. "Anyway, gotta run. I'm off to interrogate the suspect. So if you'll excuse me." Steve nodded to the men. "Director Davis. Thanks for your help."

"Anytime." Davis saluted good-bye.

Carter waited by a pile of gear. Assistant U.S. Attorney General Teresa Bouche popped the trunk before she even greeted Steve. The two men heaved tac vests, gun cases, and mobile operations bags full of every piece of gear into the trunk.

✪ ✪ ✪

Glendale, California
0446 hours, Pacific Time

PLAN B

The man in the dark green hooded sweatshirt stood at the pay phone. He stared up the street for a time. Shaking off his dismay, he dialed an 11-digit number and inserted the coins demanded by the mechanical voice. Nervously rubbing his scraggly mustache, he listened to the distant ringing repeat six times, then hung up and called back.

This time the reception clicked at once, but no one spoke.

"Mabrouk," the 5-foot, 10-inch, lightly built man offered. "Explosion and fire. The street still crawls with agents."

"Did anyone see you?" the voice on the other end asked.

Sweat glistened on Mabrouk's olive-skinned forehead. "No, no! I'm certain of it. But they've taken Abdel alive."

"I know. To the LA county jail. You know what to do?"

"The tracks?"

"Do you have what you need?"

Nodding to his distant audience, Mabrouk agreed. "I didn't keep it all in the house. I have enough elsewhere for the job."

"Set it up at once. You must start calling no later than 7:30. You understand? The chaos will show him we know where he is."

"It shall be done."

✪ ✪ ✪

Days Inn Motel
Albuquerque, New Mexico
0550 hours, Mountain Time

FADING STARS AND DREAMS

The stars above Albuquerque began to fade in the east. Thirty-two-year-old Tracy Roberts had been up for hours. The bags were beside the door of the motel. She was ready to resume the long drive to California, yet she took advantage of the quiet time and let her two sons sleep a while longer.

Wearing her old green Baylor University Bears sweatshirt and faded jeans, Tracy stared out the window of the Days Inn Motel and thought of her husband, Mike. Did he ever wake up with her on his mind? she wondered. Did he ever miss the hot summer nights when they slept on the porch of their little farmhouse 20 miles outside Fort Smith, Arkansas?

She tossed the dark hair that was evidence of her grandmother's Cherokee heritage over her shoulder. Just like Granny, who had always been strong through every hardship, Tracy vowed to resist the descent into self-pity. For the sake of the boys she would not yield to her grief and loneliness. What was done was done. Mike had said as much three months ago. Their marriage was over. He had fallen in love with another woman and would not be coming home to her.

And yet he had phoned her. Asked her to bring the boys and the dog out to California to see him. He had spoken kindly to Tracy for the first time in a year. Buttered up the boys. Promised them Disneyland and Universal Studios.

Why?

Tonight four-year-old Connor and seven-year-old Justin shared the hotel bed with their 120-pound yellow Lab, Yowser. Mike had brought the puppy home to the boys and named him Ol' Yeller after an antique Disney movie. "Nothing like a dog to keep a boy company," Mike had said. Yeller grew up to become Yowser, a much-loved member of the family and Justin's constant companion.

But no dog could take the place of a dad who rarely came to a T-ball game and didn't know what position his son played on the soccer team.

For all that, both boys adored their father. Connor, with his blond hair and bright blue eyes, was the mirror image of Mike as a kid. Like his dad, little Connor loved fast shiny cars, roaring engines, and all things mechanical.

Justin, on the other hand, was nothing like his dad. They did not speak the same emotional language. Swarthy, dark haired, and dark eyed, Justin was quiet and introspective, like Tracy in most ways. Broad shoulders and a swagger gave Justin the demeanor of his mother's Native American ancestors.

Tracy was tall, athletic, and most at ease in the quiet of the Arkansas countryside, in their little church, or among old friends and neighbors. Even traveling to the big city of Tulsa seemed like a trip to a foreign country to her. Soft country nights and gospel music ran through her veins.

Maybe those differences defined why Mike had stopped loving Tracy. After 10 years of marriage Mike had chosen a different life.

But here she was in a motel along Interstate 40 with her boys, half-way between Fort Smith and LA, wishing she were home.

The boys still had not grasped the fact that Dad and Mom would not be living together as man and wife ever again. Little wonder. Since the birth of their first child, Mike had been on the road 10 months out of 12, with only sporadic visits home. He sent good money with regularity, but Tracy always said she liked it better when he worked in the garage on Garrison Street and came home to her at night.

When Mike had roared up the long lane that led to their old house and honked to announce his arrival after months of absence, what joy! What chaos! Yowser howled. The boys tumbled out to greet him. Tracy always wept when Mike put his arms around her.

The boys said that having Dad home was better than a visit from Santa Claus! Mike would unlock the garage where his candy-apple red '57 Chevy was stored. His times at home were filled with long drives and fishing trips and campouts.

But everything had changed.

Now Mike would have another woman in the car beside him when he came back. He would load up the two boys and pack their duffels in the trunk for a monthlong vacation once a year somewhere else besides Arkansas.

And Tracy would stay behind.

Mike promised that his boys would still have a dad even if Tracy no longer had a husband. There was some consolation in that. The boys would get along. Yes. Some comfort. Not much.

Tracy hugged herself and tucked her legs onto the chair. The motel room smelled musty, like old cigarette smoke. She had asked for nonsmoking. She longed for her own bed.

She would try not to think about it. Why had she come when Mike called? *Stupid. Idiotic.* He snapped his fingers, and just like that she loaded the boys and the dog and headed west as if a happy ending waited at the end of the road.

Was she crazy?

Tracy had always loved Mike. Always. He was her first and her forever. From eighth grade on she had loved him. And he had loved her almost as long. Tracy wondered what kind of woman could make Mike forget a lifetime of shared memories.

And why had he called last week and asked her and the boys to meet him in California?

Tracy studied the ripening colors of dawn and remembered long-ago summer mornings when she lay in Mike's arms. How she wished she were home! Home with him. With him, anywhere would be home.

Oh, Lord! she begged. *Oh, Lord! I never thought we would end like this! Oh, Lord! Are you watching? Do you care at all?*

The predawn skies were silent. God's peace seemed too high above Albuquerque for Tracy to grasp it.

The ache of loneliness filled her.

✪ ✪ ✪

Brown Jug Liquor Store
Los Angeles, California
0742 hours, Pacific Time

ALLAH'S LIBERATION

Outside the Brown Jug liquor store on Soto, Mabrouk lifted the receiver of a pay phone. It was way too early for winos to be out of their cardboard shacks. Nobody in this neighborhood drank coffee on their way to work, at least not the rancid sludge left on the liquor store's hot plate since last night.

The lone clerk leaned on the counter, scanning the racing form. Licking a stubby pencil and circling his picks for Santa Anita, he had not even glanced up when Mabrouk paid for a pack of Camels with a $10, then asked for and got eight quarters in change.

Outside in the parking lot, the wail of a distant siren made Mabrouk glance at his watch: time to get under way.

From a pocket of his green sweatshirt he produced a handwritten list of numbers. Dropping coins into the slot, he dialed the first on the list.

✪ ✪ ✪

LA County Correctional Facility
South Central Los Angeles, California

Inside the LA County Correctional Facility, the pay phones on the rear wall of cell pod Alpha-3 began to ring.

A skinhead with too few teeth fretting out a third-strike arrest for B and E answered it. "Yeah? Who d'ya want?"

"You're all going to die . . . today."

"Yeah, who says so, you stupid—"

"They won't help you and you're going to die," the voice insisted.

"What the—"

"Allah will free you today."

"What kind of sick—"

The hum of the dial tone responded.

✪ ✪ ✪

Inside cell pod Bravo-4 Leroy Jones saw the clock inside the wire cage tick over to 7:45. The pay phone rang right on the dot. It had all been vicious gossip. His girl, Lawonda, still loved him after all.

Manuel Ortega started toward the phone, but a warning growl from Leroy headed him off. Leroy's massive black paw engulfed the handset. "Hey, baby! I told Fly he don't know nothin'."

"Be quiet and listen! You're all going to die."

"Get off this line, fool! My baby's—"

"No one will help you. . . ."

✪ ✪ ✪

The calls were complete inside 10 minutes.

Mabrouk shoved the phone list into the pocket of his Levi's, then unzipped the cellophane from his cigarettes.

The fun had only begun.

THREE

Basement of Suspect House
Glendale, California
Saturday, 5 September
0756 hours, Pacific Time

A SMALL OVERSIGHT

Water dripped from the soggy ground floor, adding to the 14 inches that had settled in the basement. Sump pumps hummed from beneath the surface of the pool.

Arson investigator Kristi Kross examined the scorch marks on the basement ceiling, looking for the subtlest clues in the genesis of her investigation. Even with the cause of the fire well known, it was important not to overlook details that could reveal so much about the past of the perpetrators. For example, discovering the bomb's ingredients could reveal where the materials were obtained.

In an investigation's infancy this sort of link between the bomb and other sources was but a single strand of cord stretched across the chasm of a crime. But if the cord was strong enough, eventually a rope could be pulled across, and then a delicate suspension bridge constructed.

The path across the bridge would lead from present to past, revealing other leads: names, addresses, financial transactions. Enough evidence and a more solid anchorage could be established on the other side. The footprints of those who had secretly crossed the bridge before it was burned would inevitably be discovered.

And in the construction of this bridge spanning crime and prosecution, the sum of all might reveal who lived in the secret village across the chasm, and all that their roles had been.

Despite all the jokes about her being a built, beautiful, blue-eyed blonde, she'd earned her colleagues' respect. No case was ever open and shut to Kristi Kross. Now she straddled a fallen 2-x-10 floor support, careful not to step down too quickly. Fourteen inches of water under one step might conceal a hidden trapdoor under the next.

A maroon rug, approximately 8-x-10 feet, was flung facedown across a collapsed shop table. "How did that get off the floor and over there?" she wondered aloud. The explosion above would have driven everything downward. "Maybe a blast stream ripped through the ceiling, flipping it up off the floor."

Kristi spied fibers similar in color to the carpet, hanging from a nail on the ceiling. A more focused inspection revealed three other nail holes in the rafters, spaced about the right distances for the carpet to have been nailed up like a canopy.

The underside of the carpet had not been burned to the degree that the ceiling had, leading her to believe it was blown down onto the table. This meant it probably hadn't been moved, she surmised, which also meant the space around the table probably hadn't been properly checked.

Muslim prayer rug, she guessed. Hung over a space dedicated to the work of *jihad,* "holy war"?

Concern filled her. What else might she discover?

Ever so gently Kristi pulled back the rug. Items began to slide out from under it, splashing into the murky water. Kristi dove for a yellow legal pad as it swooped toward destruction, snatching it just as the corner touched the water.

Bomb-making plans. Kristi examined the document of detailed instructions and descriptions. Clutching the notepad tightly, she bent over and reached into the black void to see what else she might find. Her fingers touched a plastic jar. There was a cap. Something slender sticking out of the top poked her hand.

She retrieved the item: A gunpowder container. She was startled to see a pair of wires with a 9-volt battery connected to one terminal. A homemade detonator!

Fear and anger flooded her at the same moment. Who knew what chemicals were mixed with the powder? How powerful—or how stable—was this explosive device?

The recovered legal pad went under the arm holding the powder can. Careful not to rattle the battery around for fear it might make contact, Kristi removed a radio from her pocket. "Chavez! Thought you guys said the basement had been swept!" Fury was evident in her voice.

"That's what K-9 said," came the reply. *"Are you down there now?"*

Kristi studied the red composite ladder that had been lowered down due to the recent removal of the stairs. "I'm holding live ordnance here, half connected to a battery!"

Water dripped from the terminals. Kristi marveled that the electric current wasn't enough to set it off under water. She continued speaking into the radio. "There's a notepad full of bomb plans. I don't think anyone has even been down here at all, yet I'm tromping around without this place having been cleared for other booby traps!"

Into a stunned void of silence the radio squawked curtly, *"On my way."*

Kristi remained motionless for a minute. The image of having stumbled into an unknown minefield was not inaccurate. She hoped Chavez could round up some guys and the bomb-barrel truck quickly.

The water mark on the wall floated lower by the moment.

Tommy Chavez's head appeared near the top of the ladder. His eyes bulged when he saw what Kristi held. "Whoa! Another one of those! Okay, stay calm. Don't let the battery touch the other contact." He disappeared from view.

"Another one?!" she called after him. The battery flopped loosely from the wire as Kristi stared at it with consternation.

A few seconds later Chavez reappeared.

"What do you mean another one?" Kristi demanded.

Chavez ignored her, giving his attention to shouting commands to someone outside: "I don't care! Just back it over the retaining wall. I want that truck as close to the ladder as possible."

Several pairs of feet trudged by, and a set of tires slowly rolled past the basement windows.

With his attention still divided, Chavez's face turned toward her again. "Uh . . . yeah . . . Kristi. That's what went off in the closet." His hands came up in a gesture of entreaty. "Don't . . . don't squeeze it. The jar. I don't know how stable that stuff is!"

"Perfect," Kristi whispered. Calm, cool, and under control, she edged her way to the ladder. Inch by inch she retraced her steps until she had reached the exit. Lifting the jar cautiously, Kristi handed up the detonator.

"Easy, easy," Chavez said, squinting, as if closing his eyes before something went *boom*! "I don't have my suit on."

"Like I do!" scoffed Kristi. "You EOD guys are so paranoid."

Chavez hurried from view, shouting, "Close it. Close it!"

The noisy whirl of electrically driven hydraulics started, then gradually slowed, stopping with a *clank.*

Kristi emerged from the basement as Chavez tightened the safety latches on the large, black, perfectly spherical cauldron that now contained the bomb. "Clear. Get this thing out of here." He smacked the truck.

Lights flashed and the siren chirped several half howls as the vehicle began to move. It drove through the flower beds on the side of the front yard to where it bounced off the curb.

That instant a muffled, metallic boom echoed from the belly of the bomb barrel. The whole truck shook, bouncing up and down on its tires.

Kristi and Chavez were stunned. Jolting the detonator had disturbed the substance enough to set it off, though thankfully the six inches of solid steel surrounding the device controlled the explosion.

The driver locked up the brakes. Leaning out the door, his expression begged for instructions.

"Just go!" Chavez waved him on. "Idiot!"

The EOD truck took to the street, sirens at full blare now, and then was gone.

Kristi looked right into Chavez's eyes, shaking her head slowly.

Nervously he began to chuckle. "What?"

A smile peeked out from behind Kristi's frustration like the sun on a cloudy day. "Don't ever do that to me again."

"I-I . . . ," he stuttered.

"Don't ever, ever do that to me again."

"I thought . . . it was those K-9 guys . . ." He began to back away in defense. "It was a small oversight."

"A small oversight? I could have been blown up! I almost got blown up!"

"I'm sorry." Chavez laughed nervously. "Do you need to sit down or—"

"No, no, I'm fine," Kristi replied, retrieving three shiny, empty paint cans from her arson-investigation supplies. "Looks like I'll be needing samples of burned evidence for the mass spectrometer after all." As she walked away, Kristi continued to talk to herself. "Small oversight! Ha! I wondered how those dogs got down the ladder! Wait'll I catch one of those K-9 guys."

✪ ✪ ✪

LA County Correctional Facility
South Central Los Angeles, California
0812 hours, Pacific Time

NO DEAL

Teresa Bouche, Chapter 16's Department of Justice connection, made sure operations ran smoothly and within the bounds of the law.

Midforties, attractive, stylishly dressed, Teresa had a set of fangs six inches long (as needed) and a wardrobe full of power suits to rival any well-known female Democratic senator in the state.

It wouldn't surprise Steve if one day Teresa decided to run for president.

While Carter was afraid of women in power suits, Steve had nothing against Teresa, since she had proven herself to be a team player. Of course it would be a lonely day on the planet before she'd accept an invite to burn some meat on the grill with the guys.

After Steve and Carter had cleaned up and eaten an awkwardly quiet continental breakfast in the hotel, enough time had passed for Abdel to be processed and moved to a holding cell.

The ride to the LA county jail was quiet too. All three avoided bringing up Anton. Small talk would have been too obvious a cover as well. As a result none of them said much of anything. And that was the way Steve preferred it.

The LAC Justice Administration Building also housed the Sheriff's Office, where parole and other court services were held.

Just south of the administration building and connected to it by a long secure hallway suspended high in the air was the maximum security LA County Correctional Facility. This safe passage kept the transportation risk of prisoners for hearings and court services to a minimum, thereby reducing the possibility of escape. Known as the Twin Towers because of its two identical figure-8-shaped, five-story structures, it was a perfect model for the modern prison. Recently built, the designers had accounted for every concern and worst-case scenario imaginable. Even the positively charged air system was state-of-the-art, with features like air locks and fire doors that automatically sealed, allowing areas unaffected by disaster to remain in lockdown.

Steve rolled up to the 15-foot steel gates and hung his badge out the window in front of a camera. "Special Agent Steve Alstead here for an interrogation by order of the Department of Homeland Security."

A deep female voice replied, *"We have you and company on the top of our list, Mister Alstead."*

A long hum sounded and the massive panel slowly opened. Steve drove into the security lock, where the gate behind him closed before the final one opened. They parked and got out of the car.

Steve unholstered his Glock 23. "Firearms in the trunk, boys . . . and girl," he added as an afterthought.

"I'm not packing," Teresa replied as she toted her briefcase toward the security checkpoint.

Carter ditched his magazines, racked the slide, and laid his gun in the trunk, along with a couple of knives and a can of pepper spray. "This right here is why I carry a big flashlight." Carter showed off his Streamlight 40XP, a rechargeable spot the length and weight of a small boat anchor. "No weapons allowed, but I can still crack somebody with this."

Steve knew Carter was trying to take his mind off Anton. Faking a smile, Steve wiggled his pocket-sized SureFire flashlight. "Betcha lunch you won't get through."

"You're on!" Carter accepted.

Carter grinned after successfully passing every one of the checkpoints in the maze of halls and security doors to the high-risk prisoner holding facility. But one of the two detention officers at the final checkpoint insisted Carter leave his illuminating impact weapon there.

Carter argued, but the slightly overweight, understimulated guard insisted, "No. A guy could easily use that to crack somebody on the head, then smash a window."

Steve patted the guard on the shoulder. "Thanks for lunch."

The guard just looked confused. Teresa rolled her eyes.

"Show off," Carter mocked, yanking the penlight from Steve's pocket. "You're obsessed with flashlights."

The three were led into a control room where the chained suspect, wearing a bright orange jumpsuit, was visible through tinted security glass.

Teresa opened her file and read out loud. "'Abdel Thind. A Saudi national, in the U.S. on a student visa in spring 2001. Disappeared from radar about the time he was asked to come forward for fingerprinting. Right now anything short of a hooded beating goes. His status is *enemy combatant.*'"

Abdel's sneer did not mix well with Steve's remembrance of Anton's charred and bandaged form.

The disgust must have showed in his body language.

"Better wait here," Teresa told Steve. "I don't want to defend you in a murder trial."

"Pretty tight in there anyway." Steve agreed to wait as Carter and Teresa entered the holding cell.

✪ ✪ ✪

Abdel didn't even look up.

Teresa cleared her throat. "Mister Thind, I am Ms. Bouche, Department of Justice liason with Department of Homeland Security."

No reply came from the long-haired, bearded man.

She continued, "This is Special Agent Carter Thomas with the FBI." Officially the FBI designation was used instead of Chapter 16 as it saved time explaining. "Do you know why you're being held?"

No reply.

Carter's blood began to boil. "America-hating punk!" Carter hissed. "Come here pretending to get ahead, when all you really want to do is chop off a few and almost blow me up in the process!"

Carter clenched his fists, managing—barely—to keep his anger in check. "Your file says you speak English. Answer Ms. Bouche!" Carter demanded.

Abdel stared at Carter defiantly. "In my country a woman would never question a man."

Teresa spoke in a calm tone, as if reading a bedtime story to a child. "Abdel, we have information from several sources that you are involved in a bomb plot."

"I don't have to talk to you! I want a lawyer!" Abdel shrieked, suddenly furious.

"Sorry, buddy. Can't have one. You're being charged as an enemy combatant." Carter leaned close enough to bite Abdel's ear off. "Do you know what that means? No lawyer and no trial. We can hold you till the day you die."

Asserting herself slightly, Teresa added, "Abdel, we know that you are licensed to transport hazardous materials but that you have never been employed to do so."

No answer.

Carter resumed his taunting. "Your friends are all dead, Abdel. Burned up by your little bomb this morning. Except for Mabrouk, and he's singing like a nightingale."

Abdel snapped, "No, he isn't! He wasn't at the house!"

"We picked him up yesterday at the mosque. He had quite a few things to say about you and the computer and the cashier's check we managed to save from the fire. . . . Said you were hired to drive the truck to the target."

"That's a lie!" Abdel spat out.

Teresa explained, "Abdel, do you see this paperwork? It says we can detain you indefinitely."

Abdel glanced at the official-looking document entitled Enemy Combatant.

"Now if you assist us in uncovering the truth, we can cut you a deal," Teresa promised.

"What scam are you speaking?" Abdel retorted. "You want to keep me forever."

"Here is our agreement." Teresa slid another document in front of him. "If you provide direct evidence in this case, aid in the capture of your superiors, and assist the Department of Homeland Security in stopping the terrorist plot you are very clearly involved in, we are prepared to offer you a 15-year sentence instead of life."

Abdel slammed his palms down on the table. "I had nothing to do with this, I tell you!"

"Could have fooled me." Carter sat on the table. "Not what

Mabrouk said, either." He raised his voice. "Who, when, where, and how, Abdel. Not that hard! Whoever sings loudest first gets the deal!"

Teresa spoke bluntly. "If you don't cooperate and this next bomb goes off, I will do my best to see you get the death penalty. Conspiracy to commit murder and murder during an act of terrorism."

Abdel, speechless and defiant, jerked away contemptuously.

Carter stood up. "Have it your way. Mabrouk is talking right now."

Leaving the documents on the table, Teresa followed Carter out.

Steve paced the tiny control room. As soon as the door was shut, he informed them that Morrison had just called. "Mabrouk has a brother."

"Is he a suspect?" Carter quizzed.

The security guard released the door.

"Don't know." Steve rubbed his stubble and shook off a yawn. "Hakim is his name. Been here . . . in the States . . . about 12 years. We're still waiting for a location. They think he works at a paint factory in North Hollywood."

Teresa brushed the bangs from her eyes. "Anyone pick him up yet?"

Steve shook his head. "Morrison thought it better to keep things with Hakim consensual. Approach him out of concern for his brother."

"Good idea," Carter agreed. "See what he knows; then tail him everywhere he goes."

✪   ✪   ✪

Back at the car the three were preparing to leave when the crashing sound of something huge and metal breaking loose erupted from outside the security wall; it was accompanied by the dying wail of a train whistle.

Steve froze as the deafening, squealing noise continued long beyond reason. "Derailment!" he shouted, grinding the starter of the already running car.

The sound of railcars colliding and jackknifing into one another went on and on and on. An explosion erupted, causing the car windows to shudder. Steve could feel the tremor in his chest. Seconds later there was another detonation, even louder. So loud that Steve thought it might rip right through the wall.

Teresa's window spidered from the concussion.

Steve slammed the car in gear, climbed the parking blocks, and sped for the exit. Holding the intercom button, he shouted, "There's been an accident just outside the compound. Hurry! Open the gate!"

Carter watched out the back window, spying a green mist wafting over the wall. "Some kind of gas released in the crash!"

Steve leaned back to see while shouting at the gate guard, "Gas is coming over the wall!"

"Hurry up!" shouted Carter. "Looks like chlorine."

Teresa Bouche grew white as a sheet watching the cloud sink into the parking compound. "Lethal! Drive, Steve!"

Steve rammed the car bumper against the gate. "Chlorine! Trigger your air-lock system, and open the gate!"

The lumbering hydraulic rams slowly pulled the gates inward, banging against the front of the car, jolting it backward. Steve slammed it in reverse, squealing the tires to get out of the way. A deafening alarm sounded.

Back in drive, he spun the wheels again, shearing off the mirrors as the gate finally opened and he cleared the compound.

✪ ✪ ✪

B-Block Rec Room
LA County Correctional Facility
South Central Los Angeles, California
0830 hours, Pacific Time

DO SOMEPIN', HOLMES!

A pulsating buzzer resonated throughout the halls and rooms of the LACJ. At any other time it would have sent the men straight to their cells if not right to the floor.

But already the word had spread like wildfire.

Not a man in the joint was deaf to the news: Allah will free all today
. . . and the guards will not help you.

The inmates were restless. Everyone had heard it. The prisoners also
heard the crashing derailment, felt it through the floor, without knowing what it was. There was no denying something big was going down.

All the guards disappearing . . .

Ventilation system shutting down . . .

Light skin, a shaved head, and vario accent made it hard to tell the
race of Junior Ramon. His mother was half Mexican; she split when he
was little. His father, a white-trash skinhead, had smoked Junior out
when he was 11. What could he say? Dope was a gateway drug. It led
to other things.

By age 14 Junior was stealing whatever he could to pay the bills. It
was a different life growing up in Receda in SoCal. But, hey, his life phi-
losophy was, get in where you fit in. Do what you please, and when the
day comes, say, "Yes, Your Honor" and "No, Your Honor," then kick
the habit for a few months, hittin' the weights and catchin' up with old
friends. Three square meals with cable TV. Life couldn't be better.

Half of the inmate population hit the deck at the sound of the
buzzer. A few of the regulars, like Junior, stood around waiting to see
what was up. He'd heard—they'd all heard. So where were the correction officers? A long buzzer like that sounded only when something
heavy was going down.

Junior threw his arms up in the air, turning slowly in a circle.
"Where are they, man?"

Several of his tough-guy partners stood fast, fists clenched, looking
around.

No guards were to be seen.

Junior flung his right hand at the guys on the ground. "Nowhere,
man! It's true. Somepin' crazy is goin' down, and they ain't gonna let
us in on it!"

A couple guys pushed slowly to their feet.

Junior continued his sermon. "I'm tellin' ya, Holmes, today is the
day they gonna let us die, man!"

The buzzer continued. More inmates stood up, but no one came. No one called out over the PA for them to lie back down.

"Terrorists! Attack on the prisons, man! And the pigs gonna let us die, Holmes." Junior flung his arms in the air again. "Do somepin'!"

The men were beginning to talk. Even the most cautious of them climbed to his feet.

The warden's voice echoed from the PA. *"Fall in line and return to your cells."* The men delayed and the warden repeated, *"Everything is under control. Fall in line."*

When Junior saw the COs appear in the control-pod windows wearing protective gas masks, he knew something really was up.

The control pod functioned as a central indoor lookout tower with a view above multiple pie-shaped blocks with stainless tables and chairs. Each prisoner pod contained as many as 16 cells, 8 doors on 2 levels, housing up to 32 inmates to a pod. Each pod contained a pay phone and a big-screen television. Each cell block of 8 pods had a dedicated rec room—an open place, often offering weights and other physical activities.

Junior pondered. No pepper gas had been thrown, and no fights were obvious, but the buzzer still hadn't stopped.

Man, maybe the crazy caller had been telling the truth.

"File in now, or there'll be a loss of privileges. Now! Move!" The warden's threat was interrupted by someone else talking behind the mike. The microphone remained open, but you had to be listening closely, like Junior, or you'd have missed it. *"Yes, boss. Confirmed. Chlorine gas."*

The warden's voice was a half-octave higher when he addressed the inmates again: *"In line! Now!"*

Junior's eyes bulged. The TV program on the big screen cut away from the canned program to a live shot from a helicopter.

It was outside the Twin Towers!

"Man, I ain't gonna die, man!" Junior gave the signal to take action, a subtle gesture. If you didn't know, you might have thought Junior was saying, "Cool it."

But he wasn't.

Inmates formed into line as if obeying the warden's instructions. But Junior, last in line, had a plan.

Just before passing the correction officer beside the door, Junior threw a hard backhanded chop to the CO's throat. The CO choked and crumpled to the floor as Junior grabbed his gas mask.

An instant later Junior's three accomplices did the same to three more guards.

"Get their masks, man!" screamed one of Junior's partners.

Several other prisoners turned to see what was going on.

Junior scrambled to pull his mask on. "Chlorine is bad stuff. Man, we mixed some and left it in a garage with my ex, Michelle's, dog for, like, two minutes." He shook his head. The air canister wobbled. The whole getup—orange jumpsuit and mask—made Junior look like something out of *Star Wars*. "Kilt it! Deader'n a doornail."

An inmate with crazy, darting, brown eyes and a nervous tick stared at Junior. "Bad stuff, man? Bad stuff?"

"Do it, Holmes! I ain't lyin'," Junior incited the others. "Better get a mask, man, 'cuz you gonna die in here if you don't!"

In a matter of seconds the entire pod began to riot. Stealing the keys from the downed guards, the men charged the stairs to the control pod. A few seconds more and they had killed two COs and taken over.

There was no time for Admin to lock out the controls.

Junior found himself a nice leather chair in front of the switches to all the cell-pod doors. He threw them open as he flipped the cell block PA microphone and announced, *"Get out while you can, 'cause Allah say you all gonna die today!"*

Inmates streamed from all openings. Men fought bloody battles over the protective masks. As soon as a prisoner seized one he was decked by the next and the mask was stolen away.

Junior leaned back in his leather chair. Arms crossed and smiling, he gloated as B-block was overrun with chaos. "But not me. I ain't goin' down."

FOUR

CHAOS IN THE MAKING

On her way to the LA Joint Terrorism Task Force offices, Teresa Bouche dropped off Steve and Carter and all their gear at the emergency staging area for the derailment. It was understood they would aid however they could.

Though it was sunny, green haze badly obscured Steve's view of where the railroad tracks paralleled the Los Angeles River. Tank cars carrying deadly chlorine gas had derailed 250 yards to the south. Chlorine gas, Steve knew, though commonly transported, was one of the most highly dangerous substances carried on road or rail. Because it was heavier than air, once released, it tended to pool in pockets on the ground, rather than dissipating.

From a distance, fluorescent green HAZMAT units fogged the air with massive fire hoses in an effort to knock the gas cloud back into a diluted liquid state.

Three of five tankers had been punctured in the derailment. Two of them streamed poison, while a third had a tiny leak. All com-

41

bined to feed a constant supply of gas to the cloud that had already formed.

Steve and Carter met with about a hundred other officers at a staging area just south of the river and the prison facility. Nearly a hundred more patrolled the streets in gas masks, evacuating residents within a one-mile radius of the chemical spill.

Steve's group, some in patrol uniforms, some in SWAT gear, readied themselves while they were addressed by the first-responding, highest-ranking officer of the LA Sheriff's Office.

"The situation is serious, men," Chief Wood explained, running a hand over his short salt-and-pepper hair. "As you know, the LACJ is a lockdown facility. After the accident, prisoners were placed in their cells and the air system was positively charged for safe recirculation. However, there was a small population of inmates in the rec yard who refused to return to their cells. They have begun to riot, smashing several windows with weights and other instruments, compromising the air seal. Word is they are also trying to gain access to the main corridor. The entire LACJ staff is on a 'hold in place' order, and there are serious concerns for their safety, as they try to regain control of the situation. Under normal circumstances we'd just wait it out . . . let the gas dissipate. But as you know, there have been deaths."

Chief Wood paused to let that sink in, then cleared his throat. "So, first order of business is to set up an inner perimeter for containment around the jail. The rest of us will make entry to assist in securing the inside." Wood gave the reins to the LAC director of HAZMAT, Rick Durrum. "Director Durrum will discuss some of the hazardous-material concerns."

Durrum stepped onto the wide rear bumper of a black SWAT van. "We have a seriously dangerous environment, as you know. The green clouds you see hovering near the facility are in fact chlorine gas, a vicious substance that can be fatal in seconds after inhaling. The prevailing winds in this area normally move north to south. This would be helpful, as the winds would then blow the gas cloud away from the Twin Towers, toward the river basin. The chlorine would sink into the basin and drift down toward the sea. Unfortunately, we have warmer weather and with it Santa Ana conditions blowing toward the northwest at about one mph. This, along with the steady feed from the tankers, has created a very challenging working environment, to say the least."

A call came over the radio: *"HR 1 to Command. We're moving in."*

Across the river 10 guys of the HAZMAT containment team, wearing bright yellow hooded suits, moved north from East Caesar Chavez Highway. As Steve watched, they fanned out along the river and railservice roads, stretching giant yellow plastic tarps.

Durrum continued to advise the first responders. "Wear proper protective clothing at all times. Don't fool with your masks because it's hot or foggy or whatever. Even after we get the area misted down, this stuff likes to hide in invisible pockets. It *will* kill you dead. Be very cautious, men. Now here's LAC SWAT Commander Werner Christi. He'll be going over the operational plans in more detail."

"Gentlemen, I'm Commander Werner Christi." An older, still very muscular man with a military-style flattop spoke to the group from atop the running board of a black GMC Yukon that was pulled up next to a silver Crown Victoria. "Right. Here's the Tac-Op side of things. LAPD and LAC SWAT teams, get with your sergeants. They have the plans for your individual squads. They'll explain where each of you will be and what you'll be doing."

The men began to swarm in small groups, scanning plans and enlarged satellite photos of the correctional facility.

Christi then spoke to the remainder of the men. "I understand that we have some law-enforcement personnel from outside the county. If you are one of them and have military experience in operating in a chemically contaminated environment, please meet with me here at the hood of my car and we'll find a job for you."

"Guess that's us." Steve slapped Carter on the back as they shouldered their Black Hawk Mobile Operation Bags. Steve often thought his MOB contained all the gear needed to survive WWIII . . . and he wanted it that way.

Spread before them on the hood of the silver Crown Vic was a high-altitude aerial image, displaying roughly nine square blocks of the affected area.

Christi passed a sign-in sheet around. Steve and Carter filled in name, rank, agency, and badge number on the sheet. There were 12 IDs on the list. Christi took roll. "When I call your name, I want you to answer 'tac rifle,' 'long gun,' or 'none,' according to what weapon you have here."

The process revealed seven guys with AR-15s and five more with Remington Model 700s in .308, including Steve and Carter. A two-minute meeting divided the men into pairs and sent the tac-rifle guys packing for an entry team.

Steve and Carter were assigned the northwest corner between the LA sheriff's building and the transportation yard. Carter put on his black rubber Scott M98 gas mask. "Boy, I wish he could have given us something closer to the train wreck."

Steve grinned. Their position was the closest of any. "That's what you get for being the most qualified," he observed, donning his mask.

Carter pulled the straps of his mask backward, two at a time. "I don't think when he read the list he said, 'Hey, here are some highly qualified HRT guys. I'll bet they'll do a fine job.' It was more like, 'These guys think they're hot stuff. Anyway, we can afford to lose a couple Feds.'"

Steve cleared his mask, covering the escape valve and blowing out. Carter did the same. Both men then covered the inlets, sucking in to seat and seal the mask properly before they began to slip into their heavy rubber biochem assault suits.

One of the SWAT guys from LAPD was having trouble sealing his mask, due to an extreme case of five o'clock shadow. Steve took a jar of Vaseline out of his bag and offered it to the guy. "Here. Glob this around your mask."

The officer stared at the opened container with unappreciative disgust.

"Go on," Steve encouraged firmly. "It may be nasty, but it'll save your life." He extended the jar.

Reluctantly the officer took the jar, grunted, then swabbed the greasy jelly around his face seal and donned his mask. Without even saying thank you, the man wandered off to meet his partner.

"Ungrateful slob," Carter mumbled before calling after him, "Hey, Scruffy! That's what you get for not shaving this morning."

"He's probably just scared," Steve said, still amused by Carter's approach to life. Carter's entire scalp was smoother than old "Scruffy's" face. "You shave that noggin every day?"

"Yep, every day but Sundays. Can't stand the stubble when it gets hung up on my pillow."

"Anybody going to the northwest, west, or southwest corners?" Christi asked from the running board of the Yukon. "Find a spot to hang on."

Fully dressed in camo biochem suits, Steve and Carter looked more like lumpy aliens than men. Long-gun rifle cases cinched on like backpacks, the HRT partners loaded aboard with eight others.

The vehicle broke traction as it sped off the dirt lot, heading for ground zero.

✪ ✪ ✪

ELFS (Electronic Lab of Forensic Surveillance) Room
FBI, Chapter 16 Offices
San Francisco, California
0927 hours, Pacific Time

TWO PARTS MILES

One part genius, one part nuts. That description fit well the six-foot-four Leonardo da Vinci of modern computer programming, Miles Miller, who now hacked away at a terminal in the ELFS room. Miles had initially named the work space Elves' Room, maintaining that the little mythical creatures did all the work. Chapter 16 Director Morrison had laughingly obliged. With a few minor adjustments he had matched the acronym to a name that worked officially and *voilà!*

Data began to stream from the T-5 uplink, connecting the San Francisco FBI and Chapter 16 offices to the world. The dual quadrallel processors made opening the mirror from the suspect's hard drive like opening a word-processor file. The on-screen command response changed from "Connecting" to "Complete" in seconds.

Wearing a thin red T-shirt, Miles leaned back with the wireless keyboard on his lap. His legs were long enough that his knees were elevated like a big four-year-old in a baby booster. He punched the intercom button connected to his headset and scratched his honey brown hair.

"Yes, Miles," Director Morrison answered tensely.

"The, ah, copy of the Glendale hard drive is here. Didn't know if you wanted to see it or not."

"I'd love to check it out," Morrison replied, "But there's too much going on down south for me to break away yet. Go ahead and look it over first and let me know when you find something."

Miles pattered away at the keys. "Sure thing, boss." The line went dead.

Socially refined Miles was not. He was still working out the details for the proper use of a napkin. "Why would I need that?" he'd say, rubbing his chin and mouth across the shoulder of his shirt.

But a genius—yes! A true savant. The only reason he wasn't worth billions due to his brilliant inventions was because he became bored too fast. Overseeing product development all the way to profitability was not for Miles.

"Hey, now. What's this?" Miles said as he opened a file entitled *Death to the West,* containing strange letters and symbols. "That's not very nice."

Miles redialed Morrison.

"Yes, Miles."

"Found something."

"And what is that, Miles?" Morrison sighed, yet his voice was kind and patient, the same way he talked to his younger grandkids.

"A newsletter from some guy saying 'Death to America' and stuff like that."

"Okay," Morrison agreed with mild frustration. "I'll come down."

Miles hung up happy. He knew that Director Morrison, once in Miles's lab, would give more specific goals. And specific goals generally made tasks easier for Miles to complete.

A minute later Director Morrison, looking presidential in a dark gray suit, entered the cozy 10-x-10 lab. "Morning, son," he said with a smile. His eyes were kind, as usual, but there were a few extra wrinkles around them this morning.

Miles leaned back, fingers laced behind his head, revealing a gold *Star Trek* emblem on the shirt that was too short for his belly. Sweat rings stained the armpits. "Oh, hey, Senator."

Morrison shook his hand. "How are you?"

"Fine. 'Cept got an e-mail today from Friends of Barney, saying I was fired and they were going to get someone else to finish the Barney project, 'cause I was four months late. Can you believe that?"

Morrison just looked at him.

"Yeah, Friends of Barney. You know, the purple dinosaur fan club. The project I was working on before you pulled me to work on this." Miles shook his head with elaborate incredulity. "I can't believe it. I chatted up the president Ralf Fuller and told him I was doing something for the Department of Homeland Security and he just said, 'You're a flake, Miles! Stop e-mailing me!' I'm a flake!" Miles displayed the same rejection a grade schooler would when nobody picked him for their baseball team.

"Speaking of national security—" Morrison spun a desk chair around and rolled up beside Miles—"what did you find?"

"I'm creating a log of the hard drive right now, but I've downloaded it to a couple different backups. Anyway, first thing I see is this Mullah Wahabi guy talking about killing Americans."

As both Morrison and Miles knew, the information could be nothing more than radical propaganda. "Hate speech," Morrison threw in. "Guy's got problems, doesn't he?"

"Yeah," Miles said. "And that isn't the only problem he has. This guy saved all these spam e-mails for free Viagra samples on his desktop."

Just then the booming sounds of Beethoven's "Fifth Symphony" chimed from Morrison's coat pocket. He reached in and removed his B-com to check it. "Looks like you've got some logging to do before we get any real news out of this." Morrison rose, placing his hand on Miles's shoulder. "Keep me up on it, would you?"

"Sure thing, Senator. I'll let you know soon as something pops."

Morrison waved, answering his phone as he left the room.

✪ ✪ ✪

SOIC (Strategic Operations Information Command) Center
Kabul, Afghanistan
2033 hours, Local Time

GONE MISSING

After the sun had dipped below the distant craggy mountains, casting cold, blue-gray shadows over the land, the temperature had dropped 10 degrees almost instantly. Weather on the high northern mountains of Afghanistan could be brutal, even in late summer. Heavy rains, flash floods, and snow flurries were not uncommon when the conditions were right.

Or wrong, as Master Sergeant C. J. Wells of the Air Force Strategic Operations Information Command imagined. Wells removed his hat as he entered the lobby of the brown brick Hotel Grand Moghul complex in Kabul, which served as the AFSOIC center in Afghanistan. The dull décor and bland colors still reflected the late '60s.

Wells was a young-faced man with slender cheeks, a bulbous nose, and clear blue eyes. He laid his file on the reception counter. "Master Sergeant Wells here for a meeting with Colonel Borland, please."

The enlisted man at the desk spun around and disappeared into the maze of cubicles behind him. He returned in a fast walk. "He'll see you now."

At the opposite end of the room a gray-haired, gruff-looking man in his fifties appeared in a neatly pressed green uniform. He summoned Wells into his office with a wave before turning around.

Wells lifted the file and briskly entered.

"Come on in." Borland reached out his hand. His head was oddly shaped, like he'd slept on it funny.

"Colonel Borland. Good to see you, sir."

Borland nodded with a tired, expressionless face. "Good to see you, Wells. I understand we've got a missing field unit."

"Yes, sir. Alfa Indigo Frank 17 of Task Force 121, sir." Wells handed the folder over to Borland. "Here's the operational history, sir."

It had been Colonel Borland's decision to send AIF 17 in for a deep reconnaissance across the Pakistani border to the rugged mountains of the Northern Quetta region. Their assignment: Make contact with friendly forces while charting enemy encampments in search of bin Laden and his men.

This unit was the best of the best. The elite of the special forces elite. Men recruited from all branches of the military—including Air Force, Navy, and Army.

Borland skimmed the pages, mumbling aloud to himself. "Seven-man unit dropped with two-man buggies and three Kawasaki 500s from a C-130 Hercules north of Quetta, Northwestern Pakistan, 92 hours ago. Um . . . hum . . . last contact at mission 3623 hours. Base camp established . . . headed out to . . . I don't know why I'm reading this when I wrote the stinking plan!"

Colonel Borland inhaled long and loud through his nose. He looked to the ceiling, then back at Wells. "Led by CIA Special Field Recon Agent Marcos Caracas and Air Force Special Operations Command Sergeant John Gordon. Do we know if they made contact with their friendly in the region?"

"According to operational intelligence," Wells reported in a monotone, "Marcos had not made contact with any friendly in the area prior to last transmission."

"Is it possible they may be in a blackout region?"

"No, sir. The SatCom CIA supplied TF 121 said that AIF 17 made a call into Langley roughly 40 hours ago."

"Who to?" Borland demanded.

"Don't know, sir. CIA's pulling the records for a communications audit today."

"Hmm . . ." Borland held his finger in the page while reaching for a map. "There it is . . . rough area." The colonel thought aloud while gently scratching the mole to the right of his chin. "Local tribesmen assisting al Qaeda, probably."

"Doesn't look good."

Closing one eye, Colonel Borland's other bright blue eye stared through Wells. "No, it doesn't. Okay, see if CIA has any intelligence on the SatCom." He clenched his jaw. "Gonna be tough. Getting the choppers that can navigate through that sort of terrain with enough range from the FOB in Kandahar. I'll look these plans over, see if we can get the logistics worked out in order to deploy a search party by tomorrow at 1200 hours."

"Very good, Colonel Borland, sir." Master Sergeant Wells saluted. "I appreciate your time."

"I'll be in contact." Borland nodded curtly before returning to his studies.

✪ ✪ ✪

LA County Sheriff's Office and Transportation Yard
Los Angeles, California
1042 hours, Pacific Time

CHAOS

This was one of the largest urban operations in which Steve had ever participated. With five to eight guys assigned to each of 17 squads, the command-and-control structure was a near nightmare. It took 15 men on different frequencies of three radio nets just to coordinate the operation. It would be impossible for one man to give orders to that many men, let alone listen to and process the constant stream of data that each OS (Observer-Sniper) Team brought in and then send it on to Charlie (Command and Control).

Working outside containment, Steve and Carter lay under the juniper bushes in full chem suits. They were behind some curbing separating the transportation yard from the prison grounds. By the time they were in place, the cloud of deadly gas had mostly subsided into nearly invisible pockets hanging near the low areas. Farther away from their spot, nearer the prison, some of the fumes had escaped the fire hoses and remained visible as a faint green haze.

There hadn't been a lot of action on the radio since the cloud had settled. Steve considered the reality of the tension that every officer must feel. His speech was muffled by the inner seal of his mask. "You know, I'd rather be confronted by a man with a gun than lay here and breathe this air, hoping my respirator doesn't fail."

"No kidding!" Carter agreed, while he took his turn on watch. "This position is redundant anyway. Nobody would chance a jump over a 15-foot wall just to run into a chlorine gas cloud. It ain't gonna happen."

"True. But somebody's got to be here if they try." A bead of condensed sweat rolled down the inside of Steve's mask. He followed it to where it pooled in the bottom, before returning his gaze to the walls and windows of the prison.

Another minute passed before Carter broke the silence. "This is ridiculous! What are they waiting for anyway?"

Steve knew Carter was already well aware of the answer, but talking helped deal with the stress. "They're setting up mobile air locks on the outer doors. Charlie's afraid that if they just go storming in, they'll contaminate the interior environment of the prison. That's why they didn't just set up C and C inside to begin with."

A frantic voice crackled onto the radio net. *"9.9.9., 9.9.9., Oz 11 to Charlie 03! 9.9.9.!"*

Steve could hear heavy coughing in the background of the transmission.

The voice continued. *"Oz 12 has been exposed!"* The sound of hacking and a gurgled screaming was louder yet. *"I repeat. Oz 12 has been exposed! Jack is choking."*

"*Stand by Oz 11,*" came the reply in a slightly elevated pitch. "*Medi-vac is en route. Confirm your position.*"

"*Directly south of the split between the Twin Towers, off the transport yard! Jack's vomiting! Oz 12 is vomiting! What do I do? Jack! Leave your mask . . .*"

Charlie 03 to OS 11: "*Keep his mask on no matter what.*"

OS 11: "*He's fighting me! Jack!*"

Steve looked west toward the place he knew the injured man must be. The situation was desperate, and Steve knew that if they didn't get OS 12 out instantly, he'd never make it. Making a decision, Steve keyed his mike: "Oz 10 to Charlie 03. Request permission to move west, to assist the downed officer."

Charlie 03 to OS 10: "*Permission granted to leave post with Oz 09 in order to assist.*"

"Oz 10, 10-4, moving southwest in trans yard." Steve left his rifle behind. It was a difficult decision, but he realized a gun would do no good while trying to resuscitate a downed officer. "Hold the position, Nine!" Steve shouted to Carter. He jumped from cover with a small pack and sprinted southwest along the chain-link fence.

A moment later the Medi-vac chopper buzzed the LAC Transportation Center. They circled once. The prop wash caused the heavy gas cloud to swirl in eddies, then the chopper gained altitude again.

Fifty more yards, Steve said to himself. He could see OS 11 wrestling around a juniper hedge similar to the one he'd taken cover behind. Before he even reached the distressed OS pair, he had swung his pack around and pulled out a small green oxygen bottle.

A pair of legs kicked and convulsed from the junipers. By the time Steve covered the remaining distance and reached the team, the body was still.

OS 11 still held the gas mask in place on his partner's face.

Steve slid to the ground. "Get him on his stomach! We've got to clear his airway!"

"What are they waiting for?" OS 11 asked.

Almost as if Charlie 03 had heard the question, the radio cut in. *"Oz 11, Medi-vac cannot get a visual of your position."*

OS 11 seemed to be in shock. He had watched his partner go into cardiac arrest—something he'd seen other times, in other settings, but likely never faced with his own partner.

Steve had to get the man's mind off his partner. "Oz 11, step out of the bushes and flag them with your flashlight!"

"Okay," was the childlike response.

Steve turned the victim and wrestled his arms under the man's chest, into a horizontal Heimlich position. He supported the body the way he had lifted the 160-pound mannequin years before during the Dummy Drag Test.

Holding the entire weight of the unconscious man, Steve thrust inward twice as hard as he could, driving the liquid out of the victim's lungs. As fluid began to drain from his slack mouth, Steve shouted, "Oz 11! I need your help!"

The sound of the chopper buzzed directly overhead.

"See that oxygen bottle?" Steve yelled. "Turn it on, pull the mouth cup off the tube, and plug it into the hydration stem on his mask."

OS 11 reacted without speaking. As the oxygen began feeding into the mask, Steve moved his hands higher on the chest, performing CPR from the modified Heimlich.

"What are you doing?" OS 11 asked.

"His lungs are filled with fluid." Steve continued chest compressions from the bent-over rowing position at a rate of about 50 per minute. "If I lay him on his back, he'll drown. We can't take off his mask, so this is the only way!" Since breathing for the victim wasn't required, Steve performed a higher-than-normal compression rate.

The chopper slowly descended. Prop wash pushed clean air downward, blasting the cloud of dust and gas away from them.

Steve's energy was flagging, but still he didn't wait for rescuers to come to him. Instead he lifted the 200 pounds of deadweight with a fireman's carry and hauled the downed officer to the chopper.

OS 11 trailed, holding the oxygen tube in place.

A pair of paramedics in bright yellow chem suits jumped from the open doorway as soon as the chopper set down. The EMTs cradled the officer's head and feet. They helped Steve load OS 12 into the chopper. OS 11 boarded behind them, still feeding oxygen through the inlet valve.

Steve backed away, panting, as the helicopter lifted off.

"Charlie 03 to Oz 10. Do you copy?"

"Oz 10, I copy you," was Steve's nearly breathless reply.

"Sending four replacements. Grab your gear for immediate departure."

"10-4." Steve staggered back to his original position. A black Suburban was there to pull him and Carter off the line.

There'd been no chance to notice before, but the wind had veered slightly. The remaining gas cloud moved toward the riverbank, where it began to settle into the LA river basin.

"Charlie 01 to all: Fans seem to be working. The last chlorine pockets are moving away from the towers."

From the tailgate of the Suburban, Steve saw eight enormous, movie-set-style, electric fan trucks blowing the air southeastward toward the river. The man-made flow was met in turn by six 10-foot-high fans on the east side of the river to keep the gas from crossing.

A Hollywood turn of events in a disaster movie.

Carter nudged Steve on the arm. "He gonna make it?"

Steve closed his eyes and shook his head. "I don't know . . ."

Minutes later the air locks of the towers were opened, allowing Echo teams to make entry with high-power and less-than-lethal weapons.

Within 10 minutes the radio net announced, *"Twin Towers 95 percent secure."*

Only 10 prisoners, including one named Junior Ramon—those who had murdered three guards in B-block control pod—continued to prolong the standoff.

The prison riot was put down with CS gas grenades and rubber bullets. With the aid of entry teams, prison officials had most of the population flattened out and resecured in a quarter of an hour.

By then Steve and Carter were well on their way to other duties, events outrunning their time to think.

FIVE

Westbound I-40
New Mexico
Saturday, 5 September
1153 hours, Mountain Time

GALLUP WE GO

The signs that flanked West I-40 out of Albuquerque were lures set to draw in travelers like fish to a hook. Tracy boomed past little towns with names reading like classic movie titles. Casa Blanca and Enchanted Mesa each promised genuine Indian treasure, rocks, pottery, fossils, silver jewelry, clean bathrooms, great food, and gas.

Probably mostly gas.

Tracy would have none of it, in spite of pleas from Justin and Connor to stop and shop at every roadside tepee. She knew that two hours strapped into their car seats of her green Chevy Tahoe were about all the boys could stand without going bonkers. But before the end of those required hours of drive time she would not pull over, no matter how they begged.

At every hole-in-the-wall she heard, "Mom! Mom! I'm hungry!"

"Hungry? How can you be hungry? You destroyed a dozen Krispy Kreme donuts 20 minutes ago!"

"Yowser ate some too."

"Then blame Yowser if you're hungry. Play I Spy, why don't you?"

Near the city of Grants the kids spied the golden arches. "Mom! There's a McDonalds! We gotta stop! We can't stand no more!"

"Connor! Justin! Listen up, boys! This morning your mama's gonna teach you boys a brand-new grown-up word. The word is *cope.* Say it with me now . . . cope. Spelled C-O-P-E. It means I'm not stoppin' till Gallup. Why don't you play paper-rock-scissors?"

Tracy slipped an old Gaither CD into the stereo and sang along as "That Old Time Religion" and paper-rock-scissors helped pass the miles to Gallup.

A little more than two hours beyond Albuquerque the sugar high from the Krispy Kreme donuts began to morph into grumpy and whiny. Third time around on the CD and Tracy stopped singing harmony. Justin's rock had broken Connor's scissors one too many times for Connor to remain calm. Even Yowser was looking mournfully at Tracy. The big dog poked his head between the seats and nudged Tracy's elbow.

It was a sure sign things were about to explode.

"Mom! Mom! I think Yowser's gotta go!"

"Mom! Mom! It's over two hours! *I* gotta go!"

"Mom! Mom! I spy a McDonald's! Cheeseburgers!"

Tracy nodded and took the off-ramp leading to a cluster of gas stations and fast-food joints on the outskirts of Gallup. She pulled into the McDonald's lot and parked beside a beat-up Winnebago. Three poodles yapped at Yowser from inside the RV windows.

Yowser drooled in Connor's hair, whined, and stared back at the creatures with the same interest a barracuda might have for a goldfish.

"Mom! Yowser's slobbering all over Connor!"

Just then Tracy's cell phone began to play "Dixie."

Mike's ring.

The poodles continued to bark. Yowser silenced them with a single deep-voiced *woof,* alerting them that he had an appetite for Poodle McNuggets.

"Dixie" played on. Tracy stared at the ID on the phone screen. Mike! *Dixie Boy.*

The boys were speechless for the first time all morning. Then Connor cried, "Answer it, Mom! It's *Dad*!"

Tracy's heart jumped into her throat. She forced herself to be cheerful as she held the phone to her ear. "Hey, Mike!"

Mike's voice was strained, weary. "Hey, Trace. How's it goin'? Y'all okay?"

"Fine. Just stoppin' for cheeseburgers."

"Where are you?"

"East of Gallup."

"Makin' pretty good time then."

"There's a playland here. I'm gonna let the boys climb around a while. Work off a little energy. Just takin' it easy, you know. Not pushin' it."

It was quiet on the other end. Had the phone cut out? Then Mike spoke. "Somethin's happened here. I can't explain it over the phone. But . . . somethin' goin' on here and I . . . I'll be glad to see you, Trace. Really . . ."

Tracy chewed her lip. How could she reply to this unfaithful, rotten heartbreaker—her creep of a husband—after he had destroyed their lives? "Yeah. Well . . . the boys'll be real glad to see you too."

"I was talkin' about seein' you, Tracy."

She swallowed hard. What game was he playing? She had heard how husbands worked to butter up wives they were divorcing so the financial settlement wouldn't be so bad. Maybe that was his game. "Don't, Mike. Not now, huh? Can't talk about that now. Gotta go. Boys are starvin'. See you soon, huh? I gotta go now."

She pushed the button and ended the call.

After a long moment Connor blurted, "Hey, Mom! Are you goin' to Disneyland with us too? After all?"

Justin whomped him on the arm. "Shut up, Connor. Can't you see she's cryin'?"

✪ ✪ ✪

Palmdale Warehouse
Palmdale, California
1058 hours, Pacific Time

CAN I BORROW YOUR TRUCK?

Lonnie Bertrand's kidneys hurt, but there was no time to think about that now. As long as there was no money for medical insurance, there would never be time to think about it. No disability coverage either.

Work when the chance presented itself was all he could do.

Every bounce of Lonnie's '96 Mack cement truck hurt like crazy, but no way was Lonnie going to turn down a job. It was tough for an owner/operator like Lonnie to get work in a hot building area like Southern California. Most of the jobs were snapped up by the giant construction outfits, with precious little left for the lone wolves.

It was not pride or ambition that kept Lonnie from signing on with Granite or one of the other large firms. Years earlier he'd tried to pick up a few extra bucks by crossing a picket line. Those union apes sure had long memories. So Lonnie had been embarrassingly eager when the call came into his office for a six-yard load.

Office was a joke. Lonnie's work space was the kitchen table of a double-wide in the Shady Grove Mobile Home Park. The caller had seemed undeterred when Lonnie answered his own phone, said he was pleased to speak directly to "the man in charge."

The caller, whose mumbled name Lonnie hadn't quite caught, had been vague about what the job was, only that he needed a load of cement immediately.

"How about forms?" Lonnie had asked, eager to sign up for more money that would mean no more work. All he had to do was call Mannie Fernandez for his crew of illegals and rake in 25 percent for locating the job.

But anyway, the answer was no.

One day's work for Lonnie and his rig.

He'd not even been asked about the cost. That was weird. Lonnie had suggested $1500 for the load, plus mileage for anything over 50 miles and got immediate agreement.

That was weird too.

"$1350 for cash."

Cash was also agreed to.

The caller had insisted on the answer to one strange question: "Is the rig an automatic transmission?"

"It's a '96 Mack, six-wheel drive, 300hp," Lonnie explained.

"But is it an automatic?"

It was. The cement truck had cost Lonnie only $17,500 at auction. Bald tires, cracked hydraulic hoses, 200,000 miles on her already . . . but after Shirley had cleaned him out in their divorce, it was the best he could afford. Besides, the drum was candy-striped blue and white, like an Eskimo barber pole. He liked that.

Lonnie spotted the industrial park right where the instructions had specified and turned right past the number sign hanging on the fence in front of the warehouse.

"Drive around to the back" was the word.

A skinny, long-haired man stepped out of a faded tan Chevy half-ton that looked even more beat-up than Lonnie's truck. He raised his hand and waved.

No forms in sight anywhere.

No work crew either.

Once introductions were complete, Lonnie asked about the job.

Longhair, who said his name was Patrick Dennison, pointed to a dirt road leading up a canyon in back of the warehouse. "That way. Mind if I ride with you?"

The jolting ride up the canyon pounded even harder on Lonnie's kidneys. Biting his lip with every pothole, sweat beaded on his forehead.

To make matters worse, Dennison kept up a string of stupid questions like a grade-school kid on a field trip. How did the dump mechanism work? How'd the wash out work? What kind of fuel mileage did the truck get? Was there any restriction on operating hours on any highways? Was it hard to drive?

Lonnie grunted and answered all his questions, including, "Power steering. How far'd you say this was?"

They turned into a box canyon. There was a broken-windowed, broken-backed shack. It—together with the weather-beaten inverted wooden pyramid of a gravel hopper near the scraped-out, 40-foot-deep quarry—was evidence of a failed sand-and-gravel pit. There was a tumbleweed-covered sandpile.

There were no forms anywhere in sight.

"Just pull around onto the grade above the pit," Dennison instructed.

"S'posed to be a one-day job, ain't it? I charge overtime after dark. Where's the forms? This the right spot?"

Dennison waved a cell phone. "S'posed to be. Some screwup. Gimme a minute." He stalked away, angrily punching numbers.

Lonnie stood above the open maw of the gravel pit. He tried not to hunch his shoulders because of the stabbing pains in his kidneys. He turned his back toward the hot Santa Ana wind. This whole setup was looking dodgy, real dodgy. He decided he'd ask for half the pay up front.

Dennison returned, looking pleased.

Lonnie didn't notice that the cell phone had disappeared or that one of Dennison's hands was in the pocket of his Windbreaker.

"There he comes now," Dennison said, pointing down the canyon.

"Who? Where? I don't see nothin'.''

Neither did Lonnie see the Taurus .38 revolver emerge from the jacket, or the bullet that entered his head behind his right ear.

Falling two score feet into the quarry and landing on his back should have made Lonnie scream with agony, but by the time he hit bottom, he was already dead.

The gun and six yards of concrete followed him into the pit.

"RIP," Dennison muttered. "And you better be right about how the rig drives itself. Now that I gotta be the driver, you'd better be right . . . or I'll dig you out and shoot you again."

✪ ✪ ✪

Holiday Inn Select
Los Angeles, California
1122 hours, Pacific Time

CAN'T REST NOW

After 23 minutes of DECOM in a fully converted fifth-wheel trailer, Steve and Carter had been given blue scrubs and a ride back to the hotel.

Carter flopped backward on his bed. "Oh, man, sleep is gonna feel so good."

"Don't count on it." Steve shook his head doubtfully, his personal cell phone to his ear.

Carter shot him a look as if he were crazy.

"I know these things, man," Steve muttered. "Our case is moving faster than you think."

Carter played the bad angel on the shoulder. "Go on. Sit down and see how good it feels."

"No way. If I sit down before we get the call, it'll be like jumping out of a car on the freeway."

Carter rolled over and belched. "Like that?"

"Something like that." Steve opened the door as his phone connected. "Hey, Cindy. Where are you?"

"Honey!" His wife's voice was filled with excitement and relief. "You're okay. Thank God. I've been praying nonstop since last night. Couldn't sleep, couldn't eat, or think about anything else." There was a pause on her end of the phone, then, "Steve? What's wrong, babe?"

Steve closed his eyes in the middle of a deep breath. "Anton got hurt."

"He did?" Cindy's voice turned worried. "Is he all right? How?"

Steve kept his answers brief. "Got burned."

"Burned? . . . Bad?"

"Pretty bad." Steve's eyes itched. He started to massage them, but remembered what the DECOM operator had told him: *"No rubbing! Even diluted chlorine's like a shot of bleach in your face."*

"Where is he?" Cindy persisted.

"He's at the UCLA Burn Center. I dunno how he is. I haven't heard."

"I'm so sorry, Steve."

"I know." Steve wanted to tell her of Anton's heroics, of how he insisted on handling the suspect himself. How he was last out and how otherwise it would have been Steve. But he didn't say any of that. He didn't want to worry her. "Just keep prayin', hon."

"Okay," she replied. "I'm pulling over. I'll pray right now."

"Pulling over? Where are you?" Steve was confused. She and their two boys weren't supposed to leave her grandmother's house until tomorrow.

"Well, babe, the kids are bored. There's nothing for them to do out here in Arizona. I hated to keep 'em out here any longer when they're already missing the first week of school."

"Oh, man—" Steve squinted with frustration—"bad timing, Cindy."

"Why? I thought you were done after the operation. Isn't it over yet? Wait a minute." Cindy's soft voice became suddenly charged. "Were you guys in the house that blew up in LA?"

"Uh, you know I can't talk about our operation." He hated not telling her the truth. But he never could hide a thing from her, especially when she already knew. "The operation is ongoing."

Cindy's concern turned to anger. "You mean you're not done yet! Steven Alstead, if the government doesn't get you killed, I'll take over the job!"

The op *would* have been concluded, Steve thought, had they caught Mabrouk and found proof of the cell's limited extent. Instead it was turning out to be an even bigger can of worms than originally thought.

"I know," he told her. "It should have been quick, but you know how these things go. Listen, where are you headed?"

"I told the kids I'd take them to Universal Studios on the way home. Tommy's waking up. Tommy, do you want to talk to Daddy?"

"Wait, babe!"

It was too late. Tommy was already on the phone. "Hi, Daddy!" his sleepy, four-year-old voice exclaimed.

"Hi, son. Are you being good for Mommy?"

"Yeah, Dad. Did you kill some bad guys? Matthew says you were gonna kill some bad guys."

Steve thought about the last eight hours. The events flashed through his mind like a DVD on 30-speed play. "No, son. We caught 'em, told 'em they were bad, and took 'em to jail."

"Oh." Tommy's voice sounded matter-of-fact. Dad routinely caught bad guys. "Love you. Here's Mom."

"Wait, son! I love you . . ."

Too late.

"Steve, I'm sorry. I already told Matthew not to talk like that to Tommy."

"Not your fault. These guys see the stuff on TV, and what else can they think? Just bust Matthew on the rear when he wakes up. And when he asks, 'What's that for?' tell him, 'That's from Dad 'cause he loves you.'"

Cindy laughed. "Some sense of humor you have, Mister Alstead."

The B-com began to buzz on top of the motel room's TV.

"Oh shoot, my other phone is ringing."

"Your girlfriend?" Cindy teased.

Steve looked at Carter, passed out on the bed. "No, she's right here. Hairy *and* bald. Figure that one out."

"Mmm, cute!"

"All right, babe. I love you. Gotta go."

"Love you too. I'll be praying for you."

"Thanks. Love." He blew her a kiss and hung up just in time to answer the B-com. "Senator Morrison."

"I wondered if you were going to answer. I was beginning to think maybe you had sat down somewhere."

"Oh no, sir. I know better than that, sir."

"Good. Carter with you?"

"Yes, sir. He's here and ready to go too."

"Teresa told me about your little sidetrack, working the off-track."

"The derailment, yeah." Steve fought back the thought of the officer he'd assisted, quickly shook it from his mind. "Pretty bad down there, but we're back in the saddle. What's up?"

"Maybe the train wreck wasn't a coincidence. We're following up on some bizarre phone traffic just prior to the event. But that's not your never-mind. This is: Got an address for this Mabrouk character's brother. Name's Hakim. He's Arab, about five-foot-eight and 155 pounds. Works at a metal-finishing factory in North Hollywood."

"Okay." Steve kicked his foot up on the nightstand, resting a notepad on his leg. "Go ahead."

"It's on Cahuenga by Universal Studios—"

"No, it's not!" Visions of Steve's last family vacation to Disneyland returned to him with new worries about Cindy and the kids. "Can't wait to break this one to Cindy . . . never mind."

Morrison finished relaying the address to Steve. "Want you to go up there and check it out. Meet with Hakim. Play it soft. You know, let him know that you are concerned about some fellas Mabrouk may be running with."

"Local law enforcement know about this yet?"

"There was some discussion ahead of time, but they don't always operate with the same priorities we do. They want to pick him up and take him in for questioning. I'd really rather follow the guy and see where he leads us. Anyway, roll on it. Can't fend 'em off long, 'specially if the connection to the derailment firms up."

"Gotcha. We're on our way." Changing the subject, Steve asked if Morrison had heard anything on Anton.

"He's been in and out of consciousness. Initial exam showed no real internal injuries, but the burns are pretty extensive. Keep him in prayer."

"Roger that."

"Okay, Steve. Keep it up. We're hoping to have this thing unraveled by nightfall."

"Big 10-4 to that."

"Let me know when you have something."

"Yes, sir, Senator."

Steve hung up and began scrambling for his clothes. Jeans and an army tan T-shirt should work nicely. He walked by Carter, who snored away. "Get up, Rogaine."

Carter hardly moved.

Steve smacked him on the foot. "Come on. We got a lead on Mabrouk's brother."

"Ow!" Carter rolled over slowly. "That'll leave a print."

"I warned ya." Steve slipped on his shoes.

Carter hurried into gear, dressing quickly. He paused with one leg in his pants, glaring up at Steve with a wrinkled forehead. "Did you just call me Rogaine?"

Pausing with a smirk on his face, Steve replied thoughtfully, "No, I said, we gotta get goin'." He began to laugh.

Carter's vengeful smile appeared permanently fixed. "I thought that's what you said. We'll see. We'll see."

✪ ✪ ✪

Nielson's Metal Finishing Factory
Los Angeles, California
1206 hours, Pacific Time

CONCERN FOR THE TERRORIST

"This is it—" Carter pointed to a semimodern, blue-and-white stucco building through the very dirty windshield of their ride—"Nielson's Metal Finishing Factory."

Steve guided the white Chevy Caprice, on loan from the LA County

Sheriff's Office, into the center turn lane, waiting out a steady stream of noon traffic. "Looks like parking is around back." He pulled into the drive that led to a large lot, the main entrance, and loading bays. Steve backed into the parking space closest to a fence dividing the property from the 170 freeway. The clunky loaner dieselled, the engine revving and stumbling even after Steve turned off the key.

Carter stared at the cracks in the dash the way a five-year-old boy looks at brussels sprouts. "Ca'piece a' junk is what they should have called it."

Steve laughed quietly. "We're lucky they even brought it by the hotel in exchange for us helping out this morning."

"Lucky?" Carter exclaimed. "I think this car is another attempt by LA county to kill us!"

Steve's snicker increased in volume when he opened the door. The sprung hinges barked so loudly he wondered if the whole thing might fall off. "Ca'piece a' junk is right!"

They made their way through the parking lot. A plan of attack had already been made on the way in: Find Hakim and express great concern for his brother, then see where that leads.

The long, low, plain building had a double set of loading docks to the north end, while its main entrance was farther south. A massive set of elaborate pipes and smokestacks comprised the burners and reburners for scrubbing paint fumes out of the air exhausted from operations.

The pair of agents approached concrete steps that led to the glass doors of the main entrance. A very petite Asian secretary peeked over the desk at them as they entered. Then in a tiny, almost childlike voice, she spoke. "Hi! My name is Kim. Are you here to pick up or drop off??"

Carter grinned broadly as he unfolded his badge wallet. "Not today."

"Oh my!" the receptionist exclaimed, almost flirtatiously. "How can I help?"

Steve made a quick inventory of the room. Two hallways led from the entry—one west to the street entrance off Cahuenga and the other north toward what he assumed was the factory floor. Seeing no one else around, Steve held his badge on the counter in front of her. "Agent Alstead of the FBI. We're here to speak with a Hakim Ziad. Is he here by chance?"

"Goodness." Kim covered her mouth with her hand. "I knew he was bad."

Carter flashed his best Mr. Clean smile. "Got a good sense about people, do you?"

Steve interrupted. "Actually, we're worried about him. Can we speak to him, please?"

Kim screwed up her face suspiciously. "Probably running with the wrong crowd. Certainly. I'll call him up."

Steve shot his hand out over the microphone as he realized too late that perhaps he'd overreacted in fear of what Kim might say. "Uh, just tell him he has a visitor."

Winking, Kim said, "Silly boy. If I tell him about you, he might run away." Turning to the microphone, she announced, "Hakim Ziad to the reception desk."

By then Carter was grinning widely, smacking his gum. "She's somethin' else, ain't she, Alstead? She's somethin' else."

Kim batted her eyes.

Steve wouldn't let himself be even the least bit distracted by her. Many times, when the shooting had stopped and all was quiet, a man poked his head out, only to have it shot off. The trick, Steve knew, was never stay put long enough to let the bad guys get a bead on your position. It was true what they said: Curiosity killed the cat. And sure as shootin', if he even turned his attention toward her for a minute, that would be the moment Hakim split.

"Your friend isn't as nice as you," Kim complimented Carter.

"That's 'cause he's shy. It's tough bein' second."

Steve rolled his eyes. What if they were close to getting a lead on Mabrouk, a possible arrest that could dismantle the cell? And Carter was chatting up some girl for a date? What a numbskull.

When Steve didn't even acknowledge Carter's comment, Carter said, "See? No personality."

Just then a man in a blue cotton coverall who fit Hakim's description—short Middle Eastern man of small build—entered the reception area.

Steve knew immediately that he wasn't who Hakim expected to meet. "Hakim Ziad?" Steve presented his badge again.

Carter cut short the dialog with the cute receptionist.

Hakim approached slowly, apprehension stretched across his face. "That is me."

"I'm Agent Alstead of the FBI."

Hesitantly Hakim asked, "How can I help you?"

For starters, you could register with Immigration, like you should have after 9/11, Steve considered saying. But instead he said, "We are very concerned about your brother."

Hakim began to look sickly. "My brother? What is it? What has happened?"

Steve cleared his throat. "Can we speak in private?" His voice expressed concern.

"I think the lounge is empty," Hakim replied.

"Talk to you later." Carter winked at Kim, who replied with pouty lips.

Steve and Carter followed Hakim into a room. Aside from a simple rectangular table, a few folding chairs, a small microwave, and refrigerator, the lounge was indeed empty.

Hakim faced them, worry in his eyes. "What has happened to my brother?"

Steve took on a very soft approach. He eyed Carter, as if laboring over what he was about to say. "He may be in great danger."

Oddly, Hakim almost seemed to cheer up. "Great danger?"

"Yes." Steve swallowed hard. "He was the victim of a hate crime last night."

"A hate crime," quizzed Hakim, curiously acting relieved. "Uh, is he all right?"

"Well," Steve added, "we don't know. Last night a racist threw something into his house and burned it down."

Dread flooded Hakim's face once more. "Burned it—"

Steve interrupted. "Mabrouk wasn't there, but one of his housemates was killed."

Hakim stood wide-eyed and speechless.

Carter added, "We're looking for him to make sure he's warned."

"Killed . . . burned down . . ." Hakim stared in disbelief.

Steve rested his hand on Hakim's shoulder. "I know. It's very scary. The anti-Islamic movement has taken over the actions of a few Americans. I'm sorry."

Hakim's face grew serious and more stern. "But Mabrouk wasn't there?"

"No," continued Steve, "and we need to know if there is anyone who might have threatened him or anywhere he might be. We are concerned for his safety."

Hakim stared at Agent Alstead in an effort to read him. One eyelid dropped a bit. "The mosque."

"The mosque?" Carter questioned. "LA Mosque?"

"Yes," Hakim agreed. "The LA Mosque. This is where he must be."

Steve handed him a business card, knowing it would be very unlikely Hakim would ever dial the number. The bait had been set, but Hakim hadn't taken the hook yet. "We'll continue to search for him, but when you see him, you must have him call us right away. It's possible that whoever set the fire is still a threat to you *and* your brother."

Hakim's eyes began to dart around. "Yes. I will call if I learn something."

"Very good, sir." Carter patted him on the arm. "We're sorry for the bad news, but thank you for your time and assistance."

"Thank you," Hakim replied, exiting the employee lounge without even looking back.

Steve and Carter followed him out, passing the receptionist.

"Thank you, miss." Steve pressed the glass door outward.

"Thanks, sweetie." Carter winked.

"Bye-bye," Kim called sadly as they departed.

After Carter had finished blowing kisses, he smacked Steve on the back. "Bet you lunch at Quiznos he makes a run for it in about ten minutes."

"Large honey-bourbon chicken?" Steve eyed him.

"You're on."

"Deal." Steve looked back over his shoulder about halfway through the parking lot to the car. "He won't call."

"Oh really, genius? What gave you that idea?"

"Well, obviously, he wouldn't, but I always like to search for tiny clues in their words."

"And?"

"If—" Steve raised his eyebrows as if that one word had life-changing significance—*"if,* instead of *when.* That's what he said. Hakim had already decided he was never going to call us. Of course he'll find out something about his brother. He'll be making phone calls right now. But anyone who was genuinely concerned, not afraid of trouble but concerned, would have said, 'I'll call you *when* I find something.'"

Now back at the car, keys in hand, Steve paused for dramatic effect.

Carter gave off an aura of one suitably impressed. "Oh, Hakim," he mocked. "We're so worried for your poor sweet brother, the terrorist."

"I'll admit, it's a liberal's agenda if ever I heard one," Steve jabbed.

Carter took a verbal shot back. "You know, you're pretty smart for someone with no personality! Now open the door before I break a window."

"Wouldn't be that hard." Steve pressed down on the glass. To his satisfaction, the window slipped a few inches . . . just enough for him to reach inside and unlock his door manually.

With one eye closed, Carter harassed him. "Now you're just showing off."

Steve released the other door lock and immediately began to dial out on his B-com. A moment later the call connected. "Senator Morrison?"

"Hey, Steve. How'd it go?"

"Well, he didn't swallow the bait, but he's nibbling. Got a possible lead pointing to the LA Mosque."

"Already under surveillance," Morrison noted. "Thanks for the confirmation. And I've got Miles on a wiretap. We just got authorization about five minutes ago to tap and record all the phones at Nielson's Metal Finishing Factory, as well as trap and trace the calls."

"Nice." Steve bobbed acknowledgment toward his distant boss. "If Hakim knows where Mabrouk's hiding, he'll be itching to call and find out what's going on."

Morrison coughed. "Let's just hope he isn't smart enough to use a coworker's cell phone."

"Possible, but I doubt it. He seemed scared. I'll bet he leaves work early to track his brother down." Steve squinted through the dusty windshield. "We'll find a better hiding place so we can follow when he leaves."

"Sounds like a plan. I'll let you know if we get anything interesting on the phones in the meantime."

"I appreciate it, Senator."

"You bet, Steve." Morrison disconnected.

Steve started the car and pulled out in search of a better place to park. "Would have been better if we'd walked up."

"Tell me about it." Carter leaned on the window. "Didn't count on a stakeout. How 'bout that hotel parking structure there?" He pointed.

"Dark enough to back into while still leaving a view of the parking lot exit." Steve waited for traffic before speeding off down the road. A few blocks over he flipped a U-turn and headed back, quickly ducking into the shadows of the parking garage.

SIX

VOICE FROM THE PAST

Middle-aged Coleson Specter pressed his broad tortoiseshell-rimmed glasses higher up the bridge of his nose as he strode down the endless empty corridor. His combed-over hair and tweed jacket and the fact that he worked for the Agency made him a perfect character from any of the '70s spy flicks.

As a young man Coleson had been unpopular, except for a small group of friends on the cross-country team at Kenmore High School in Akron, Ohio. Due to his small-framed physique, his frumpy dress style, and his overbearing intellectual approach, females rarely, if ever, found him attractive. The jocks called him Coleslaw. Even his male friends considered him a little too self-important to hang with much.

When he wasn't running or studying, Coleson had spent his time reading spy novels. Lots of them. Anything and everything he could find. At 18, he imagined himself one day cracking the Soviet super-computer, while disguised as a visiting Romanian dignitary, thus causing the USSR to crumble from within. With a name like Specter,

Coleson was destined to be a national hero. Everyone would love him, Coleson fantasized.

But now he was 46. The Soviet Union had long since crumbled—no credit due to him—shortly after he was recruited to Langley Headquarters as a low-level analyst. Working for the CIA had been nothing like he imagined in his younger days. In reality, he sat in a basement cubical, reading data and graphs; sometimes strings of numbers were all he saw. After 17 years of service, he still knew little about that to which he had dedicated his life.

Sure, he'd reached G-14 pay rate when he moved into the Communication Auditing Division, though it made little difference to the women he knew. After all these years, Coleson was still the same self-important, nerdy guy he had been in high school. Mostly people saw him as Coleslaw rather than Specter.

Coleson's flap of hair bounced in smooth rhythm with his unnaturally lengthened stride as he approached his office. He held up his security pass on its metal bead necklace and pressed his lips together, making his best Clint Eastwood face. *Firefox*, a film where the famous actor sneaked into Russia to steal the world's most advanced aircraft, had truly changed Coleson's life.

Now he was both nerdy *and* he sneered. It was not an attractive combination.

The unimpressed security guard waved Coleson in without speaking.

"Hi, Linda." Coleson swayed as he waited at the counter for the secretary's response. "Busy saving the world today?" His laugh was clumsy, distractingly so.

The plump brunette wearing a red blouse continued to type away on a keyboard without so much as an acknowledging glance. Her response was subdued. "Hey, Specter."

Coleson waited a moment longer, swinging his head as he considered the sheer wit of his own greeting. "Okay—" he conceded defeat—"I'll be in my office."

His words must have floated right over Linda's head, for she never responded.

The 12-x-12-x-10-foot white walls of his government office were empty. His superior had told him when he moved in, "No nail holes!" Probably believed—or hoped—that Specter wouldn't be around long enough to warrant decorating.

Coleson stared briefly out his third-story window at a miniscule, concrete-floored courtyard, which functioned more for drainage than for viewing pleasure. He sighed before turning to his desk.

A stack of documents lay waiting to be analyzed. The word *Priority* stamped in bold letters on top of the first page caught his attention. He read the report objectives: "Compare and contrast call data from missing SatCom and incoming call logs. Determine final extension of originating call."

It never occurred to Coleson to ponder how easily he could be replaced by a computerized scan of spreadsheets. His job was not to reason why.

Coleson began comparing data on the CIA satellite phone log with the incoming logs for all of Langley Air Force Base in area code 757. Last call on the phone log was made to prefix 931. He searched the Langley AFB incoming logs, a stack about half an inch high, matching the date of the last call on the SatCom. Discovering the 931 section, Coleson pried the staple from the thick document, removing the section of interest, before restapling the documents in two separate stacks.

"Hmm." While scanning, Coleson ran his hand gingerly, one direction only, over his hair as if he were stroking a cat. Then back to the SatCom record.

Aloud he murmured, "Looks like whoever made the call dialed the security encrypted line . . . 931-0000, entering the pass key code at . . ." Coleson, already tired of his own voice, subsided into unuttered thoughts.

He refined his search further on the list of Langley incoming calls, stabbing a forefinger at a listing like he was reprimanding an unruly subordinate. Coleson folded back the newly stapled pages. He held his finger at the top of a list of 23 calls that were logged near the same time the SatCom registered the outgoing call.

At what moment did he enter the encryption key to get into the system? The phone-system log at Langley AFB was accurate down to the hundredth of one second. The SatCom, however, was not. Its record was complete only to the second. A dilemma surfaced like a splinter too short to pull out. Coleson was temporarily stumped.

As a communications auditor, he knew the specifics of his job were not always appreciated by others. In fact, most people hated him for it, since most of his efforts revolved around busting employees for making personal calls to friends and family around the world at the department's expense. He couldn't just start dialing the list of extensions to ask the random individuals, "Did you get a call from a SatCom a couple of days ago?"

Not a good idea.

He tapped his fingers rapidly on his desktop before lifting the telephone. "Hi, Linda. Get me Com-Data, please." Coleson leaned back in his chair, one hand on his small potbelly and the other again stroking his flap of hair. The receiver was held in place by his bony shoulder.

When a voice answered, Coleson quickly sat up, as if he'd been caught sleeping on the job. "Yes, this is Coleson Specter, Communications Auditing. I'm working on a trace for SatCom." He rattled off a series of numbers. "Can you tell me if this phone was issued to anyone with another extension at the 931-0000 number? I'd like to cross-reference commonly called numbers with it to see if any of them match my list."

"Sure, Mr. Specter," an eager, young voice replied. "I can do that for you right now. I'll compile a list and send it electronically."

Coleson recognized the voice of Melvin Ritchie, another numbers guy who made great lunch company. *At least somebody respects me,* Coleson thought to himself while waiting.

"Should be there now," Ritchie informed him.

"Thank you, Melvin," Coleson responded politely.

Opening the e-file, Coleson compared the list of names and numbers for the extensions. No matches. He pored over the chart again.

His phone rang. It was the young man from Com-Data. "What's up, Melvin?"

"I'm not sure if you needed the name of the person who was issued the SatCom or not, but I thought I'd ask."

Resourceful young man should know better, Coleson considered. How could an auditor be objective if he knew the name of the person he was auditing? Might be someone he knows.

But Coleson Specter was stumped this time. He thought a moment before agreeing, "Okay, give it to me."

"Marcos Caracas; he called extension number 2349, but you didn't hear it from me."

Coleson wrote it down. "You got it." He hung up, thinking, *2349 . . . 2349 . . . why does that number sound familiar?* He checked the sheet of incoming destination extensions again. "That's why." He nodded to the pigeon on the window ledge after spotting the same number on the sheet. "Wonder who that is." He considered calling the number, but what if someone answered?

This time he dialed Melvin in Com-Data directly.

"This is Melvin Ritchie."

"Hey, Melvin, Specter here. One more favor . . ."

"Sure. Whatever you need."

"Need a name for extension 2349."

"One minute . . . Caracas, Marcos."

Odd, very odd, Coleson pondered. *Why would this guy be calling himself?* "Uh, Melvin, one more thing?"

"Anything. You got it."

"I need a voice-mail pass code for him." Expecting resistance, Coleson cringed.

Melvin's voice crackled. "But, sir, you know I'm not authorized to release that information outside my department."

Coleson coaxed, "Melll-viiin! Come on, buddy. Gotta bend a little if you wanna be a super spy. You know auditing supercedes regular channels." Coleson was impressed by his own resourcefulness.

Silence on the other end.

"Come on, Mel," Coleson wheedled. "You know when you promote next my recommendation is going to be five-star. . . ."

Melvin gave in. "Okay, sir. 2349, but I never talked to you about this." Ritchie hung up.

Coleson considered his plan of attack. "I can dial and if anyone answers, I'll just hang up. Yeah." Coleson dialed the number, finger over the kill switch. Five rings were followed by Marcos Caracas's greeting. Before the beep, Coleson entered the pass code.

The phone system clicked, and a female voice told him, "You have one message."

Coleson reclined in his preferred position to savor the result of his detective work.

"First message: 'This is Marcos!'" The recorded voice was frantic, hoarse, and overlaid with grimacing pain. "'This is Marcos! AIF 17. In Quetta region . . . in gorge . . . ohhhh! I met . . . informant . . . gave me proof—audio tape of UBL . . . al Qaeda.'" The sound of panting, then, "'Stuffed in cleft . . . before I fell. Someone . . . trying to kill me!'" Then a gunshot echoed.

Coleson heard the sound of a leaden smack and a groan. There were a few more seconds of ambient noise and a final, definitive *beeeep.*

Coleson could hardly believe his ears. This might be the biggest intelligence find of the year. He listened to the recording two more times, just to be sure of what he had heard.

Someone had intercepted a communiqué and been killed! But the tape was hidden! Now Coleson Specter was possibly the only one in the world to know about it!

Illusions of grandeur from Coleson's younger days glowed like embers, awakened by a new breath of excitement in the ashes of his mind. This information might unravel an al Qaeda plot . . . or bring them down altogether!

"Linda!" Coleson shouted into the intercom. "Get Section Chief Dixon on the phone!" He didn't even wait for her to reply. "Never mind," he yelled at the intercom, while snatching up the stacks of papers. "I'll find him myself!"

Coleson rushed out the door, headed for stardom and . . . a medal?

Old Coleslaw might be a national hero after all!

✪ ✪ ✪

Westbound I-40
Arizona
1319 hours, Mountain Time

ANYTHING FOR LOVE

Signs for *Painted Desert Visitors' Center* loomed ahead. Tracy glanced at her cell phone. No service. She had promised to phone Mama around lunchtime.

New Mexico in her rearview mirror, Tracy drove through country that looked like something right out of an old John Wayne/John Ford movie. Arizona. Real different from Arkansas. Barren. Red rocks and pinnacles. Beautiful. Rugged. Tracy liked it. It made her feel proud to be an American.

All these years Mike had told her she ought to come along with him, see the country. He had been right. Why had she refused? When he asked her to join him on his trips, she had trembled at the idea. She'd never even been in an airplane.

Tracy had lived her entire life in Arkansas. She had not traveled farther west than Oklahoma City to see the National Memorial honoring those who had died in the bombing there. On her thirteenth birthday her daddy and mama had taken her to Opryland in Nashville, where she got Loretta Lynn's autograph. That was a big deal. Enough excitement, Tracy always said, to last her a lifetime. Then she and Mike went to Branson, Missouri, for their honeymoon.

And that was pretty much it.

No wonder Mike had gone off and found himself another woman. A French woman. Somebody who liked to travel with him and see America.

So what was Tracy doing now? What? Home was a long way behind her. This time, at Mike's request, she had done something she had never done before. She had left everything familiar in hopes of finding his love still waiting for her at the end of the journey.

How gullible could she be?

Was it really possible? Tracy wondered. Could Mike really believe—actually imagine—that he could snap his fingers and she would come running now after so many years of refusing to budge?

Well, yes. He could. He did.

And he was right. Tracy *had* come running.

Desperate for love, she lowered the sun visor and drove faster on West I-40.

The boys, smelling of fries and burgers, were asleep in the backseat. Yowser snored in the very back of the SUV.

Tracy listened to Dr. Laura's radio program through two call-ins from women who were as stupid about their husbands as Tracy was. No help there. Men like Mike really were total jerks. Tracy had not needed Dr. Laura to point that out to her.

Three months ago, after Mike announced he wanted a divorce, Tracy's mama shook her head and prayed and prayed that Mike would come to his senses. But if he didn't, Mama said, then Tracy was indeed a "grass widow," but a widow nonetheless. Not her fault or her shame. No different than any woman whose husband had died. Only Mike was still alive.

What was it Mama always said? "Life is all about the journey toward heaven. When you get there, it means life on earth is done. Better enjoy what comes your way, or you'll blink, and the trip will be over."

For the sake of her boys Tracy would have to keep living and trust the Lord to see her through! She would have to rely on Jesus to meet her needs in spite of the outcome!

So when every aspect of their marital disaster was dissected and analyzed for the thousandth time and Tracy was still abandoned for another woman, her life all came down to one grown-up word: *C-O-P-E.* Tracy would survive without Mike. After months of tears and recriminations, she knew that now.

Mama said she could survive and be bitter. Or she could survive and be happy. Happiness required that she make choices. Move on. Build a new life. Like it or not, circumstances propelled her down a road she had not chosen and could not have imagined.

Cope. A grown-up word for grown-up Christians. It meant "trust and keep on keeping on." There was no way to get off the ride until she arrived at the gates of heaven. Nobody said it would always be fun or easy.

Suddenly back in the cell-phone service area, the ringer began to play "Dixie." Tracy exhaled loudly and picked up the phone. No mistake. The letters on the screen spelled "Dixie Boy."

She couldn't help the song that began to flash through her mind:

> *I wish I was in the land of cotton,*
> *Old times there are not forgotten!*
> *Look away! Look away! Look away. . . .*

Justin awoke. "Mom? It's Dad. You gonna answer it?"

Tracy pushed the button, ending the call. "Nope. Guess not."

The highway sign read *Painted Desert Exit ¼ mile.*

Justin asked, "Hey Mom, can we stop?"

"Not two hours yet," Tracy replied.

Then she remembered: It's all about the journey.

The Painted Desert Visitor Center was just ahead. Tracy put on the blinker, slowed, and followed a silver van to the exit. *Okay,* she told herself, *so maybe Mike is waiting at the end of the interstate.*

But in the meantime she would stop long enough with her sons to see what was along the way.

ELFS Room
FBI, Chapter 16 Offices
San Francisco, California
1219 hours, Pacific Time

QUACK!

Miles switched between two keyboards the way a primate swings from tree to tree. At times he even made primal noises, grunting and snuffing.

Lines of code, indecipherable to anyone but Miles, streamed across the screen on his left. He slurped his watered-down fountain soda. A puddle of condensation marked the counter. Swinging back to his right, he entered the print command. An instant later sheets of paper began to shoot from the printer. Miles examined the phone records from Nielson's Metal Finishing Factory.

A list of phone numbers and names, some businesses and others private individuals, were marked by date and time and categorized as Incoming or Outgoing. The documents were quite similar to a cellular phone bill, except that Miles had cross-referenced all the numbers in a database to produce a list of the names and addresses tied to each number.

He rang Charles Downing, formerly with the CIA but now working exclusively for Chapter 16 as their profiling specialist.

Three minutes later, Downing, sharply dressed as usual, with not one black hair out of place, arrived in Miles's ELFS room.

"Good work, Miles," Downing complimented the resident ape man. "This is really handy. It will literally save hours of research. The guys in the call center have enough to do, monitoring Nielson's calls."

"Glad you like it," Miles responded without looking up. He grabbed hold of the desk, then flung himself and the gliding office chair across the room. He skidded to a stop beside a third terminal. "Oh yeah, we've got action from the Web trace."

Downing glanced over the printouts.

"Somebody sent another Viagra e-mail to this guy's account."

Downing's face remained expressionless. "Anything else?"

"Nope." Miles clicked the e-mail open. "Just another spam with gibberish. I think it's voodoo to make you buy the stuff, but the link just goes to some nonexistent Web site."

"There's a link?" Lowering the phone log, Downing made his way over. "But it doesn't go anywhere?"

"Nope." Miles contorted his face by squinting and puckering. "I don't know why someone would keep sending spam with an address to nowhere. Quack doctor must be crazy." He interrupted himself. "Ever really listen to the word *quack*?"

"No, uh . . ." Downing's interest in the spam e-mail had been piqued. He was trying to keep Miles on task. "You got a lot of these then?"

"Least one a day. *Quack!*"

Leaning forward, Downing quizzed him. "All from the same address?"

"*Quack!* Yep." Miles interlaced his fingers and stretched. "That's a really funny word. *Quack!*"

"Did you check out the sender?"

Miles shook his head. "Everybody gets these. These and links to pornography Web sites."

Downing pulled up a chair. "But they usually come from different addresses. I rarely, if ever, notice getting one from the same e-mail."

"I'll run a trace. See if I can find out where this crummy doctor is. You know, he prob'ly doesn't have any Viagra to sell anyway. You know? Prob'ly just runnin' a scam." Miles handed Downing a stack of all the printed e-mails from the last month. "Anything older'n that'll take a day to dig up. *Quack!*"

Even though he was annoyed, Downing calmly turned to Miles. "Miles, would you mind please not doing that?"

Miles clenched his jaw and showed his teeth. "Oh. Sorry."

Downing leafed through the pages, skipping over the propaganda, comparing the spam e-mails for similarities. Strings of random words filled the background of the messages, each group capitalized at the front and punctuated at the end. "Somebody acts like they're writing complete sentences." He handed the documents back. "You might be on to something."

"Keep 'em," Miles offered with a warning. "Just don't use your credit card if you decide to order."

Downing blinked, unsure if Miles was serious or joking. Serious, he decided. "Sounds like good advice, Miles. Thanks."

"Anytime." Miles grinned with squinted eyes before he glided back to the first keyboard, his feet paddling like a duck's. *"Quack!"*

✪ ✪ ✪

Hotel Parking Garage
Cahuenga Boulevard
Los Angeles, California
1234 hours, Pacific Time

GRAB IT WHILE YOU CAN

Perhaps the greatest irony of working for the FBI's Hostage Rescue Team, or any other elite law-enforcement outfit, was the downtime in the field. Steve was a guy who trained for eight hours a day to shoot and fight, jump out of aircraft, and climb rock walls. His whole life revolved around getting the call that would vault him into action on a mission to save the world. And here he was—on a mission to save the world—sleeping in a stinky old car in a parking garage. For all the time dedicated and all the responsibility, how funny was it that so many operations involved so much downtime?

The most serious crises produced standoffs that might last days or even weeks. The standoff at the Branch Davidian Compound in Waco, Texas, lasted for 51 days. It happened before Steve's time in HRT but was still noteworthy. A couple hundred FBI people shuttled back and forth from hotels for weeks on end. Each day they rode in a Bradley armored carrier through a field to a pile of sandbags in a shop overlooking the compound for 12-hour shifts.

How boring and frustrating was that? Lying behind a rifle for 51 days, away from home and family, while nothing happened.

In Steve's line of work, one never knew how long the job might last or how long it might be before he'd get a proper night's rest. Like free drink refills or a fumbled football, Steve's motto regarding sleep stood paramount: Grab it while you can. So leaning back in the driver's seat, with his arms crossed and a black ball cap pulled over his eyes, Steve snored through Carter's watch.

✪ ✪ ✪

From the shadows of the parking garage, Cater could survey Nielson's Metal Finishing Factory's main entrance and the exit door on the side street. For the last 35 minutes he'd been listening to a classic rock station; currently "Juke Box Hero" played on the lone working auto speaker.

At the first sight of the street-side door opening, Carter jolted forward. A man wearing traditional Muslim garb with a head scarf and robe walked a bike out of the building. Carter scowled. "Hakim, is that you, you dirty sucker?"

Thick dirt on the windshield badly obscured his view. Carter reached over and slapped the wiper control stick, before backhanding Steve.

Steve woke with a start, instinctively swinging up his right arm to guard his throat. "What? What!"

Dirt clumped around the edges of the wide arcs on the windshield, before sliding downward.

"Look at that guy." Carter pointed as the man swung a leg over the seat. "Is that Hakim?"

A rush of traffic intermittently blocked their view. There was hardly time to discern if the face was the same as their quarry's as the man pedaled away. The clothes had obviously changed. Steve looked to the shoes as a last resort. "Brown Rockport-style hiking boots. That's him!"

"I knew he'd try to sneak out!" Carter fastened his seat belt.

"Maybe you should have bet on that," Steve kidded Carter. Steve adjusted his hat before cranking the ignition. The starter ground, its gears clicking and stuttering, before growling down to silence. "Battery's dead." Steve snapped off the radio with exasperation.

Carter punched the dash. "I'm not gonna chase this fool on foot!"

"Carter, now is a good time to consider prayer."

"You gotta be kiddin' me."

"Not saying you have to," Steve countered. "Just saying it's a good time." Concentration caused wrinkles on his face as he said out loud, "Please, Lord. This may be important. Maybe for the safety of innocent American lives. Please let this car start."

Carter looked on sourly. "And that's gonna do it?"

"Wait a minute." Steve hesitated with his hand on the key. "Gotta work, please God." He twisted. The engine lurched—once . . . twice—then it caught, igniting with a roar. "Told you. Get Morrison on the phone."

"That was luck. No—" Carter corrected himself as he began to dial—"that was science. The battery just needed a minute to rest."

"Believe what you want," Steve argued, "but you'll never know how often prayer helps until you try it." He slipped the car into Drive and slowly pulled out of the garage to recover a view of Hakim. "Faith in small miracles first, Carter. Good practice for when you need the big ones."

"This is Morrison." Steve could hear the senator's cheerful voice from the driver's seat.

"Senator, this is Carter. Got an update. Hakim just left the building on a bicycle."

"Bicycle. Very tricky." There was a pause and a sigh.

Steve caught sight of Hakim about a quarter mile down Cahuenga, headed northwest. "Tell him we've got a little time, but if we don't get a Ped team out here to follow him, he may slip away."

"I agree," Morrison replied, evidently overhearing Steve. "Okay, stick with him. I'll get Special Operations Director Davis on the phone to get some help ASAP."

"10-4." Carter ended the call. "Just follow real slow, bubba."

"I don't know if this car has any other speed." Steve pulled out into traffic. "Hakim could probably outrun the old Ca'piece." As they passed his favorite sandwich place, Steve called out, "Hey, Quiznos. I almost forgot. You owe me two."

SEVEN

Canyon Hills Mall
Los Angeles, California
Saturday, 5 September
1249 hours, Pacific Time

COLD LEAD

Steve let the vehicle coast a safe distance behind Hakim, careful not to reveal themselves to him. Steve was certain the suspect had fresh images of himself and Carter plastered across the front of his mind.

Hakim searched his surroundings nervously as he chained the 21-speed mountain bike to the mall's bike rack. He fumbled with the combination lock, pausing frequently whenever he saw something that made him nervous.

"Look at him squirm." Carter nodded.

"He knows something. That's for sure." Steve guided the Caprice slowly through a stop sign.

Hakim was temporarily lost from view by a passing double-trailer UPS truck. When the truck no longer obscured their view, Hakim was gone.

"He's gone inside!" Steve swerved toward the curb, stopping a couple feet past a wall, where any view of their car would be blocked. Slamming it in park, he snapped, "Get out."

Carter snagged his light blue Windbreaker from the backseat. "Give me your hat."

Steve tossed it out the window as Carter shut the door. "You follow him. I'll keep driving around out here. Set your B-com to 'radio' and let me know when you spot him."

"10-4." Carter slammed the door, hurrying off as fast as he could without looking like he had someone to chase.

Steve flipped open his B-com like a sunglasses case. When the concealed miniature keyboard and screen were faced down, the phone was set to speaker mode. Steve dialed Morrison. "Senator, Agent Thomas has just entered the Canyon Hills Mall on foot, following Hakim. What's the status of the Ped teams?"

"Just one team, Steve. When I notified LAPD we were pursuing a cyclist, they sent a pair of bike cops."

Steve slapped his forehead. "Not gonna work in there."

"I got Dispatch on the phone right now. Hang on." Morrison's voice grew distant while he talked to someone else. "Yes, he's in the mall now. Thank you, but understand that it's critical this man not know we're trailing him. He's a person of interest we hope will lead us to Suspect No. 1. Thank you. Please advise all officers to hang back. Thank you." Senator Morrison returned to Steve.

"I got it." Steve checked over his shoulder before whipping the car away from the curb to head toward the back of the mall. "Now, let's hope they do it." Steve's B-com beeped. "Senator, I've got Agent Thomas here."

"10-4."

Steve clicked over to Carter. "Alstead to Carter. What's your 10-20?"

A few seconds of silence followed before Carter replied in a whisper, "He's keeping a good pace, almost halfway through the mall. My guess is—" His voice suddenly stopped.

"Agent Thomas?" Steve waited. Had Carter been spotted or jumped? Was he lying low, or had something else happened?

The short silence was agonizing as Steve determined the best course of action. "Agent Thomas, do you copy?" Without a reply, Steve couldn't know if the reception was bad inside the building or if things had broken into a foot pursuit.

Steve hopped on the gas to circle the sprawling structure, headed for the opposite side toward where he guessed Hakim might emerge.

"Agent Thomas..." In a whisper Carter was back in radio contact. "Almost spotted me. Had to play dumb. Suspect moving south toward rear, 100 yards from the opposite entrance."

Steve's quick thinking had been right on the money. "I'm more'n halfway there."

"Two bike cops at the door. Idiots," Carter lamented. "They're looking and pointing right at him. Wait a minute. Suspect has turned left. He's now headed into Macy's."

Steve saw the store's sign just down the way. "I'm rolling up on it now. I'll hang back in one of the parking rows."

"10-4."

Steve noted one of the bicycle cops round the building, rolling full speed down the sidewalk. "What does he think he's doing?" Steve worried aloud.

The officer barged right up to the door, arriving the moment Hakim burst out. The glass panel flung open, smashing the cop in the head. His helmet protected him from serious injury, but the force was still enough to knock him over on his bike and disorient him.

"Here we go." Steve gunned the Caprice just as Hakim broke into an all-out run. Steve swerved in front of him, causing Hakim to tumble over the fender and lurch along the driver's side.

Steve slammed the car into Park, reaching out the window toward Hakim. Steve snagged the robe. He heard a ripping sound as Hakim tore free and sprinted off. Another instant and Steve was free of the seat belt and dashing after him.

Hakim approached the main street. Steve called on his peripheral vision to search the traffic for approaching danger. Hakim hurdled the hedge and a low block wall, crashed through a line of commuters waiting at a bus stop, and bolted into the street. Cars swerved and skidded, temporarily polluting the atmosphere with tire smoke and blaring horns. Hakim spun halfway around to view the chaos in his wake.

But his concern was too late. As he swung back around, a public transit bus was skidding to avoid him. The right front tire bounced up on the curb at the same moment Hakim did. Without even time to scream, he shielded his head before impact. The massive vehicle collided with him, knocking him 20 feet into a light pole.

Still sliding out of control, the bus crashed into the pole a moment later, pinning Hakim somewhere between the bumper and the sidewalk. The light pole flew through the air and crashed into the hood of a pickup in the nearby parking lot.

Steve paused at the edge of the street to take it all in. He shook off the shock, flashing his badge to traffic as he came to his senses.

Carter joined him as they loped toward the accident.

The bicycle cops arrived shortly after, one of them speaking into a walkie-talkie. "One Berry 3 to Control 1, request immediate EMS at the corner of . . ."

Near the front of the bus, Steve and Carter knelt, afraid of what they might find. Even after all his training, the grisly sight stole Steve's breath away. Hakim had been crushed between the sidewalk and the front axle. *Stay calm,* Steve told himself.

Passengers were rushing toward the exits of the bus. He realized that witnesses would be wandering off, even mixing with people who had other perspectives of the incident. The urgent need to stop them from leaving the bus distracted his mind from the brutal reality underneath.

Steve rushed to the front door as people began to exit. "Ladies and gentlemen, please remain in your seats. Keep calm."

People stared at him as if he were crazy. "What do you mean sit down?" one passenger demanded. "We just ran over a guy."

"Please return to your seats. Someone is badly hurt, and it will help if you stay calm and be patient. Do not exit the bus."

Sirens approached in the distance. An ambulance.

Steve left the bus and tortured himself with another look at Hakim's body, hoping it wasn't quite as bad as he'd first thought. But halfway down on his knees this time, Steve knew for certain that Hakim would not be leading them to Mabrouk today . . . or any other day.

✪ ✪ ✪

FBI, JTTF (Joint Terrorism Task Force) Technical Investigation Lab
Los Angeles, California
1324 hours, Pacific Time

HIDDEN LIVES

Special Agent Kristi Kross removed a tray from an evidence-drying unit. The unit was a stainless-steel box, like an oven, but with more sensitive controls and a much lower operating temperature. It was an invaluable replacement for the old clothesline when it came to processing evidence.

Swinging her long blonde hair aside, Kristi placed the tray on the white Formica counter. In it was the cashier's check for $2300 recovered in the raid, the check now sporting a reddish hue caused by soaking in the chemical Ninhydrin. Dark circular images now stood out like bacon-grease spots on a futilely washed tie.

Fingerprints.

Kristi smiled; her aqua eyes flashed, displaying her delight.

Prints everywhere! Wonderful, lovely paisley-patterned prints! All over the check.

She imagined whose they might be. Already the story of the lives the check had passed through appeared in her mind. From its printing to its capture, the secrets held by this single scrap of paper were about to be revealed.

A clear set of perfect thumbprints—one on both right and left sides—were probably made by the handler as he carried this check on top of a stack of similar ones before placing them into a machine. Somewhere out there in the world his other eight prints were on the back of another check that had been on the bottom of the heap.

Four fingerprints of a left hand also shone brightly around the bank's identification area. Judging from their small size and dark clarity, they were probably made by a young cashier with small hands, freshly moistened with lotion. Kristi imagined a young college student pressing firmly as she wrote in the details. An interesting mark in the center of the ring finger almost jumped off the rouge paper. The design looked like a tiny rose surrounded by circles.

Another set—and the one that interested Kristi the most—was similar to the four smaller ones, except they were lower on the check and larger in size. This group was made by the left hand of a man, Kristi deduced. They were marked up, flawed by the nicks and scratches caused by hard labor. Someone with rough, dry hands.

Kristi looked at the signature line. She'd bet he made those when he signed. "I'll be lifting those first," she resolved aloud.

A few other faint sets had painted the check at random all over. The buyer's, the bank manager's, the receiving clerk's prints, Kristi knew, were all on there somewhere.

Kristi slipped on her latex gloves, grinning. She loved to discover the story a single document could tell. Hopefully all the characters in this story would have faces and names, identified somewhere in the vast database called Identex used to store and compare fingerprints.

Placing the check into a scanner, Kristi waited for the image to process onto her computer screen. An invisible curtain wiped slowly from left to right across the monitor, revealing a blown-up copy of the Kool-Aid-colored check.

She sighed deeply, settling in at the keys. With a complex formulation process the computer program would allow her to separate the image into layers, lifting away each set of prints. Each individual's mark could then be isolated and fed into Identex singularly.

In a couple more hours, like ghosts caught in a jar, all of these lives, once held together by a single sheet of paper, would be free and separate again . . . and perhaps recognizable.

✪ ✪ ✪

ELFS Room
FBI, Chapter 16 Offices
San Francisco, California
1331 hours, Pacific Time

MILES, PHONE HOME!

Miles Miller had tried everything, explored every possible avenue of tracing the e-mails through the Internet. His conclusion was that, without detailed legal authorization or some serious code-breaking software and a whole lot of time, the perp would be nearly impossible to track.

The sender of the messages had used proxy servers to send and route these messages similar to what the terrorist mastermind Khalil had done in his e-mails about Prussian Blue and the resulting Chapter 16 operation, Firefly Blue.* Miles had been able to defeat that encryption device and crack the e-mail by using a program he created. Firefly filtered e-mail for target words in the subject line. Once the program found a match, *bing!* Firefly contacted Carnivore, the FBI's supercomputer.

But this case was different. The sender was using proxies, which made things difficult to trace, but not impossible. The real difficulty in tracking the Viagra spam e-mail was the fact that it *was* spam. There was no signature text string in the messages that Miles could program Firefly to find. Literally tens of millions of e-mails for vitamins and drugs were sent out over the Internet every day, making spam the perfect hiding place for secret messages.

The fact that the sender had gone to such lengths to keep his identity secret made Miles certain he was onto something significant. "You can't sell something to people if they can't buy it," Miles hypothesized. If not to hide something illegal, why would someone go to such lengths for a message that was essentially worthless?

And so Miles had spent the previous hour lifting gibberish out of e-mails and into ET, his Encryption Translator. ET, aptly named after the extraterrestrial creature that had appeared in the movie, indeed

---

*For more heart-stopping action and suspense, read book 2—*Firefly Blue*—in this series.

seemed to have extraterrestrial powers and a mind of its own. It could take just about any string of coded letters and numbers and, with enough time, find the common threads, one strand at a time. Eventually a new alphabet was born that made perfect sense to ET and in the very next instant . . . *bang!* The encrypted message would become as clear and simple as the ABCs.

Miles highlighted the messages in the e-mails and, with an Aladdin Switcher, dragged them over onto another screen. He dropped them in an export box that read *ET.*

Though working alone, Miles made his voice raspy like the alien in the Steven Spielberg film and chortled, "Miles, phone hooooome! Phone home! Phone home! Phone home!" He clicked *Send.* The export file visually flattened out on the screen, then shot out of view like a rocket. An instant later a small chime sounded from the silver-and-gray box that served as the electronic home of ET.

Shifting his chair wheels and body to ET's terminal, Miles began feeding it the text strings to process. The machine seemed to slurp them up as it began the complicated process of deciphering. A small visual of an alien wearing a sad, homesick expression while watching spaceships fly overhead appeared in the *Waiting* box on the screen.

"Do your thing, little buddy." Miles patted the monitor and winked before rolling back to his other workstation.

✪ ✪ ✪

Bus Station
Palmdale, California
1337 hours, Pacific Time

THE WHEELS ON THE BUS GO ROUND AND ROUND

The bus depot in Palmdale, California, dated from the 1950s when the spacious, drafty, fluorescent bulb–lit hall had been the epitome of modernity. Its front windows had enough greasy handprints and dead flies to easily represent over half a century's hard use. Tired gray plastic chairs competed with scuffed gray linoleum tiles for dreariness.

The Los Angeles bus was late. Patrick Dennison shoved a fourth quarter into a candy dispenser and pulled the tab to drop a Reese's Peanut Butter Cup into the tray. When he shoved his hand through the narrow vending slot, his fingers plunged into a half-inch of sticky cola someone had poured into the tray as a joke. His candy was bathed in it too.

Yanking his hand back, Dennison wiped it angrily on his Levi's and glared around the room to see if anyone was laughing. There were only a handful of other occupants. A cleaning lady pushed a dirty mop in circles. What appeared to be a Mexican family of six clustered together, their luggage all tied up with twine.

No one laughed or even smirked.

The prank was probably a plot by one of the bus-terminal workers—someone as fed up with this plague hole as Dennison was.

Control! he told himself. This was not the time to lose his temper or shoot off his mouth. Besides, blow this place up and who would miss it?

The arriving bus finally tooted its horn and slid into the driveway out back. Bald-headed, fortyish Mohammed al Krefa was the last of four passengers to emerge from the coach. His skin was mottled olive and dirty brown, as if he'd tanned through a screen of leaves. His build was muscular, especially through his biceps and shoulders.

Dennison was not even supposed to know The Bombmaker's name. Mabrouk had let it slip once, then theatrically warned Dennison to never repeat it on pain of death.

Walking toward Dennison's pickup truck, al Krefa spoke in bullets. "The cement truck? Where?"

"Warehouse. Couldn't pick you up in it, could I?"

Al Krefa appeared to digest this assertion, then said, "The driver may be missed. Move it."

"Let's get the sucker truck on the way. No sense making two trips. We'll hide both of 'em up the canyon."

Al Krefa's eyes bored into Dennison's, as if testing his loyalty. "It's good. Everything moves. The apartment is clean; the papers burned."

Dennison was exultant. "One day left! Just one day more!"

EIGHT

Bus Accident Site
Los Angeles, California
Saturday, 5 September
1348 hours, Pacific Time

NOT MY SCENE

The commuter bus passengers had been emptied after the wreck, interviewed, and sent on with another bus. Since Steve and Carter were in plainclothes, the decision had been made by the controlling officer on scene that they couldn't conduct the interviews. "It might confuse the already frightened passengers," the self-important sergeant had declared.

During his years with the FBI Steve had conducted hundreds of interviews in much more complex investigations than this, but his reply was, "Whatever. Your scene, your paperwork." He released control of the scene to the officer and dismissed the challenge as nothing more than interagency rivalry.

So Steve waved the busy afternoon traffic around the scene. Six flares burned in a wedge, leading vehicles away from the right two lanes. A Caltrans crew with a hydraulic hoist prepared to lift the bus off Hakim's body.

Why did he run? The question rolled over and over in Steve's mind.

He must have been guilty of something, but what? Hakim wasn't living with his brother. From the looks of it the man hardly even associated with Mabrouk.

Could his failure to register with the Immigration and Naturalization Service have prompted him to fear Steve enough to run away? Or did he know something about his brother's plan? A more logical scenario, but why hadn't they seen it coming?

Or was it just fear of any authority? Was Hakim trying to contact his brother without anyone official knowing?

For whatever reason, he had run at the expense of his life. The lesson: Never run from cops. They seldom chase people without a good reason.

Steve was a firm believer that incarceration, even if wrongful, was better than death.

His B-com buzzed. "Special Agent Alstead."

"Steve—" Senator Morrison sounded out of breath—"just got a message from Downing. Have you got the accident scene cleared up enough to get away?"

"Nearly," Steve replied as the workers covered the body in black plastic.

"Good. Listen: Miles ran the call records for the paint factory. Downing's team looked them over and found several calls to and from a *synagogue*. Started about the time Mabrouk disappeared."

"Synagogue? Isn't Mabrouk Muslim?"

"Sure," Morrison persisted. "But what better hiding place could there be for a Muslim terrorist to hide out than in a synagogue? Now I've already called SOD Davis. He was a little ticked off we didn't let him know about your pursuit—at least before we chased Hakim to death—but I explained it was LAPD that botched this one. Anyway he's going to help out. Got guys on the way to set up covert surveillance on the synagogue right now."

"How 'bout the mosque?"

"Still watching that too. Davis said he'll see that you can make your statement about the accident by phone. Get Carter and buzz me once you hit the road."

The discussion ended. By then the accident cleanup was mostly finished anyway. Steve waved Carter over and let him know what he'd heard.

The commanding officer showed resistance in letting go those he referred to as "the guys responsible for this."

Steve didn't bother arguing. "Call Special Operations Director Davis if you feel it's necessary."

Carter threw his two cents in. "We've got more pressing matters than mopping up, street cop."

Steve grimaced as Carter walked the edge again. There was an instant when Steve thought the sarcasm would blow up in their faces, but his repeated references to SOD Davis worked.

The investigating uniformed officer bit his lip and muttered under his breath about "hotshot Feds" but dismissed them anyway.

Coalition Headquarters
Kabul, Afghanistan
0101 hours, Local Time

OPERATION ROCK AUDIO

Within 10 minutes of Coleson Specter's phone call, word traveled like an electrical fire on an overloaded wire without a fuse. News of Marcos Caracas's message and the location of the audio tape burned through walls and phone lines from the Pentagon to Afghanistan. Every person around the world who was even remotely involved with Task Force 121 was called back from lunch or rousted from bed.

From the moment after the hot electronic bullet hit Colonel Borland in the ear at 2401 hours, he had the engines on and the screws turning. There hadn't been time to completely finalize the specific plan for Operation Rock Audio, but neither was there time to labor over a drafting table. Contingency plans were yanked from the stored worst-case files on the way out the door with climbing gear.

Colonel Borland was determined. He was going to find Marcos and the rest of the men of AIF 17, recover the audio, skewer al Qaeda on a pole, and have the leaders back in time to roast them for breakfast.

At that very moment Apache attack choppers were preparing to lift off from the air base in Kandahar. Equipped with advanced night-vision and thermal-imaging devices, as well as surface-to-air countermeasures A to triple Z, the Apaches would burn a hole in the ozone, right to the spot. They'd look for any sign of enemy life and quickly stamp it out before the Black Hawks arrived to deliver four squads of men.

Two C-130 refueling tankers would be circling at 30,000 feet, ready to swoop down with enough fuel to keep the birds flying for days, if necessary.

Master Sergeant C. J. Wells, of Air Force Strategic Operations Information Command, had devised the plan with Borland. MSGT Wells strapped on his Omega assault vest and patrol pack, and grabbed two extra bandoliers of loaded M-16 magazines and his weapon. He left the warm Quonset hut for the cold tarmac, leading 27 others similarly armed and geared up.

From a run Wells heaved his kit into the Black Hawk and leveraged himself onto the bench seat. Like four rows of dry cleaning, all on moving racks, men floated up and into the choppers as the screws ramped toward full speed. They strapped themselves in.

The doors were slung shut, and immediately they lifted off, headed out on what could be the most significant military operation of the year.

Temple Beth-El Synagogue
Fairfax Street
Los Angeles, California
1402 hours, Pacific Time

BLACK AND WHITE

Heat waves danced off the hood of the rough-idling Chevy Caprice. Steve Alstead's B-com baked atop the cracked dashboard. The B-com was their only communication device, since the LASO loaner radio had long since conked out.

Quietly Steve and Carter waited, watching the windows at the back of the little apartment at the synagogue 100 meters away. After the lone-eagle stunt they'd pulled earlier, the pair was condemned to operate on the outer perimeter of the stakeout.

How ironic it would be, Steve considered, to find a Muslim terrorist living on the charity of his worst enemy. He scanned the hands and faces of every pedestrian in all directions.

The long wait gave him plenty of time to think of Cindy. "Oh no!"

Startled, Carter jumped. "What?"

"Cindy! I forgot to call her back and insist that she not come out here. She said she was taking the kids to Universal Studios." Steve's eyes continued to scan the distance, scrutinizing a man walking with a backpack. "With the operation going on and LA law enforcement on Red Alert, I just don't think it's a good idea."

Carter took a long peek through the side mirror at someone approaching up the sidewalk, before offering his usual choice words of wisdom. "See? That's why I'm not married."

Good thinking, Steve mentally responded. The 36-hour-no-sleep doldrums had set in, preventing him from bantering back with *Thanks for the helpful suggestion*.

Steve debated calling Cindy. To maybe even explain the recent jump to Threat Condition Red due to the imminent danger in the LA Basin. The last thing he wanted was for Cindy to show up with the kids and be right in the middle of the action again.*

He should call. He must. But he knew that as soon as he got her on the phone the shooting would start. Then he'd be stuck explaining while bullets were flying overhead.

"Alstead, Thomas," Morrison's voice called to them via the radio feature of the B-com.

"What's up, Chief?" Steve glanced over his left shoulder to get a

---

*This story is told in *Shaiton's Fire*, book 1 of this series.

better look at the dark-skinned, middle-aged man across the street. Too old to be Mabrouk.

"I got word from the investigators who made contact with the manager of the apartments. Guy took one look at Mabrouk's photo and said, 'Yeah, I know this man, but he calls himself Nathan Gold.' Witness is on his way to the room with detectives right now. Also says he hasn't seen Mabrouk too much over the past couple of months, and lately hasn't seen him at all, or the two others who lived there."

"Two others?" The new information surprised Steve.

"That's what he said, but he never learned their names," Morrison added.

"Thanks for the heads-up. Since our radio doesn't work in this piece of junk, don't know how much good we could do for the stakeout anyway."

"You sound tired, Steve."

Steve looked at the radio with only one eye open. "You could say that."

A distant voice cluttered the line on Morrison's end. "Hang on, boys . . ." Unintelligible cross talk filtered through the speaker, then Morrison returned. "Steve, that was them. They've opened the apartment. Mabrouk's gone."

"We'll go in and check it out then. Call you in a bit."

They left the synagogue, and Steve drove up and parked across the street from the apartment building. They made their way up a narrow concrete path through a star-jasmine arbor, and then down a dark cement-and-stucco hallway where a few officers pooled around the door of apartment 3A. Steve held out his badge. Apparently the bags under his eyes were more obvious than the shiny brass.

A fresh-faced detective with a bushy mustache slapped him on the back. "Hey, FBI? Last again, ah?" He laughed.

At that point Steve was uncertain if the man was joking or taking the opportunity for an interagency stab. Even Carter was too subdued to bite back. So the two of them walked past without speaking.

Dirty brown carpet, dull-looking shades, and flat-white enamel walls . . . it wasn't a place Steve would hang around on vacation. More notable, though, was the tiny kitchen, where ashes cluttered the stainless-steel sink. Near the charred remnants, the exhaust blower over the range still hummed. *How they got rid of the smoke*, Steve surmised.

He silenced the fan at the switch. In the basin a black-and-white checkerboard pattern on a scrap of partially burned, glossy magazine paper caught his eye. He dared not touch it. No doubt it was evidence of something Mabrouk wanted to conceal.

Carter wandered toward the back rooms. "Alstead," he called a minute later.

A few steps beyond the kitchen Steve found a hallway leading to two bedrooms and a bath.

Carter had already pulled several drawers from a shoddy dresser in one of the rooms. "Nothing but a few clothes and a Bible, man."

Steve nodded as he glanced around. "Cleaned out."

"Yep." Carter yanked out another drawer, dumping a pile of mismatched socks on the floor.

"That isn't a Bible." Steve pointed to the copy of the Koran, which lay open on the barren mattress. Arabic symbols were completely foreign to Steve. He couldn't even tell what page number the book was on.

Steve felt it. The definite presence of evil. It swirled in the room, as if Mabrouk himself were still there. It was tangible, like no other presence Steve had ever felt—like an icy cold blanket draped across his back. It filled the room and stole his breath away.

Steve was struck with a concrete reality. "Mabrouk isn't comin' back."

The same understanding seemed to hit Carter. "Gone for good. He's on his way to die."

"Burned everything that might link him to anybody." Chills ran down Steve's spine. Even in the muggy 85-degree temperature, goose bumps popped up all over his body. "Now is the time to start believing in God, man, 'cause this isn't just about stopping some psychopath who wants to blow himself up—alone."

Carter had been quiet for several minutes. But this time, in the presence of such palpable evil, he seemed to respond to Steve, or at least to want to. He certainly didn't react with his usual lighthearted banter that so easily dismissed the existence of God. This time he listened intently and then whispered, "It's real. Evil is real."

"Oh, it's real, all right." Steve's eyes widened to meet the spiritual confrontation head-on. "We're right in the middle of a battle between heaven and hell, fought for the souls of men. Terrorists like Mabrouk are nothing less than the physical incarnation of vile spirits. The spirits of fear and suffering and despair. People want to paint the whole 9/11 scene as just a competition between religions. But this war goes way beyond that. The people who choose to become terrorists are possessed by demons who want to break the spirit of mankind. They want to make us give up, give in. And it's working too. You see it all the time in some of our own leaders."

Steve paused. "'No war,' people say—" he waved his hand—"'Just let 'em be' . . . as if 9/11 never happened! Man, Carter! I'm telling you: This evil wants us to sit back and watch. There are powers that would love it if we decided not to stand up for what's right . . . love it if we adopted the attitude of sacrificing the weak so we can live in comfort and peace. But I'm telling you, unless we confront it for what it is—lies—we're history!"

Steve pointed at the book on the bed. "Satan is called the Angel of Light, the Deceiver, the Accuser, the Enemy. Do you know what the name *Allah,* the god of the Muslims, means in Hebrew?"

Carter threw up his hands. "I don't know. What? God?"

"No." Steve shook his head. "In Hebrew *Allah* means " 'curse, swear, desecrate.' That's what their own prophet Muhammad named their god 600 years after Christ walked the face of the earth. Muhammad didn't intend it that way, I'm sure, but that's what the word means. Satan set out to reinvent the wheel in an attempt to eliminate the one and only true God from life."

Steve's voice was charged with conviction. "Maybe Satan actually believes that in a world of free will, if he can get enough souls to choose him, God will have to spare him from the eternal suffering that will come to him on Judgment Day."

Steve kicked the bed. "Satan and those who choose his way want us to fail. They want people to blame the president, blame anybody and everybody, except the true perpetrators of evil. This kind of evil has no limit to its appetite. If we let it go, it'll come back. Only next time it'll come while we're sleeping."

At that very moment Steve felt convicted—to pray more, to be more watchful, and to be as passionate about his faith as the misguided and evil Mabrouk was about his.

Steve placed a hand on Carter's shoulder. "Look, I'm not asking you to pray, but would you kneel with me?"

"Uh . . . sure." Carter agreed without offense. It might have been awkward for him, but out of respect he hit a knee next to Steve.

Steve closed his eyes. "Heavenly Father, Lord of all the universe, I need to ask your forgiveness on us today, so that we will be pure and strong and completely in your will. Lord, we have a task that seems way too big for us alone. But I know—I *know*—that we can do all things through you. God, I give myself to you fully, and I ask your protection over all of us in this great country. Open our eyes to reality, Lord. Let us see and live and be completely within your truth. Amen." Steve opened his eyes. He smiled at Carter.

"Wow, man." Carter smiled back.

"Pretty heavy?"

"Hey, it couldn't hurt," Carter admitted.

As Steve stood up, something beneath the bed caught his eye. "Couldn't hurt . . . what is that?" He pointed to a slick brochure half buried in the mess.

Carter pulled out a colorful pamphlet that displayed a happy couple working out together. "'Offer for a free gym membership at 24-Hour Health Club,'" he read. He opened the trifold. "And it's signed 'good for one friend for one month.'"

"That's interesting!" Steve reached for the brochure. "I wonder if he's already signed up."

"Gower Street. Only a few minutes from here." Carter rubbed a hand over the stubble on his head. "Maybe another chance to catch up."

The pair agreed to follow the tenuous new lead. There was nothing more to see at the apartment to help them in their quest, but they left the scene energized, possessing a new resolve to locate Mabrouk and stop him.

NINE

SOUL SEARCHING

Once the fingerprints on the check were layered and scanned into the system, Kristi began the tedious process of marking the various points with tiny yellow dots. These dots functioned as constant placeholders, where precise measurements could be made and exact distances between them compared against hundreds of thousands of other records.

Senator Morrison believed strongly that time was of the essence, that this group of deadly killers was most definitely tied to other organizations already on the battlefield, readying their attack. So certain was he that their plan was near to unfolding that Morrison charged Chapter 16, mental bayonets fixed, full into the investigation.

There would be no rest and no pausing to reload until the enemy either dropped their weapons or laid down their lives.

Kristi was a model not only of beauty but of innovation and efficiency. She operated two Identex systems simultaneously, having started with the sets of prints that she most strongly believed would reveal a new lead. The purchaser of the cashier's check was a man with ties to money and others higher up in the terrorist organization called Allah's Will.

Kristi liked to think of her job as soul searching. . . .

A fingerprint was a unique signature. Its presence may not have been left voluntarily, or even consciously. But without a doubt, every print was unmistakably left by someone—someone who had a life, a name, and a soul.

Kristi began with the larger set of four, made by the left hand of the one she believed was a working man and the one who'd purchased the check. The waypoints were set and the prints were shot out into the Identex universe to find his soul or his evil spirit, as the case might be.

Images strobed across the computer screen, judging the unknown's identity against the masses in instantaneous trials. It was entirely possible that the individual for whom she searched had never been processed into the system.

Her brow wrinkled in the hope that it was. She had begun to send out a second query when her B-com rang. "Special Agent Kross."

"Special Agent Kross, Morrison here."

She was happy to hear his voice. "Any news?"

"Yes!" Morrison was ecstatic. "We ran the routing numbers off that check. Got hold of the issuing bank in Glendale."

"Uh-huh."

"They've taken all morning but managed to come up with the security footage for the date and time that check was written. It's on its way in now, but I just wanted to give you some bits of description that might help to narrow your search."

Kristi gently bit her lower lip. "Is the image good enough to run a facial print from?"

"I'm not sure," Morrison answered. "From the sound of it, the guy never looked up. He must have known where the cameras were. Had a ball cap on to boot, so it doesn't sound like we've got a real good image of the suspect."

Frowning, Kristi rested her forehead in her palm. "That's too bad."

"But we did get word from JTTF's white-collar-crime unit that the young lady working the counter remembered the fellow. Said he was Middle Eastern and had a deep scar high on his right cheek. I guess he stared her down when she looked at it. Scared her."

Kristi awoke from disappointment. "That's wonderful! Perfect! I can feed it into the system with the prints. It'll save hours, eliminating the need for a complete search. Thank you, Senator."

"Figured it would help. Keep me posted."

Kristi's fingers flew over the keys before she'd even disconnected, entering the elements of physical description into the blank fields for additional information: "Country/Region of Origin" and "Marks, Scars or Tattoos."

A few more seconds and it became a race between machines. Which one would be first to reveal the mystery man's soul?

✪ ✪ ✪

Painted Desert
Arizona
1527 hours, Mountain Time

TWO GUNS AT DIABLO CANYON

So the Painted Desert was indeed miraculous. Tracy decided it had been worth changing the schedule to see. It gave her an appetite to see other sights. Maybe someday, she promised the boys, they would head north to Monument Valley and stay where all the great John Ford Westerns had been filmed. Someday. But not now.

Justin, sad and thoughtful, stared out the window at the blur of scenery.

Connor opened his blue Hot Wheels box and gazed down contentedly at forty tiny metal NASCAR replicas. He plucked out his favorites: Dale Earnhardt Jr. in the red BUD car. Jeff Gordon driving blue with red flames. Kevin Harvick in his black-and-silver Goodwrench car. Matt Kenseth zooming around the track in yellow and black. And so on.

Thanks to Mike, little Connor had memorized the names of the most famous NASCAR drivers in America. If knowing NASCAR Cup cars had been a subject in prekindergarten, Connor would have been top of the class. Back home at Willie's Barber Shop Mike had frequently demonstrated Connor's brilliance to the men in the chairs by playing Name That NASCAR Driver as they waited to be shorn. Without fail, Connor astonished every fan with his ability to match number, Cup car, and colors with the driver's name. Not bad for a four-year-old. He done his daddy proud.

Tracy chose to go yet another round with the Gaither CD over the heartbreaking tunes of Garth Brooks.

Hot Wheels roared around Connor's car seat like race day at Daytona. Now and then Ryan Newman or Jimmie Johnson flew off the track and onto the floor, requiring Justin's help to retrieve them.

The wrecks and explosions grew more violent as the miles slipped past. The game of race-chase-pit-stop-crack-up-send-the-ambulance-pick-'em-up-give-'em-back-now-do-it-again got old.

Justin finally protested. "Mom! Newman rolled under the seat! I can't get him without taking off my seat belt!"

"Don't take off your seat belt," Tracy admonished. "It's dangerous when you're going 180 miles an hour."

Connor wailed, "Pit stop! Pit stop! I can't race without Newman! Harvick's gonna whomp him! Tell Justin I need Newman so Harvick can whomp him!"

Tracy now understood why she had instinctively refused to ever go on a long road trip with her children before now. She also realized she would probably never really return to vacation in Monument Valley until the boys were at least in their twenties.

"Pit stop! Pit stop!" Connor demanded.

Justin moaned, "Mom! Please, Mom. I gotta get out or I'm gonna kill him."

The sign at the side of West I-40 read *Diablo Canyon, Two Guns, and Meteor Crater Natural Landmark.* All three names were written in big white letters on the large green board. Together.

No kidding.

Tracy figured that such a billboard must be a sign that things really could get worse.

Then the cell phone began to sing "Dixie."

Silence from the NASCAR fans in the backseat. Waiting. Watching. Listening. What would Mom do?

She pushed the button and held the phone to her ear. "Hey, Mike."

Mike's voice crackled, threatening to break up. "Hey, Trace . . . how's it . . . where . . . y'all?"

"Just about to have a two-gun shoot-out at Diablo Canyon. Aren't you working?"

"Trace . . . few minutes between . . . wanted you to know . . . important. I'm a . . . wrong . . . I . . . you. Something . . . goin' on . . . don't know yet. . . ."

"What? Mike! You're breaking up! Mike?"

"Can't hear you . . . Trace? Breaking up . . ."

The phone went dead. Dead! How could it be that at that exact moment he had chosen to tell her something important? Something. But what? And his last words had been *"Breaking up."*

Tracy grimaced at the pulsing message on the phone screen: *Call ended.* Right.

Connor was quiet for the first time in 90 miles. And Justin resumed staring out the window.

Tracy asked, "Y'all want to see the meteor crater?"

Connor spun the wheels of Harvick's car. "What's that?"

Justin muttered sullenly, "A big hole in the ground where a rock fell out of outer space and killed all the dinosaurs."

"Oh." Connor solemnly replaced the Cup car in its slot and snapped the lid of the Hot Wheels case shut. "Mom?"

"Yes, Connor?"

"How come Dad don't love us no more?"

Out of the mouths of babes. Talk about a meteor! Right out of the blue. *Oh, Lord! Jesus!* she cried silently. *Help us! Help me! Does he believe his daddy doesn't love him?*

Tracy moderated her tone. *Easy does it.* "Dad does love you, Connor. And Justin too. Very much."

Connor rephrased the question. "But, Mom, how come he don't love you no more?"

Tracy swallowed hard and put on the blinker. She pulled onto the off-ramp for Diablo Canyon. Devil's Canyon. Yes. Just the right sort of place for such a question to be asked. The road sign had indeed been a sign, she thought. How could she tell a four-year-old that a blazing rock had fallen out of nowhere, smashed their family, and left a gaping hole where her heart had been?

She had no answers.

Why didn't Mike love her anymore?

It would take a lot longer than one road trip from Arkansas to California to explain.

ELFS Room
FBI, Chapter 16 Offices
San Francisco, California
1446 hours, Pacific Time

MAN VS. MACHINE

"There must be something to it, Miles," Charles Downing argued. "I don't know why anyone using their modus operandi would save this kind of junk e-mail unless it was worth something."

"I don't know what else to tell you." Miles threw his hands up. "ET will get it eventually."

"But we don't have until eventually!" Downing stated forcefully. His desire to crack the code had begun to overwhelm his usual cool sense of purpose. "We have 'til tomorrow. The intel says something is going down tomorrow. That's it! Did you try the Arab-to-English translator?"

"I tried it." Miles pointed and clicked his way to the program. "It just comes back with nothing. Watch." He copied one of the gibberish text strings into the translation box and clicked *Enter*. "See, I told you. Nothing!"

Downing stared at the answer blankly: "0 matching results."

"The text strings are real words. They just don't make any sense. It's like someone pulled them out of a dictionary randomly." Miles scratched his head and sighed as if completely lost for any further ideas. "We just have to wait."

Downing squinted at the screen. "What did you say?"

"We'll just have to wait . . . wait for ET."

"No, before that . . . about a dictionary." Downing leaned out of his chair and pointed to an icon of the suspect's computer desktop on Miles's display. "What's that?"

Miles gave him a glance proclaiming, *Duh!* "Looks like a dictionary."

Downing twirled his finger in circles at the image. "Open it; open it."

Miles double-clicked it before reading the words in a dialog box: "Cannot open the file you have selected. File may have been deleted or moved." He turned to Downing. "It isn't there, see?"

Wrinkling his handsome face into massive thought, Downing paused with his mouth open. "Did the file not come when they sent the computer? Or . . ."

"The file may have been old or corrupt, or maybe it was a CD-ROM. They may not have sent it, or we don't have it because . . ."

Downing finished Miles's sentence. ". . . because it's a factory-made CD-ROM dictionary."

"Right, but if you need a dictionary, I have one." Miles reached for a CD jewel case.

"No, that's not it." Downing attempted to clarify his hunch. "When you talked about words from a dictionary, it made me think. What if they used a dictionary for coding. Here, look at the text string again."

Miles pasted the text string on a blank word-processing document. "READING CODE –23."

"Stop! That's it!"

"I'm sorry, I—"

"Minus 23!" Downing exclaimed. "What if these guys were using a dictionary to encode their stuff? A positive or negative number, in this case, minus 23, was the encryption key. What if they wrote the original message, then counted the words forward or backward in the dictionary to construct a gibberish text string. Unless ET had that exact dictionary in his programming, there wouldn't be a source code for a complex mathematical encryption formula that ET could break! This may be electronic, but it's also old-style, low-tech!"

Miles stared at the computer awhile before answering. "It could work."

Downing snatched the phone up. "Get me LA JTTF, Technical Investigations, Electronics Unit, please."

Miles seemed confused. "Why are you calling them?"

Downing covered the phone. "See if maybe that CD-ROM is still in the drive."

The wait of a minute or two seemed like an eternity. Downing watched the little alien figure on Miles's ET screen scan the starry sky for his spaceship—one that would never land. "Yes, this is Chapter 16, Special Agent Downing. I'm working with Miles Miller to decipher some messages found on the desktop of the suspect's drive that came in a couple of hours ago."

"The stuff in the Viagra e-mail?" the distant voice replied. "Yeah, we looked at those too."

"On a long shot," Downing continued, "you guys wouldn't by chance have a CD-ROM still in the drive?"

"Nope, nothing in any of the drives. We sent everything we had."

Doubtful, Downing added, "Anything else come in from the house?"

"Sorry." The voice registered disappointment. "Looks like everything else was burned up."

"Last question."

"Shoot."

"You wouldn't by chance have a copy of a—" Downing motioned to Miles—"what version is that?"

Miles selected the properties menu on the dictionary icon. "Webster's 0.1 for Windows 95."

Downing repeated the name.

The man on the other end of the line laughed. "Version 0.1? Buddy, that stuff is a 10-year-old beta. What would you need it for?"

Downing blinked, remained silent for a moment. "Never mind. Just, uh, let us know if you find anything."

"You bet." The man hung up.

Downing replaced the receiver. "Miles, we've got to find that version of Webster's Dictionary!"

"Gonna be tough. Wasn't ever in wide circulation."

"I'll be in the call center." Downing flung his coat over his shoulder. "Why don't you see if the version is still floating around out on the Net somewhere? I'll get the boys to make contact with Microsoft and Webster's both, to see if we can come up with something soon."

"Okay." Miles scratched his head as he looked sadly at ET. "Sorry, guy. Unless your ship comes in first, I guess it's man vs. machine."

✪ ✪ ✪

24-Hour Health Club
Los Angeles, California
1502 hours, Pacific Time

IT AIN'T DRUGS

Steve and Carter waited by the check-in counter. The assistant manager, a beefy jock type in blue sweats with a name tag that read *Guy,* towered over them.

Steve was flustered. He really resisted making a request to see Mabrouk's records in front of the whole world. "Yes, I realize you could help me, but I actually need to speak directly with the manager."

In a resonant but dense-sounding voice, the jock demanded, "Tell me what this is regarding."

Steve sighed and shook his head. Looking at Carter, he said, "There may be no way around it."

"Fine," Carter replied, anger and impatience welling up in his voice. "All right, Guy!" Carter whipped out his badge. "Special Agent Thomas with the FBI. We're conducting a steroids investigation. Is that something you want to help us with? Shall we go talk with you first, or would you like to get your manager for us?"

Guy was dumbfounded. His face turned from tough guy to worried sick as the thoughts percolated through his muscles to reach his little bitty brain. "I'll g-go get Sheila," he stuttered and left.

"Good work." Steve rubbed his face, considering the ridiculous nature of certain people. He looked at his watch. Being tired never helped.

"Thank you," Carter replied proudly. "Glad it worked. Next I was gonna gas and cuff him."

"So you can do *some* things right." Steve referred to their needlessly lengthy trip here that was supposedly only 15 minutes away from the suspect's apartment.

"Hey, we're here, aren't we?"

Steve consulted his watch again. "An hour later . . . I was beginning to feel like Gilligan."

They stopped the banter when an athletic black girl with shiny black hair appeared wearing the same workout getup as Guy. "Hi, I'm Sheila, manager here at 24-Hour Health Club. Guy tells me you need to speak with me about a steroid investigation." She appeared calm and unconcerned.

"Special Agent Alstead with the FBI." *Bet she's seen everything in Hollywood,* Steve imagined. "This is Special Agent Carter."

Carter grinned, greeting her with a handshake.

Steve continued, "Actually, it might be better if we speak in private."

"Sure." She motioned for them to come into the club. "Right this way, please."

The floor was packed with treadmills, stationary bikes, climbers, free weights, and other machines. It appeared to be a great place to work out. Much cleaner than Steve's usual haunt.

Steve followed Sheila into her office, a room just off the cardio floor. "You wanna keep an eye through the blinds?" Steve prompted his partner.

Carter nodded, lifting a slat from the metal miniblinds to keep watch for Mabrouk. A moment later he began to laugh.

"What?" Steve took a seat.

"You won't believe the way these jocks are streaming out of here with their gear."

Probably fearing the worst, Steve figured. "Thank you, Sheila. We're actually not here to look for steroids. But we are looking for some information about a possible client of the club. Due to the seriousness of the investigation I really can't say why we need this information, only that it's critical and also very important we keep things quiet."

"I see," Sheila replied. "But you must know we're not allowed to share information about our clients—"

Steve politely cut her off. "I understand, and we've accounted for that. I have a telephonic search warrant."

"What is that?" She crossed her legs, resting her chin on her right hand.

"A telephonic warrant is used when there isn't time to go before a judge. When the situation is critical and time is limited, a judge will permit a specific search to occur while the paperwork is being processed, as he has in this case. You can take down my information, and in fact, if you have a fax machine, I'll bet the docs will be ready soon. I can have them sent right through."

"I see. So who is this individual and how can I help?"

Without breaking off his gaze through the window, Carter passed a file folder behind him. Steve removed a photograph of Mabrouk and handed it to her.

She frowned while examining the photo. "This is him?"

"Yes. He goes by the name Mabrouk Ziad." Steve pointed to the name on the bottom. "Sometimes he uses Nathan Gold as an alias."

Sheila spun 180 degrees in her chair to face a computer. She entered both names. "Here it is. Looks like he signed up under Gold about three months ago. No address. Paid cash for a six-month membership. No racquetball or aerobics. He really hasn't come more than—" she counted—"six, seven, eight times total. And he has a locker."

"He does?" Steve raised his eyebrows.

Carter let the blind snap as he turned away. "Can we look at it?"

"I don't see why not, if your warrant will allow it," Sheila offered helpfully. "It's locker M36. We can go right now."

"Wait—one more thing," Steve interjected. "When was the last time he was in?"

Sheila glanced at the screen again. "Looks like his card was swiped around 4:45 this morning."

Steve's stomach dropped as he doubted Mabrouk was here to work out. A meeting maybe, or else the locker. He might be using it to hide things. "Let's have a look at that locker."

The three were making their way out as a rotund Samoan, topping 400 pounds easy, almost ran them over. The man stumbled back. "'Scuse me." He hurried off, wiping the sweat from his face.

Sheila led the agents to the male locker room. She flagged Guy over. "Guy, I need you to make sure the bathroom is empty. Put up a closed sign."

"Sure," he replied sheepishly. Guy led Steve and Carter in. "So what's this really about?"

Pretty bold, Steve thought, nudging Carter.

Carter stepped up to the plate. "You just cooperate with us and we'll see you get full immunity." He winked at Steve, fighting the urge to laugh.

"Sure, sure! Anything you need."

Steve and Carter stopped in front of the locker wall while Guy checked to see if the room was empty. Steve scanned the numbers. "M36. There it is!" He examined the combination padlock. "Guy. Room empty?"

"Nobody else here."

"You sure?" Carter interrogated. "All right, go get your bolt cutters. Know you got 'em."

"Okay, sure." Guy trotted off.

The instant he disappeared, Carter and Steve burst into laughter.

Carter's eyes watered. "For being as big as he is, poor fella's scared spitless."

"That'll teach him," Steve added before abruptly straightening at the attendant's return. "Thanks, Guy." Steve took the long-handled, orange bolt cutters. "Did you put the sign up out front?"

"Oh, yeah." Guy hurried off again.

Steve called after him, "Then just go ahead and wait outside" before mentally shifting gears with a long sigh. To Carter he noted, "Now we've got to make sure this thing isn't booby-trapped."

"I'll bet you lunch it isn't."

"You don't want to do that, you two-time loser. Of all the bets to make, right before I open this thing up." Steve shook his head.

"What? Are you superstitious?" Carter yanked the cutters away. "At most he's using this as a hand-off point."

Steve remained reluctant. The little voice in his head jangled alarm bells like a hammer on a metal table. "Sure you don't want to wait for a bomb dog?"

Carter clenched his jaw, closing one eye. "Let's do it." He pressed the sharp jaws of the cutter to the puny metal ring. The metal snapped. "Like butter."

As soon as the lock was removed, the door bulged, trying to swing open.

Steve involuntarily blinked rapidly.

Carter held the panel in place, handing the cutters to Steve. He leaned his head on one side, attempting to peer in. "Give me that puny flashlight of yours."

Steve handed over the extremely bright but compact SureFire E1E. "See anything?"

"Looks like a duffel bag. No wires or switches. Looks pretty safe."

"Okay. Go slow." Steve couldn't help but think of the explosion that almost took his life and nearly killed his best friend this morning. If there had been more time, Steve would have called in a K-9 team. At the moment, though, keeping a lid on the investigation in order to prevent panic and avoid tipping their hand to the bad guys was top priority.

Steve didn't want to send Mabrouk running to light his bomb prematurely.

Carter eased the door open. A black duffel slumped out into his arms. "Pretty heavy. Maybe this guy is stealing weights." He set the bag down on the tile seat, looking to Steve before he opened it.

"Ready when you are," Steve acknowledged.

"Here goes." Carter pulled the tab slowly, revealing some clothes.

Just as Steve began to feel relief, he spotted a pair of wires . . . and then another set. "Stop! Wait! I see a possible threat!"

Carter saw it too. He cursed, letting go easy. "He's got a whole explosives cache in here. Now what are we gonna do?"

Steve looked around. "Have to clear this place out. Like now."

"You want to let Sheila in on the little secret?"

"Have to." Steve raised his index finger. "I'll wait here, while you go make sure this locker room is really clear."

Seconds seemed like minutes to Steve as Carter was gone, checking all the stalls.

"Clear," Carter replied.

The pair made their way to the front of the locker room.

"I'll wait here," Steve instructed. "Go get Sheila to clear the women's room. Sic Guy onto the folks on the workout floor. Everybody's gotta be out."

Carter hustled off while Steve evaluated the meaning of safe distance. He called Morrison on his B-com. "Senator, we found a bag of bombs in Mabrouk's locker."

"This case is getting messier, Steve. Are you able to keep things quiet?"

"So far." Steve ran his fingers through his hair.

"That's the way it needs to stay if we're going to catch the big one."

"The big one?"

"Yes, the big one," Morrison replied. "Agent Kross got a positive hit from Identex on a set of prints made by Mohammed al Krefa. He's a known terrorist with ties to our old friend Khalil."

"Al Krefa!" Steve was shocked. "I thought he operated overseas. Afghanistan? Saw him on the Most Wanted list."

"He was." When Morrison's Southern accent came through more pronounced than usual, Steve knew the director was under stress. "We got a positive ID from the bank teller too. Doesn't look good, Steve."

A second later the lights went out and the locker room went completely dark.

"Senator, we've just lost power in here. I've gotta go."

"I'll get EOD on the road for you."

"Thanks." Steve signed off, wondering aloud, "Now what?" He took out his slightly larger 6P flashlight.

The emergency lights illuminated, and after a few more seconds Guy's voice came over the loudspeaker. "We're sorry, ladies and gentlemen, the power has gone off due to an electrical problem in the locker rooms. We need all of you to grab your things and head for the parking lot. Do not go to the locker rooms. You could be shocked and killed."

Not bad for a big meathead, Steve decided. Of course, if there had really been a power failure, the PA system probably wouldn't work. Fortunately the facility was filled with jocks just like Guy. They bought the story and hit the highway. The place was empty in a matter of a minute.

Carter reappeared. "EOD is on the way. I told 'em to head around the east side, where there's an emergency exit from the men's locker room."

"Perfect. Senator Morrison was going to alert them too." Steve made his way toward the front of the building. "Bombs at the gym?" he mumbled to himself.

"I know. Most guys use *drugs* to blow up around here. But good thing we're in a gym," joked Carter.

"Why?" Steve was entirely too focused to read Carter.

Carter began to laugh in anticipation of his own humor. "At least you know everything around here . . . *works out!*"

Steve snarled his disgust. "Corny, Carter . . . very corny. Pitiful stuff. Did your last partner die from it or just get sent up after trying to kill *you*?"

TEN

MAMA'S ADVICE

Just east of Flagstaff, Arizona, Tracy's mama called from Mansfield, Arkansas. Justin and Connor were dozing in the back of the Tahoe.

Mama's thick country accent twanged over the miles, irritating Tracy. "Me and your daddy was just down at your place. Watered the houseplants."

"Thanks, Mama."

"Fed the cats. Fed the goldfish."

"Thanks."

"Everything's fine. Fine. Locked up tight. Mary-Belle wanted to know where y'all had got off to. How come you're a-missin' the salad lunch. We all been prayin', you know."

"What'd you tell her?"

"Said praise God, you was goin' to California to have a long talk with Mike."

"Oh, Mama, I don't think this is a 'praise the Lord' kinda trip."

"'Course it is, baby. It's about time you pried yourself loose and went out to see him. Him travelin' all the time, like he's a engineer for the railroad. If he was, he'd still be gone, but he'd make more money."

There was a silence, and Tracy could tell her mama was forcing her thoughts back to the present situation.

"He's been after you to come along with him for years," Mama said. "'Rejoice in the Lord always'; Tracy's goin' out to see her husband at last!"

"Mama . . ."

"We're all a-prayin'. That's all I'm a-gonna say to you."

"You promise?"

"Well, I'm your mama. You don't expect me to go easy on you now, do you? You go where he is, that's what I've been a-sayin'. Lots of pretty girls out there making his life a whole hill of temptation without you. That's what I've been a-sayin'."

"Mama, not now. Please. Not now."

"And that's all I'm a-gonna say. You know that boy always loved you, Tracy. Oh, Lordy! I never saw a boy look at a girl with such love in his eyes."

"It's not me he's lookin' at now, Mama."

"Well, you just turn his head right back around then! You put on that little see-through number you bought over yonder in Tulsa at that Victoria's Gossip store—"

"Mama!" How could Tracy end this conversation without blowing up or throwing the cell phone out the window? What would make Mama want to end the lecture on feminine wiles and ways to entice an unfaithful husband back to the farm? An idea! "Hey, Mama, this call is costin' a lot of money."

"Oops! Well, then. Sorry. Better get off. It ain't God's plan those boys don't have their daddy. Sometimes it ain't a woman's fault. But Tracy, Mike's a man, and you haven't been there for him. That's the truth, baby. That's all I'm a-gonna say about it. Your daddy and I are a-prayin'. Love you."

And that was plenty enough said. Tracy bit her tongue as they signed off. How—*how*—could her own mother say such things to her?

This wasn't just about putting on some slinky see-through thing and enticing Mike back to Arkansas! He had made a choice. Chosen a life that she could never share. He was the one who gave up summer nights making love on the porch under the stars to go chasing off around the country, not her!

Tears of indignation brimmed in her eyes. How could her own mother say such things to her with everything she was going through? It felt like a betrayal! And how could Tracy ever rejoice in such a circumstance? How could she hold her head up if she and Mike were the subject of gossip at the Christian women's salad luncheon?

Flagstaff was five miles ahead. Not for the first time, Tracy wondered what she was doing, driving all the way out to California. Maybe she should just get a good night's sleep, turn around, and go on home.

✪ ✪ ✪

Northern Peshawar Region
Western Pakistan
Sunday, 6 September
0231 hours, Local Time

FIREPOWER

Lifting off from the forward air base in Jalalabad, Afghanistan, two AH-64 Apaches sliced through the Afghan-Pakistan border escorting four UH-60 Black Hawk helicopters. Operation Rock Audio had begun.

The eerie early morning sky was still dark. The moon had long since gone to bed, but it made no difference for navigation. Using the Pilot Night Vision Sensor system, thermal images of the landscape below were fed to the pilot's eye through a one-inch TV tube mounted on the right side of his helmet. Wherever the pilot looked, the external night sensor moved, turning the darkest nights into broad daylight.

Armed to the teeth, the Apaches tore past the craggy peaks and over the barren valleys, heading into the lawless tribal-run region north of Peshawar, east of Asadabad.

Each Apache was operated by two men—a pilot and a gunner,

whose fingertips commanded 1200 rounds of 30mm ammo for the nose-mounted chain gun. Roughly the diameter of a fat marking pen, the blue-and-red, high-explosive ammunition could easily penetrate light armor.

The Hellfire missiles, the laser-guided antitank weapon of choice normally carried by the Apaches, had been traded for two rocket pods and extra fuel tanks. The detachable pods held 38 2.75-inch Folding-Fin Aerial Rockets (FFARs), suitable for blasting away at fortified positions.

The Apache was the ideal high-speed, low-drag, quick-assault chopper. It was perfectly suited for laying down heavy suppressive fire to protect the four Delta squads inside the Black Hawks, whose mission was to find Marcos and the hidden tape and capture or kill any al Qaeda resistance.

Riding in the lead UH-60 Black Hawk 1, AFSOIC Master Sergeant Wells reviewed the coordinates provided by the intelligence on Marcos's last communication. Wells was not one of the pilots, nor was he part of the seven-member Delta Squad 1 who silently waited. The only one of his kind, Wells had been appointed Mission Specialist on Operation Rock Audio.

Wells marked their destination on a map illuminated by a red light. His forefinger circled a narrow valley 23 miles east of the Afghan border. He tapped the natural bottleneck in the terrain where the mountains narrowed, near their planned Landing Zone. "This is probably where AIF 17 encountered some problems," he called to the Black Hawk navigations technician.

Wearing a flight helmet and suit, Crewman Colbert nodded, shouting over the hum of the aircraft, "Looks like a good ambush spot. I recommend we swoop up from the east side and drop in. Less time for anyone to hear us coming."

"We don't want to be any deeper in the country than necessary," Wells argued, knowing full well the Pakistani government had been less than fully cooperative about smoking bin Laden's gophers out of their holes.

The political situation was tricky. Prior to Operation Enduring Freedom in 2001, Afghanistan had been run by the Taliban, who refused to aid the United States in its mission to dismantle the al Qaeda terror organization.

So be it.

Along with a coalition of the willing, America had stormed in with more than probable cause and taken over. The Taliban leadership had tumbled into the pit of history, power was given back to the Afghan people, and an international coalition set out to accomplish its original mission to rid the world of al Qaeda.

No problem.

Except . . .

Pakistan, though not an enemy of the coalition, was still not quite an ally. It was also the one country truly backing Taliban rule, and had reservations about supporting the United States in the War on Terror. Pakistan's population was primarily Muslim, and though in many respects a modern country, its politics still bordered on Old World backward.

Once Afghanistan fell to the forces of democracy, surviving al Qaeda members learned of Pakistan's desire to remain semi-independent of the international coalition. There was a mass migration of enemy forces. Al Qaeda terrorists and Taliban officials fled Afghanistan like refugees, digging their way out through the porous border into nearby Pakistan.

Complicating matters was the threat of nuclear war. At the same time the border leaked terrorists like a sieve, huge numbers of Pakistan's armed forces were massed on another border, the one with India, in a nuclear standoff. Even if the forces had wanted to cooperate, they couldn't. As a result, al Qaeda, already adept at survival in the rugged mountainous regions of Afghanistan, moved into the lawless areas of Pakistan and set up camps.

The Pakistani government was not completely unhelpful though. They allowed certain provisions for small units of soldiers from the international "Coalition of the Willing" to operate within their territory. But the hoops through which the U.S. was required to jump in order to mount such a mission made it impossible for forces to operate on the whim of a flimsy tip or unconfirmed intel.

These limitations, combined with the recent news that Pakistani scientists had proliferated nuclear weapons to some of the world's most dangerous rogue states, made the strained ties between the United States and Pakistan even more tense.

All these reasons shaped the plan that required AFSOC to drop in clandestine seven-man units to begin with. They also led to Wells's response to the navigator's suggestion. Master Sergeant Wells didn't want to be part of making the political situation any worse. "We need to head north up this valley and then in from the west over this range."

Crewman Colbert disagreed. "Mountains on the west side are too high. These Hawks have a ceiling of 11,000 feet. It'll be too dangerous. Plus we'll be more exposed when we come into the LZ."

Wells studied the map over and over, searching for another way. "Sorry. Too many villages along the southern route for us to be invisible."

Colbert shook his head in frustration. "Politics before mission safety! It's ridiculous!"

Wells passed the navigation plans along to the pilots.

Colbert's rant grew into a cursing tirade. "You know, we shoulda done the Paki's the same way we shoulda' done the Russians in World War II!"

"So?" Wells responded, unwavering. "But we didn't and we aren't gonna fuel the fire now. We got our orders. Let's stick to them."

The men fell silent again as the column of choppers swooped north through the craggy peaks of Pakistan.

FBI Call Center
San Francisco, California
Saturday, 5 September
1554 hours, Pacific Time

LOST FOR WORDS

Downing, red-faced, leaned forward at the small desk in the cubical. The phone was pressed to his ear while he waited on hold. He had spent the last two hours trying to get through to the right people. Downing got as far as the dictionary's consumer beta test assistant director.

"Mr. Downing, this is Mr. Fielding," a voice finally said on the other end of the phone.

"Yes, sir." Downing lifted his head, hoping to at last hear a good, helpful word.

"I'm sorry for the delay. I did manage to reach the division director, who's in New York at a convention. He said he was actually in product development around the time that software was released, and he vaguely remembers the version of Webster's you mentioned."

Downing interjected, "Version 0.1? That's great!"

"Yes, Version 0.1. He said it was released on only a few hundred machines."

Downing could hardly sit still. "So is it available? Can you get it for me, please?"

The man on the other end of the line sounded regretful. "Unfortunately, that type of material would be archived. We just don't keep old betas around. Not that old."

"So you can get it from the archives, then?" Downing pressed.

"I'm afraid no one in that department works during the weekend."

"Call them!"

"Sir, I tried. I can't reach anyone."

Downing bit his lip. "Then try again. Please understand that when you do this for me, you are doing it for the sake of the country! This may be critically important."

"As the government has been so helpful to Microsoft . . ."

Downing was infuriated—coldly furious. "If we ever meet in person I'll pretend I didn't hear you say that. This isn't the time to gripe about the antitrust case. Thousands of lives could be at stake here!"

"No, sir, hardly what I meant." The man, extremely apologetic, backpedaled and clarified himself. "I meant that we at Microsoft are certainly grateful for all the United States government's business and if there is anything we can do . . . I'll continue to try, sir. And if I can get someone down here tonight, I will definitely call you."

Growling to himself, Downing closed his eyes and pounded on his desk.

"Mr. Downing?"

Downing was silent for a few seconds as he collected himself. "You have my numbers?"

"I have your numbers."

"Please call me if you hear anything."

"I'll do it. Thank you. Oh, and one more thought."

"Yes!" Downing sprang back to life.

"You might try a local computer technician. They may have some of the older versions lying around."

"That's a good idea, Mr. Fielding. Thank you."

"Good-bye, then."

Downing hung up the phone in defeat. Hours wasted chasing what might amount to nothing. He sighed and stood, addressing the call center operatives. The eight other agents placed their calls on hold to listen. "All right people, anyone get through to Webster's?"

No reply.

"How about Hewlett-Packard? Anyone getting anywhere?"

Nothing.

"All right, new plan. I want you all to get in the phone book and call all the computer sales and support numbers you can find. Divide them up. Get every local who answers the phone to go digging in the box under the stairs. We need to find this thing tonight!"

It was like unpausing a waterfall. All the agents crashed back into work at once. Downing had lifted the phone again himself when a man walked up behind him.

"Charles?"

Senator Morrison. Downing blinked and turned around.

The senator's smile was bright and his voice optimistic, though Downing spotted a faint dullness in his eyes. "No progress, eh?"

Downing clenched his jaw. "I was just about to call Miles to see what he found on the Internet, but I figure he'd have called me first if he had anything."

Morrison nodded. "I just talked to him. Nothing either."

"Agent Downing." A young man in a blue pin-striped suit popped his head above the wall. "I've called two of those places and so far they're closed. It's Saturday, sir."

Downing snapped, "I know what day it is! Keep trying!" He lowered his face into his hand.

Senator Morrison patted him on the back, squeezing his shoulder as he offered a little fatherly pep talk. "Charles, you can only do what's within your own power. Don't waste your energy worrying about the things outside of your control." He patted him harder. "Spinnin' your wheels isn't worth it."

Downing looked up. "You're right, sir."

"I know I'm right. That's why they call me Director and pay me the big bucks!"

The agents had a laugh before Morrison added, "Why don't you get a couple dictionaries—old-fashioned, paper ones, that is? Webster's from the year before the software was released. Just start flippin' through the pages."

With a slow, steady nod Downing agreed. "Good idea. I'll send some guys out to Barnes & Noble to pick up every dictionary they have. We'll get right on it, soon as they return."

"Thata boy."

Downing dispatched a couple young agents with a Bureau credit card, while he got back to the phones.

✪ ✪ ✪

FBI, JTTF Technical Investigation Lab
Los Angeles, California
1603 hours, Pacific Time

RECIPE FOR DISASTER

Kristi Kross removed a shiny gallon paint can from the shelf seconds before her phone rang. "Hello?"

"Miss Kross. I'm glad I caught you." Morrison's Southern drawl carried an urgent note. "I called to congratulate you on the fingerprint processing. Besides the ones we already knew of, the big hit was Mohammed al Krefa."

"And he would be the big fish then?"

"That he would. A known terrorist associate of a Khalil—"

She interrupted, "The wealthy shipper. I remember!"

"You got it," Morrison continued. "Al Krefa's been pretty high on the list since he busted out of prison in Yemen, or was let out. Anyway, his passport hasn't been used, for obvious reasons, but your work and the bank's surveillance video proves that he's right here, right now, somewhere in LA."

Kristi leaned her head to hold the phone, brushing back her long blonde locks. "That's great, Senator. Bad news, but thank you for the compliment just the same. How else can I help?"

"I speak for many when I say that the news is startling. It's beginning to look like this operation is much bigger than we anticipated and may be every bit as close to the punch as we imagined. I was hoping you could tell me a little about the explosives that went off in the house this morning."

"Just working on that when you called." Kristi picked up a printout. "I ran a preliminary test of the material through the Mass Spec Analyzer—"

"Speak English for me," the senator teased.

Kristi dropped the printout on the desk and then pried the lid off the top of the paint can with a screwdriver while she explained. "Mass Spectrum Analyzer, or MSA, is a device used to tell us all of the core elements present in a sample." Using tweezers she pulled a tiny black strip loose from inside the can's lid. "I let the sample material soak, as we say, into a charcoal strip inside an airtight container, usually for a minimum of 24 hours. The strip absorbs fumes from the substance."

She placed the charcoal strip in a shallow dish. "We then insert that controlled sample into the MSA, and the machine reads with such precision that only one atom of each element is able to pass through the system at a time."

Kristi slid the small dish into a slot in the countertop machine in front of her. "MSA then logs those atoms, keeping track of the amount of each element as read from the controlled sample. The end result is a graphic that displays recorded amounts for all known elements present and their proportions."

"Very interesting," Morrison replied. "So you've got some results?"

"In fact I do," Kristi said, lifting the paper again. "The samples I ran showed high levels of nitrates, ammonium, aluminum, and some of the complex hydrocarbons found in fossil fuels."

"Now, Kristi, I'm just a layman, but from the sound of that shopping list, we've got a little recipe for ANFO."

"Correct. Ammonium Nitrate Fuel Oil." Kristi nodded calmly as if they had been discussing cookie dough. "It makes for a nasty explosive."

"And you're positive . . . that machine is 100 percent accurate?"

"Senator, nothing in science ever is, and these tests are all very premature, but the levels of those substances are so high it'd be tough to argue with the conclusion, even this early."

Morrison paused as he considered the possibilities. "Not good."

"Sorry, Senator." She pushed several buttons on the MSA device, canceling three blinking lights. "Not good."

"And did you get the—"

Anticipating his next question, Kristi interjected, "Get the black powder bombs that almost blew me up today?"

". . . is what I was gonna ask."

"I sure did. I was about to run another prelim MSA on them. I checked one out. Looks like pistol powder, reduced with acetone to make a nitroglycerin charge. The ones found were dehydrated right in the plastic jars. An electronic detonator, with wires and all, was buried in the middle of all three brought in from the basement. Heard Alstead and Carter found a few more?"

"Yes. In a locker owned by Mabrouk."

"Mmmm." Kristi sighed with concern.

"I know . . . six or seven of these little packages. Makes you wonder what they might be planning."

Kristi leaned on the counter. "My assessment is, with the results from the MSA and knowing what I do about ANFO—it's easy to make and the materials are easy to procure—I'm sure they're working on more of the same. And all the powder jars . . ." She began to explain. "You see ANFO is a pretty stable substance *on its own.*"

She lifted her head, waving her hand as she explained to the unseen student. "It usually needs a real punch; otherwise it could just burn without exploding. Ammonia, nitrates, and fuel oil by themselves are deflagrating substances. They burn below 3300 feet per second. In order to achieve bursants, explosive detonation, a burn rate higher than 3300 feet is needed for ANFO. Once that critical burn-rate velocity is achieved, the chemical bond in the ANFO is broken and a new one is made."

Kristi closed her eyes. "That's how Timothy McVeigh did it. The explosives train is the most critical part of the bomb, not the ANFO. So I'd bet that these guys are planning to use the little powder cages as detonators to initiate the bigger explosives train."

"Boy, you said a mouthful." Morrison sighed. "From the evidence so far, these fellas are going to set off a bunch of these. And the one at the house was only a test run."

"That's my take." Kristi stared blankly at the wall.

"Okay, we'll factor for that." Clearing his throat, Morrison wrapped up. "Let's be in touch then."

"Senator?" Kristi delayed Morrison from hanging up. "Have you heard any news on Anton?"

She could hear his deep inhale before he spoke. "I'm still waiting to hear his exact condition but . . . it doesn't look real good."

Kristi fell silent. The little device she had so casually described in a matter of minutes had done so much damage in a single instant. Reality set in. A tear ran down her nose and she sniffed.

"Kristi, you okay?" Morrison's tone was of genuine concern.

"I'm fine—" she snuffled—"I, uh . . . sometimes forget what we're up against. What the real cost is in lives."

Morrison's voice lowered to a gentle whisper. "I know. I know it. We are definitely up against some real evil. Pray for Anton and . . . for the team. We need all the help we can get."

Kristi wiped her eyes, smearing a faint trace of mascara down her cheeks. "I will, Senator. I will."

✪ ✪ ✪

Northern Quetta Region
Western Pakistan
Sunday, 6 September
0321 hours, Local Time

SAFETY VS. POLICY

During the latter part of the Cold War, the Soviets had battled the Afghans. Operating on the basic assumption that the enemy of my enemy is my friend, the U.S. military flooded the local tribal leaders there with weapons, including the venerable surface-to-air, heat-seeking, Stinger antiaircraft missiles.

The mujahedin and what later became the Taliban had used these weapons and others very effectively against the Soviets. Eventually the USSR became bogged down by years of slogging it out over what amounted to little more than a pile of rocks and heroin fields and gave it up. Remnants of destroyed Soviet tanks still rusted away on the hills and roads of Afghanistan. Relics of a forgotten war, left as reminders.

But blown-out tanks and burned-up armored personnel carriers weren't all that was forgotten and left behind. A huge surplus of Stinger shoulder-fired missiles remained at large, stockpiled in caves and mud houses.

A terrible irony emerged when the U.S. found itself on the other side of the Stinger's infrared sensors. Americans were now threatened by the very weapons they had perfected and supplied.

Normally groups of low-flying aircraft would distance themselves from each other in order to avoid forming a tight flock that might make them easy targets for Stingers. The spread was also to allow room for antimissile countermeasures.

This time, however, the squadron stayed tight. The requirements to keep their presence as little known as possible and the desire for surprise kept the four Black Hawks and two Apaches closely knit. The concealment offered by night made it more difficult for an observer to know exactly how many aircraft there were. The sound from each chopper's prop wash melted together into an indecipherable whirl in the rocky canyons.

Seconds after the column had topped the ridges and descended toward the LZ, a sizzling orange beacon sailed through the night sky. A Stinger missile was headed directly for the last bird of the bunch.

The formation split, choppers peeling out into four directions. Electronic countermeasures engaged automatically. Chafing flares exploded, generating artificial heat signatures that lit up the night, but it was already too late.

The Stinger collided with the tail section of Black Hawk 4. The explosion practically ripped the bird in two in midair. The UH-60 spun out of control in a fiery spiral toward the valley below.

The pilot fought the controls. Every warning light on the board was lit up. There was no saving it. Nothing to do but hang on and ride it down as the world spun into a blur and into oblivion.

The wreck struck near the base of the mountain. In a mushrooming fireball it tumbled down . . . down . . . down the hillside before coming to rest 150 meters from the scheduled LZ.

All the birds spread out while both Apaches spun around to face the attacker. Stinger shoulder-launchers are single-shots and take half a minute to reload, but guard birds Alpha 1 and Alpha 2 weren't about to wait to discover if the shooter had a second one.

Aided by the NVS—the Night Vision System—the copilot gunner homed in on the launch spot. A single man in a white robe and checkered head scarf scrambled up the hill. Alpha 1 cut loose several rockets from under the stubby wing before also tearing up the side of the mountain with the 30mm chain gun.

The explosive-tipped rounds pocked the darkness with brilliant flashes just as the rockets cratered in orange, white, and blue explosions.

Alpha 1 banked hard in a maneuver to throw off any other contenders, leaving the target momentarily to reassess the danger.

Master Sergeant Wells had been slammed against the cockpit wall when Hawk 1 had banked out of formation. He shook off the impact to figure out what had happened. One of the Delta crew had flung open the door and was busy rattling the 50-caliber chain gun at every inch of earth.

When no other Tangos were spotted, Hawk 1 circled in again. This time Wells could see the flaming wreckage of Hawk 4 below.

Colonel Borland, back at Air Force Command and Control, was contacted, but there was little to be done. The wound had been inflicted. There would be no denying that an American military aircraft lay at the bottom of a ravine in Pakistan.

Was Colonel Borland to blame? No, for he'd planned for everything. Was he surprised? Yes, and in his words, "After taking out one unit, why would anyone be fool enough to stick around and wait for the search-and-rescue teams?"

Sadly, Colonel Borland found out why.

Crewman Colbert had also been right in his navigational argument with Wells: War is a nasty business, where team-member safety and policy don't run parallel.

Still, it wasn't Wells's fault either. He had his orders.

Anticipated, yes, but no one could have prevented the ambush. It was a skill terrorists had mastered: Lie in wait. Attack from behind. Increase the damage inflicted by attacking those sent to rescue the first to fall.

But even in the face of grave danger, American military doctrine doesn't change: "Leave no man behind."

And so, the Delta teams' mission remained:

Find Marcos and his squad.

Recover the audio tape hidden in the cliff face.

Capture or kill al Qaeda operatives and anyone who resists.

Once an exhaustive aerial search of the surrounding hills was performed, Hawks 1, 2, and 3 set down in the Quetta region of Pakistan. Alpha 1 and Alpha 2 remained airborne, flying top cover for the mission.

Wells and the surviving 21 Delta men spread out. One squad fanned toward the wreckage. The other two teams took cover on the opposite hill, hoping to discover the gorge where Marcos Caracas's final words had been recorded.

ELEVEN

Holiday Inn Express
Flagstaff, Arizona
Saturday, 5 September
2022 hours, Mountain Time

HARDHEADED IN FLAGSTAFF

"Hey, Mom! A pool! This place has a pool!"

"Mom! Can we go swimmin'?"

"Mom! A pool! Pizza Hut right next door!"

"Pizza Hut! Can we?"

Tracy rolled their luggage up to the check-in counter of the Flagstaff Holiday Inn Express and asked for a nonsmoking room overlooking the pool.

After checking her in, the clerk slid the folder with the key cards across the counter and circled a number on a floor plan. "You're here at reception. Room 202 is there. Two double beds. Nonsmoking. AAA discount. Continental breakfast from 6 to 8:30 A.M."

Her cell phone beeped, signaling voice mail as Tracy dumped the luggage on the floor of their room and sniffed suspiciously at a whiff of stale cigarette smoke. With a sigh she switched on the window air conditioner and sank down on the bed while Justin and Connor dug through their bags for swim trunks. It occurred to Tracy that kids surely did react differently than adults after traveling eight hours. They suddenly had energy. All she wanted to do was lie down awhile.

"Come on, Mom!" Connor, already dressed in red trunks with his little white potbelly hanging out, swung her bathing suit around his head like a lasso.

She sighed. "Okay, Con. Lemme check messages first." She dialed the access number and waited for the cue. *"Please enter your password. You have two voice messages."*

Tracy followed instructions. *"Message 1:* 'Hey Tracy, honey, this is your mama callin'. Just wanted to tell you I'm still a-prayin'. I know the Lord's gonna speak to you directly 'bout what you need to do. I had a word from the Lord when I was a-prayin'. "Put your trust in God," the Lord said to me. "Trust in God and she'll see the answer when she takes head in hand." Now, I reckon that means the Lord put a good head on your shoulders even if you are a mite hardheaded. But you're no fool. So use your head and figure it out. And that's all I'm a-gonna say about it. So . . . this has been your mama talkin'. Daddy and I love you, honey. And the boys and Mike too. Bye now.' "

Tracy glared at the phone and pushed *Delete.*

"Message 2: 'Hey, Trace. It's me. I was tryin' to tell you, hon. Tryin' . . . I'm . . . so, so sorry for what I have done. Sorry. Bone-deep, wash-my-soul-in-the-blood-of-Christ sorry. Some of the guys here, they're Christians. They seen what kind of woman she is. Knew about you and the family. They been talkin' to me. Prayin' with me. And then there was somethin' that happened. Got me spooked. Maybe it don't mean anythin' to you anymore, but I seen what I done. It's worse than I ever dreamed. I need you, Trace. I love you, and I need you to help me figger out what to do now. Okay? Call me. If you want to.' "

Tracy punched the number to save the message. She snapped her black swimsuit out of Connor's hand and retreated to the bathroom to listen again and again until at last the boys' demands for a swim could not be ignored.

✪ ✪ ✪

UCLA Burn Center
Los Angeles, California
1937 hours, Pacific Time

GOOD-BYE, FRIEND

An hour earlier Steve and Carter had still been wrangling with news
reporters and spectators at the health club. The media had begun to
piece together the events of the day, including the explosion at the
terrorist's house and the death of Hakim.

Morrison had hoped to keep things quiet, crack the cell and foil
their plan without the public knowing, as the JTTF frequently managed to do. Even spectacular disasters, if explained as accidents,
wouldn't arouse the public's fears, promote panic, or alert links in
terror networks that law enforcement was closing in.

This strategy worked as long as the occurrences were compartmen-
talized and remained singular in public perception. But this time, from
the house explosion to the train derailment to Hakim's death and
finally to the bomb squad's descent on a gym, the secrecy of the operation had shattered like a busted water pipe in a wall.

There was a flood of speculation and a whole lot of mess to clean up.

Just when Steve thought things couldn't get worse, Morrison called.

"Steve, Anton is pretty broken up inside."

"What's wrong? I thought he was doing better."

"It's not just the burns, Steve. He's got some internal damage."
Morrison had trouble speaking. His voice was hoarse. ". . . heart is
operating at 25 percent. Kidneys are down and—" the senator's
voice cracked, and he paused to clear his throat—"life support just
isn't holding, Steve. I'm sorry. Anton may not make it through the
night."

Steve swallowed hard and tried to be analytical. How well he knew
that the devastation to a human body caused by the force of an explosion isn't always visible. Often the crushing impact of overpressure
critically wounds victims internally. One minute a conscious survivor

is thought to be fine. In the next instant the doctors realize the victim with unseen symptoms is in the worst shape of all.

"Life support not holding? How could that be? I just saw him this morning." Steve's world slipped into a downward spiral as the words sank in. He had to sit down on the curb to keep from collapsing.

Life felt like a detached dream. Steve watched reality pass by him like scenes in a movie. He felt disconnected, distant.

Carter drove Steve to the hospital . . . to say good-bye.

Weak and nauseated, Steve paused to sip water from a drinking fountain and splash it over his face. The cool water felt good. He closed his eyes as it washed over his cheeks. His body ached from all that had happened today. His feet felt heavy, his heart even heavier.

Anton . . .

Steve's heart skipped a beat.

For years Anton Brown had been more than just his partner. Anton was his best friend. They had been through almost everything together—including family picnics, births, and bringing down a major terror cell. They had saved each other's lives many times, and even rescued Steve's son Matthew when he was kidnapped.

Anton and Steve had functioned symbiotically, helping each other through life and loss.

Steve lifted his dripping head. The water concealed his tears, but still he didn't turn to face Carter. He spoke slowly to hide the trembling in his voice. "I'll be back in a few minutes."

Carter sat down in a lobby chair. "Take your time," he replied with deep concern, not wanting to intrude on Steve's apparent grief.

The map on the hospital directory instructed Steve to follow the red stripe on the floor all the way to the critical burn unit. He staggered along slowly and gave a heavy sigh.

It had been a long, wearying day. Yet as hard as it had all been, Steve would have done it over a thousand times if he could have changed that one single moment. . . .

Anton.

Steve's head hung as he traced the red line, step by tired step, into the elevator. Doors and hallways, nurses and therapists, doctors, visitors and patients, all floated by, completely invisible to Steve. He couldn't take his mind off Anton. *I wonder how he's doing. Will he be awake? Will I even be allowed to see him?*

The elevator opened on the third floor, where the red line resumed. At the nurses' station, Steve asked one of the attendants, "Anton Brown?"

He didn't even hear her answer but walked in the direction she pointed. Light blue curtains blocked his view inside the room. Pausing for a shaky breath, Steve blinked back the tears. "Please, God, save my friend," he whispered.

Pulling back the drape, Steve entered and was frightened by what he saw. Covered in loose bloodied gauze, Anton lay facedown on a special gurney. Every inch of his body was wrapped. His back had been burned so badly there was no other way to position him. Reflected in a mirror beneath the rig, Anton's swollen eyes were barely visible through slits in the bandages while he slept.

A heart monitor ticked away the remaining seconds of his life. Blood-filled tubes carried life to and from the dialysis machine. A breathing machine forced air through the tube taped to his face.

Steve was in denial. This wasn't Anton. This wasn't the man he knew. Prior to the accident, Anton had been big and strong, able and willing to shoulder the burden of any two men. In shock, Steve simply couldn't accept the reality. This feeble, dying man looked nothing like his friend. There must be a mistake. This must be someone else.

Steve wished to God he could go back in time. Part of him believed he could. In slow motion he relived glimpses of his memories with Anton:

Anton's big laugh while riding in Steve's old Mustang, crossing the Bay Bridge on the way to Oakland.

Anton's gentle smile that promised Steve he wasn't really alone, even when Steve was separated from Cindy. "You've got family," Anton used to say.

Anton's spirit, tough and determined in practice and on missions, yet ready to protect the team with his life at the moment any threat emerged, as he had proven.

Anton's compassionate soul on the day Steve's son, Tommy, was born . . . and soon after, the way he cradled the tiny child in his big arms.

Anton's prayers for Carter, who seemed so cavalier about life and death. For each team member as they faced a new mission.

Anton was angelic. A big-hearted, courageous, muscular angel. No wimped-out, harp-playing angel for Anton Brown.

Steve remembered how he had been there for Anton too. When Anton's daughter had drowned. Steve saw again an image of Anton at little Alyssa's funeral . . . Anton's face buried in his hands as his whole body shook. Trembling . . . sobbing. Wishing he could turn back time . . .

Just as Steve wished he could turn back time today.

The day of the funeral Steve had stood by him like the brother he was. He had grieved with Anton when neither of them understood why.

Just as Steve didn't understand why now.

Tears streamed again from Steve's eyes. His body began to shake. He reached out to touch his friend but could find no place that wasn't bandaged. He wanted to comfort Anton but couldn't.

The feeling of helplessness that surged over him was overtaken by anger. "I promise you, buddy," he said, struggling to speak, "I'll get them." He swept his hand over the bandages. "I'll finish the job, so help me, God. I'll get them for you."

Steve stood, mute, by Anton's bedside for several more minutes. Then he turned and walked toward the doorway, realizing that the next time he saw Anton alive might be in heaven.

Nielson's Metal Finishing Factory
Los Angeles, California
1949 hours, Pacific Time

THE DEATH STAR

The drive from the quarry to Nielson's Metal Finishing Factory was no more than 45 minutes in the light Saturday evening freeway traffic.

Even so, Patrick Dennison was sick of Mohammed al Krefa's griping in less than half of that time.

"It is not my place to do this," al Krefa protested for at least the fiftieth time. "I plan; others execute. I send; others go. I do not drive. I do not—"

"Yeah, well, why are you here then?"

Al Krefa narrowed his eyes. Frowning, he grudgingly allowed, "My plan is good. Too good to waste. Too far along to postpone." He thumped Dennison's shoulder with a clenched fist. "But no more changes!"

"We're here anyway."

The streetlight at the entry to the alleyway was out. The narrow lane behind Nielson's was unlit, bordered by windowless walls at the rear.

Dennison nipped the chain from the gate, shoving it out of the way for al Krefa to drive through before closing it again. The truck was backed up to the loading dock and parked inside 20 seconds.

Nielson's Metal Finishing Factory had been in business for over 30 years, surfacing metal and other media. They had forged a connection to the film industry by doing special set treatments for the original *Star Wars* trilogy and had enjoyed Hollywood's business ever since.

At present there were no secret projects underway in the shop, and nothing in particular worth stealing . . . to anyone except a terrorist.

As promised by the well-paid man on the inside, there were no guards, no dogs, no exterior alarms and no lights. The loading dock was shrouded in darkness.

Using a red light-emitting diode key-chain light, Dennison squinted at the scrap of paper on which was written the alarm code for the rear security panel. A six-number sequence turned the amber *Armed* light to green and the duplicate key opened the metal-core door. Moments later the metal loading-dock door rolled up with a clank.

Dennison located the barrels exactly as agreed upon. One was marked *Powdered Magnesium* and the other *Powdered Aluminum.* Both 55-gallon drums carried the warning symbol *Explosive Hazard.*

Widely used in metal finishing and in the production of metallic paints, magnesium and aluminum in finely ground form had a range of legitimate uses.

It was also true they figured in pyrotechnics. The powders increased the detonating power of explosive charges by a factor of 10. An unenhanced charge big enough to destroy a house would level a city block with the addition of the powdered metal.

Each barrel weighed over 400 pounds. Fortunately, a loading dolly rested against the wall. Dennison grabbed it, nudged the lip against the first drum, and waited expectantly.

"You gonna help me here or what?" he demanded.

"I don't—"

"You wanna get out of here some time tonight?"

With al Krefa jockeying and Dennison doing all the heavy lifting and straining, the first barrel was soon trundled into the bed of the pickup. The Chevy's well-worn leaf springs sagged under the weight of the second keg, then recovered.

"There's another half-full one here," Dennison reported.

"What?"

"Magnesium. Yep, more of that."

"Good. Load it."

"You done helping?" Dennison asked.

"Get it done," al Krefa ordered tersely. "I'll be back." Without explanation, The Bombmaker twisted shut a 12-inch-diameter water valve on a red-painted pipe. Toting a worn leather satchel he'd produced from the cab of the Chevy, he disappeared into the lightless interior of the factory.

By the time Dennison had the three drums lashed securely to the cargo tie-downs, al Krefa had returned.

"What was that about?"

"A small surprise."

"Listen," Dennison suggested as they exited the alleyway. "I been thinking. We're all the way in town here, see? Why don't we go pick up the detonators on this same trip?"

"Don't think! It's not your job!" al Krefa said gruffly. Then, relenting slightly, he explained, "Remember this: Keep components apart till last possible moment—especially detonators. Anything can be explained . . . except them. Without them nobody can prove nothing! Now drive! We stick to the plan."

TWELVE

Royal Palms
Hollywood, California
Saturday, 5 September
2023 hours, Pacific Time

FIFTEEN MINUTES OF FAME

The eight bungalows comprising the Royal Palms dated from the 1920s. Looking over the bedroom, four-foot-square bathroom, and miniscule kitchenette, Mabrouk was certain the place had not been updated since then. Dust from the plastered walls and ceiling settled like fine ash whenever he shut a door. The two-ring gas range required a match to light.

The bed on which he was propped was lumpy where it didn't sag. But in every other way the antique motel suited Mabrouk's needs. When he checked in, the Korean clerk, who barely spoke English, merely grunted when Mabrouk declared that his ID was missing. The man had happily accepted a two-night cash deposit in place of a credit card for one night's lodging.

Mabrouk glanced at his watch: less than 18 hours to go now. Time to prepare himself mentally and spiritually for what lay ahead.

Eighteen hours to Paradise, but that was not the aspect of the immediate future that most held Mabrouk's attention. Instead his thoughts focused on how different the world would be for Americans by this time tomorrow night. These smug, complacent, egotistical Americans. How could they be so gullibly stupid, so blatantly infidel, and yet remain the richest nation on earth? It was an injustice long past due to be righted.

Mabrouk intended tomorrow's blow to be another rallying cry for the resurgence of the Islamic Empire, a step toward its eventual destiny, replacing America as the greatest force anywhere.

What were Americans thinking about tonight?

As much as Mabrouk hated the shallow, self-centered lives portrayed in the American media, he felt himself drawn to see what caught their attention this last night of security.

The television had no remote. The set hummed for a while before a picture appeared. Even then the newswoman had a distinct greenish tint to her skin, but Mabrouk sat on the edge of the bed to watch.

First came five minutes of sex to sell everything from automobiles to diet sodas. This was followed by an ad urging viewers to rush to their doctor and demand a new heartburn remedy.

When the news returned, there was the usual political nonsense. American leaders squabbled. Talking heads pontificated. Video footage showed American flags being burned by Americans to protest their government's decision to send more troops to shore up the new tribal council in Iraq.

The irony was not lost on Mabrouk. As much as such scenes gave comfort and encouragement to terrorist bombers in the U.S. and overseas, Mabrouk knew democratic protest inside the rising Islamic fundamentalist governments of the world would never be permitted. Instead of being feted as peace loving and progressive, any demonstrators would meet swift and harsh retribution. Most would simply disappear . . . permanently.

Mabrouk snorted and switched the channel. The change carried him from national programming to a local news bulletin already in progress. The scene displayed an aerial view, apparently from a helicopter, showing a building surrounded by police and firefighters.

Mabrouk started. He recognized the place: It was the locker room where his detonators were stored! Hurriedly he turned up the volume.

". . . has been called a false alarm by authorities anxious to prevent panic. Los Angeles county officials stress that this was not a terrorist act. But suggesting that more is going on behind the scenes than the brief official announcement indicates, a joint press conference by the Los Angeles Sheriff's Office, the Los Angeles Police Department, and the FBI publicized a Most Wanted warning for this man. . . ."

Mabrouk found he was staring at a photo of himself. The grainy picture showed a man five years younger, with different hair and beard, but it was still unquestionably him.

The news report went on: "This man, known as Mabrouk Ziad, also known as Nathan Gold, is wanted in connection with the death of his brother, Hakim Ziad."

Mabrouk's photo was replaced by a snapshot of The Bombmaker.

"This man, identity unknown, is also being sought for questioning. The public is cautioned that both men should be considered extremely dangerous. If you think you know their whereabouts, contact law-enforcement authorities immediately."

"Al Krefa!" Mabrouk snapped off the set. His mind raced. How had they gotten anything on The Bombmaker? His identity was the most closely guarded secret in the cell.

The fact that somehow he and Mabrouk had been linked proved that the raid on the health club had turned up the detonators.

Mabrouk would have to replace them—and quickly.

But how?

He did not dare phone The Bombmaker or attempt to meet with him. What if The Bombmaker was already compromised? What if part of the news flash was a ruse to draw Mabrouk from hiding?

From this moment Mabrouk was in charge. Prepared or not, he would see the plan through to the end.

✪ ✪ ✪

Gravel Quarry
Near Palmdale, California
2037 hours, Pacific Time

PIXIE DUST

There had been no sign of activity at the alley beside the warehouse, none where the gravel road led back into the hills, nor any indication anyone else had passed that way recently. Around each bend Dennison and al Krefa watched for headlights. The next few hours were critical. If anyone chanced on the waiting cement truck, they would have to be dealt with, or the plan abandoned.

Back at the quarry both men relaxed. The cement mixer loomed up out of the darkness like a slumbering elephant. Dennison had driven it into a low spot, beside the old wooden loading hopper. From the bank above they could step across some planks, then use the catwalk of the hopper as a ledge from which to pour the metallic powders into the drum of the mixer.

Al Krefa informed Dennison that the transfer required moving the magnesium and aluminum in buckets, by hand.

"But I can back my truck right up to the edge, man," Dennison protested. "We can dump the barrels over, right into the mixer."

"Dump over?" Al Krefa slapped Dennison in the chest with a bucket—a *plastic* bucket. "You wish to be martyred before the time, to no purpose? There is grease and oil over the fittings. When mixed with our cargo, one spark and *whoosh*!" Al Krefa pantomimed the whole hillside going up like a skyrocket. "No dumping of metal on metal . . . no metal shovels. By hand only. Quickly now."

The hot east Santa Ana wind blew in their faces as they worked. Had the hopper and hillside faced the other way, the dust would have blown away from them as they laboriously emptied bucket after bucket of powdered metal into the cement mixer.

As it was, bits of magnesium flicked into Dennison's eyes, no matter how carefully he poured. They itched at first, as if gritty with sand, but soon it felt like metal shavings were under his eyelids.

"Don't rub them," al Krefa warned. "Men go blind."

Plastic buckets, but no goggles, Dennison thought with disgust. And what was this stuff doing to their lungs?

A particularly strong gust swept a handful of aluminum into al Krefa's face. He sneezed violently, and the resulting bobble spilled half a bucket on the catwalk. "Hurry," he urged, his voice croaking.

Dennison's eyes were pinched shut, partly through defense and partly because they had swollen that way. It was getting harder and harder to work by the headlights, to see a safe path from pickup to plank to catwalk.

The 4-x-24-inch beam by which they moved from hillside to hopper had seemed plenty wide and plenty sturdy when they began the task. Now it became a test of nerves to place each step carefully and not plunge off into the pool of darkness beside the cement truck.

Somewhere down there Lonnie's body rested under a congealing blanket of concrete. One more handful of the agonizing dust in the eyes, one missed step, and his killer might fly off to join him.

"Hurry!" al Krefa urged the cautious younger man.

"Shut up!" Dennison retorted. "If you think you can go faster, why don't I just watch and you show me how it's done?" Tears streaming down their faces, both men hacked and coughed and spat and sneezed.

When the work was finally completed and the barrels of powdered aluminum and magnesium emptied inside the mixing drum, they took turns pouring bottled water into each other's eyes to clear them. Even so, it took 15 minutes of weeping and blinking before either could see to drive the cement truck on to the next phase of the plan.

✪ ✪ ✪

B&B Surplus
North Hollywood, California
2057 hours, Pacific Time

LAST CALL THERE, BUDDY!
Mabrouk, wearing blue coveralls, hopped out of his car. His long hair was pulled back and tucked beneath a Raider's cap. He almost looked

Mexican—a good thing for him. LA was crawling with cops looking for him.

The streets were busy for being almost 9:00 P.M. Mabrouk ran around the side of the blue metal building and managed to get an arm through the front door just as it was being locked.

Mabrouk pleaded with the clerk to let him in for some reloading supplies. "Please, man. I just got off work. I'm having some guys over for reloading night."

The thin, pock-faced man with a greasy ponytail seemed to understand. "All right, man, but grab a number and get it quick."

"Thanks! You don't know how much this means to me." Mabrouk smiled as he thought of what he would really do with the supplies.

He entered the large showroom of B&B Surplus. It was the store where the infamous robbers of the bank in North Hollywood had stocked up on body armor and 50-caliber ammo. It was also the store where the cops involved in stopping those same robbers bought better armor and 50-caliber ammo.

Mabrouk glanced at all the last-minute customers in different locations around the glass horseshoe-shaped counter. He wondered if anyone might recognize him from the television blaring in one corner, but he managed to keep cool. Searching their faces, he realized there wasn't a pretty boy among them. All the men appeared to be gun-toting rednecks from the NRA, he surmised. Most of them looked more like criminals than he did. Who were they to judge?

He decided his timing was perfect. The employees were scrambling, helping these customers and tidying up the pistol cabinets that spanned the perimeter of the showroom floor. Mabrouk suspected they wanted to get home as much as he did. He walked to the counter and pulled a number.

A fast-speaking guy who looked like Tom Cruise said, "I can help ya' right now."

Mabrouk crumpled the number. "I'm going to be reloading some pistols tonight."

"Okay, sure. We've got stuff for that."

Mabrouk didn't want to ask for Green Dot powder for fear it might trigger a response. Every white-trash Okie in the place might draw down and shoot him. He quickly came up with a plan. "I need a good efficient powder that only takes a little bit. Do you recommend one?"

"Oh, buddy. You're lookin' for somethin' hot—3, 4 grains for 40 cal 'stead of 6 or 8."

"That sounds good. Three pounds." Mabrouk was already staring at the keg he wanted.

"How 'bout tryin' some Green Dot? Good stuff." The attendant pulled a plastic jar from the shelf at the exact moment a Wanted Poster of Mabrouk appeared on TV.

Mabrouk's heart dropped. He quickly called the attendant's attention. "Hey, uh . . . can you show me this gun here?"

"Sorry, buddy. Heard you say you wanted reloading stuff and that's it. We're closed. Maybe next time, huh?" The man hadn't glanced at the TV anyway.

Mabrouk sighed. "Okay." He swallowed hard as sweat trickled from under his cap. He suddenly realized he had no way of setting off the powder. "How about some hobby fuse then?"

The salesman made a face, like he'd just eaten a green lemon. "What are you gonna do with that?"

Frightened, Mabrouk thought the clerk was onto him and remained silent.

"What? You got a little cannon or somethin'?"

"That's it." Mabrouk gulped, thinking he might be sick. "You guessed it. That'll be all."

The attendant gathered the powder and the fuse and began to ring up the sale when he noticed Mabrouk's face. "Hey, uh, you don't look so good, man. Feelin' all right?"

"Bad Mexican food." They were the only words Mabrouk could come up with.

"Yeah, hits me like that too sometimes—" the man did a double take at Mabrouk—"hey, you look familiar. Don't I know you?"

"I don't think so." Mabrouk spoke slowly.

Pausing at the register, the clerk insisted. "Maybe I sold you a gun or somethin' a while back?"

Mabrouk played along. "Yeah, that was it." He read the name tag. "Danny, right?"

"Yeah!" Danny laughed. "You got a good memory. Was it a Sig 9 or a Beretta 92?"

"Beretta 92," Mabrouk answered through a forced smile.

"Yeah! Thought so." The cash-register drawer hit Danny in the belly. "That'll be $53.63."

"Here you go," Mabrouk said, dropping a $50 on the glass surface. He had to dig for some singles, so he decided he'd better keep up the charade. "You've got a good memory too."

"Hey, well thanks, man, and thanks for shopping at B&B." Danny handed back the change and the bag of powder and fuse.

Mabrouk raised his eyebrows as he turned. "Thanks."

The biggest challenge was keeping himself from running through the door. *Slowly, slowly,* he told himself. *Don't do anything crazy.*

He reached for the handle. *Locked!* His heart jumped. *Do they know?* Footsteps echoed behind him.

What if they know? He wanted to turn around swinging. Eyes wide, Mabrouk realized it was Danny close behind him.

"Let you out there, buddy?"

"Thanks" was all Mabrouk could manage before rushing out the door.

Holiday Inn Express
Flagstaff, Arizona
2208 hours, Mountain Time

HEADS OR TAILS

Even after sundown the temperature in Flagstaff hovered just above 100 degrees, but it was a pleasant dry heat, not muggy like back home.

A beat-up Bible open on her lap, Tracy sipped a cherry Coke poolside at the Holiday Inn. Connor and Justin took turns with three other young travelers swimming to the bottom to retrieve a quarter. Yowser, replete after a dinner of mushroom-and-olive, deep-dish pizza, dozed at Tracy's side.

After Mike's voice mail, Tracy had turned off the cell phone. She needed time to think, to figure out what it was she really wanted. Who would have thought the most important decision in her life would be made at a motel in Flagstaff, Arizona?

Should she go home to pick up the pieces of her life alone?

Or drive on to see if maybe she and Mike could work it out somehow?

But even if she still loved him, how could she forgive him for what he had done to her and the boys? More to the point, how could she ever trust him again? How?

Was it easier just to accept that the marriage was at an end than to spend the next 40 or 50 years looking at his face and wondering if he was lying to her? *What's he gone and done, Lord? And what is it to me? Shouldn't I just turn around, go home, and never look back? It's a coin toss. Heads, I use my head; I go to California. Tails, I listen to my fearful heart, turn tail, and run home. Which one, God?*

Either way I lose, she thought.

She gazed down at her Bible. Psalm 112: "Happy are those who fear the Lord. Yes, happy are those who delight in doing what he commands. Their children will be successful everywhere; an entire generation of godly people will be blessed."

But Tracy wasn't happy. Her sons would be scarred by divorce for the rest of their lives. So far nobody she knew had ever been really blessed by Tracy's life.

So, if the Lord was right here beside her, what would he tell her?

All right, Lord, I'm listening. Heads or tails? What?

Justin, his dark Cherokee skin golden in the pool light, dove down to retrieve the silver coin. Beaming, he burst to the surface and shouted, "Hey, Mom! Fastest time! Ten seconds! Want to see me do it again?" He raised his arm to throw it.

A big kid who had been playing with them for the last 20 minutes took offense that Justin's recovery time beat his. "No! We're done! We quit after the last one, remember?" The boy lunged and knocked the quarter from Justin's fist. The coin flew into the air, arched, and spun directly at Tracy. With the instinct of a shortstop on the Arkansas State girls' champion softball team, Tracy made a one-handed grab.

"Good catch, Mom! Is it heads or tails? Tails means quit. Heads means go for it."

Tracy blinked dumbly at Justin, then slapped the coin down on her wrist. *Heads or tails. Quit or go on.* Could it be that God was speaking to her? That his answer would come in this way? If so, the Lord surely had a sense of humor at times.

"Heads or tails?"

She removed her hand to see George Washington in profile. And there it was, just like the Lord had told Mama. Tracy held head in hand. *Liberty* was engraved at the top, and *In God We Trust* was tucked under Washington's chin. She had never noticed that before. Couldn't have told anybody which side of the coin *Trust God* was written on, but there it was, plain as anything, commanding Tracy to trust God, quit goofing around, and go for it. No kidding.

"Heads. Heads it is. In God we trust." She threw the coin back into the water, setting off a mad scramble to fetch it. She whispered, "All right, Lord. All right. I heard you. Mama's been really talking to you, I reckon. Okay. We're goin' on to California."

FBI Call Center
San Francisco, California
2112 hours, Pacific Time

DICTION

The tense code-cracking atmosphere, along with the mingled smells of cold pizza and fresh coffee, reminded Charles Downing of his days at The Farm, studying for exams. The Farm was the CIA's once-secret name for their private grounds in Langley, Virginia, where recruits were brought in to train and study.

"Ah, the good ol' days." Downing sighed, puffing his cheeks out.

One of the other agents who worked in the San Francisco FBI offices looked up from his sheet of pencil scratches. "When was that?"

Downing remembered the importance of the course of study, before computers had become really common. It had been a time when the good guys used their wits alone to find what bad guys had used theirs to hide. "The Farm. Cramming for finals in our Cryptology–Mathematical Equations class."

The agent nodded. Almost everyone who worked in a high-level law-enforcement agency had been through something like it.

Downing scratched his head and lifted his paper to read the string of random words again:

amice ninety frustule often sentiment sirup quotation

After a certain point, belaboring the words made little sense. Downing called out, "Okay, time to reset."

Most of the seven other people in the room dropped their pencils.

"We know—or at least we assume with great certainty—that the words are based on some kind of phonetic code." Downing read the first letter of each word slowly. *"A . . . N . . . F . . . O . . . S . . . S . . . Q."* Clearing his throat, he ran his fingers through his hair. "With the contributions made by Miss Kross and the rest of LA's JTTF guys, we know that ANFO is Ammonium Nitrate Fuel Oil and is something these guys used—and may be planning to use on a larger scale." He frowned before flipping the lock of dark hair from his face. "What we don't know is what the letters *S, S, Q* stand for."

A young agent in a short-sleeve white shirt with a cheap tie pulled away from his loosened collar raised his hand as he began to speak. "How about *Sixth Street* . . . uh . . . *Question*." He stumbled. "A question . . . maybe the sender is asking a question: How about an ANFO Bomb on Sixth Street?"

"I came up with *Sixth Street* too," a thin, very tall agent with red hair and narrow glasses added softly. "But I came up with *Quadrant*, meaning location, or possibly even *Quake* or *Quarter*, as in quarter of the day, meaning 6:00 A.M." He shrugged. "I don't know, maybe . . . ?"

Downing furrowed his brows, clicking his tongue. "Pretty good, pretty good. I'll send that one out. We'll see what happens on Sixth Street and six . . ." His voice trailed off. "Six, street, six." The numbers reminded him of the biblical mark of the beast, from the book of Revelation.

Miles Miller raised his hand. "I've got one." He read from his paper. "How about ANFO . . . *September* . . . *Sixth* . . . *Quran*."

The chill that ran through the room was as palpable as an icy wind. Miles had struck a raw nerve. After all, the terror-cell members were Muslim fanatics, with the Quran—the Koran—as their holy book. Current intel suggested an attack was imminent . . . making the date a likely fit.

But still they were no closer to discovering the truth. None of the other messages revealed anything even remotely translatable. Letters could be transmuted through phonetic clues into words, but the team would have to consider nearly every word in the dictionary. At a hundred thousand entries, the string of letters could create just about any meaning in the world.

Downing rubbed the permanent wrinkle in his forehead. He was worn out. "Until we get the right copy of the dictionary, I just don't see how we can come up with anything more definite that this." His voice registered defeat. "Maybe we should break for the night, make it an early morning when we have a version of the dictionary to work from—"

"Wait!" a muscular agent shouted from the back of the room as he jumped up with his paper. "*Quod*! It's British slang for prison!"

Downing blinked as he considered it. "ANFO . . . September Sixth . . . at the Prison. Wow!" he exclaimed. "Abdel, the man who survived the Glendale 5 house explosion, is at the prison!"

The agent searched the ceiling for inspiration. "I'll bet the train derailment was nothing more than a warning, or a hint. The terrorists might be planning another attack with a large ANFO bomb!"

"Bombs!" Downing corrected. "We have evidence they were planning to set off a bunch of these things." The nuance of what he'd just heard struck him. "Possibly at prisons around the county or state." Downing grabbed the phone. The room was quiet enough that he could hear the agents breathing. He waited. "Senator Morrison! I think we have it!"

Morrison sounded startled. "What? The target?"

"Yes. We've been working on the codes here. We believe we can make sense of one of them by translating them into the phonetic alphabet. ANFOSSQ."

The muscular, clean-cut young agent handed Downing his sheet of paper.

"And what does it mean?" Morrison asked.

Downing lifted the page. "Ammonium Nitrate Fuel Oil attack on September Sixth at the Quod, which is another word for prison. It's British. Isn't Mohammed al Krefa from Britain?"

Morrison silently considered the plausibility of their discovery. "And isn't Abdel—?"

Downing cut him off. "In the LACJ, where there was a train derailment today. Did we ever find out what caused it?"

"No, but I can check into it further." Morrison offered energetically. "And I'll let Special Operations Director Davis know what we've got. And alert the prison."

"Or *prisons,* sir," added Downing.

"Prisons, right. I'll discuss sending out an All Points Bulletin to all the correctional facilities in the state. Let me get back with you." Morrison sounded distant, as his mind raced ahead. "Go get some sleep fast. I'll be in touch."

Downing agreed, hanging up the phone. Everyone in the room stared at him with bulging eyes.

Finally Miles asked, "So what'd he say?"

"He said he's sending out an APB. Go home and get some sleep!"

The people in the room cheered. A breakthrough. Success. Finally what had been a very long workday for most of them had at last come to a close.

The agents stood, slapped each other's backs, and shook hands as they headed for the door.

Miles was the last to shake Downing's hand. "Guess I can take tomorrow off then."

Charles Downing laughed. "I don't know about that. I still need your help finding the proper version of the dictionary. We still have a lot to clear up."

Miles pursed his lips. He wore the disappointment of a five-year-old who had been told "no balloon." "Okay, then."

"I'll pick you up outside your apartment at 0730."

Miles winced. "Okay, 7:30. Can I get a ride back to my place?"

"Sure, Miles. Anything. You deserve it."

THIRTEEN

FBI, Chapter 16 Offices
San Francisco, California
Saturday, 5 September
2124 hours, Pacific Time

FUNERAL PYRE

It couldn't have been more than 15 minutes since Senator Morrison had hung up the phone with Special Operations Director Davis that Davis called back.

Morrison replaced a stylish silver pen into the drawer of his walnut-inlaid desk. "Director Davis, what did we forget?"

"I sent out that APB, but that isn't why I'm calling." The tone of Davis's voice wasn't promising. "I wanted to catch you before you left. Give you a heads-up on something."

Morrison slowly slid the drawer closed as he stood. "Certainly. What about?"

"Literally 10 . . . 12 minutes ago, the factory where Mabrouk's brother, Hakim, worked, the one who was killed by the bus . . ."

"Yes." Morrison, anticipating, leaned over the desk.

"It just blew up. Still blazing."

"Mmmm." Morrison sat back down on the edge of his seat.

"I've got to be honest. It doesn't look too good."

Licking his lower lip, Morrison asked, "What sort of place was it?"

"Metal finishing factory. They use materials like powdered aluminum and bronze. Anyway, I know we've been talking about ANFO here . . ."

"Yep."

". . . and through my experience up north as a bomb tech, I know that possible key ingredients to make this stuff more volatile are certain metal powders, even crumpled aluminum foil. The news is all over this already. The coverage is live right now. It's on LA channel 5, if you get that channel on cable up there."

"Hang on a minute." Morrison grabbed the remote off his desk, rotated his chair 90 degrees, and switched on the television. Scanning through the channels, he stopped on the aerial view of a factory fully engulfed in flames. Periodic small explosions sent brightly colored embers showering over the parking lot and nearby buildings. Portions of the sheet-metal roof melted and sagged, eventually falling into the smoke. "Oh no . . . ," he breathed aloud.

"I'm watching right now too," Davis confirmed. "Those little flashes burn at 4- to 5000 degrees F. Pretty hairy when used as an accelerant in a bomb." Davis spoke softly and thoughtfully as he continued with his concerns. "Anyway, I find it too coincidental that the day this guy Hakim ends up dead, and his workplace, which happens to have this stuff in it, gets burned down."

Apprehension covered Morrison's face. He rubbed his forehead. "*Suspicious* would be a significant understatement," he drawled.

Davis added, "I heard from Dispatch that the alarm company recorded a brief power failure, right around 8 o'clock tonight."

"As if someone broke in?"

"Inside job?" Davis speculated further.

"You think?"

"No way of telling right now, but my guess—this is arson. If it isn't just a funeral pyre for Hakim, it was probably set to cover up something else."

"Like the theft of some of the materials—" Morrison shifted gears—"once the fire is out, will we be able to determine if anything has been taken?"

"You're asking the wrong guy here. You might try that bright arson investigator of yours."

"Even with Kristi sifting the ashes, it'll be almost impossible to inventory after the fact."

Morrison practically heard the mental nod of assent from Davis. "That's what I think too . . . anyway, thought I'd let you know."

"We're on it," Morrison said. After he hung up he added to himself, "I only hope we're on it . . . in time."

✪ ✪ ✪

7-Eleven
Fontana, California
2128 hours, Pacific Time

PARDON MY FRENCH

Thirty-four-year-old Mike Roberts stared blankly into the picked-over ice-cream freezer at the 7-Eleven. Only the weird Ben & Jerry's flavors were left. No Chocolate Chip Cookie Dough ice cream. Mike ran a hand through his close-cropped blond hair and shook his head in frustration. How could Joseph be out of Chocolate Chip Cookie Dough at such a moment? When he'd taken this quick break because the guys were desperate for inspiration?

"Hey, Joseph? What's the deal with the ice cream, man?" he called to the olive-skinned, Lebanese clerk who seemed to always be behind the cash register no matter what time of day or season of the year. All the guys on the crew knew Joseph. He'd worked at the 7-Eleven for as long as anybody remembered.

Joseph shrugged. "You guys. You guys. Man! Like a flock of grasshoppers swooping down on Ben & Jerry's. Don't you eat other flavors? I thought you guys liked Cherry Garcia. I got lots of Cherry Garcia."

"Come on, now. You remember. Chocolate Chip Cookie Dough. It's a good-luck thing for us. You know that. Last year you had a ton of it laid in for us."

Joseph squirted Windex on the countertop and wiped it with a paper towel. "Cherry Garcia. They named the flavor after that guy from the Grateful Dead who died. You remember him?"

Mike noted two entire shelves of ice cream dedicated to the late Grateful Dead guitarist, Jerry Garcia. Mike drawled, "We're gentlemen from Dixie, Joseph. Not into that hippie kind of music. Or hippie ice cream either. Now I'm gonna have to drive somewhere else for it."

Joseph's eyes sparkled with amusement. "Won't do you no good. None left nowhere. You know who come in here an hour ago lookin' to buy up the world's supply of your good luck? Bought every quart of Chocolate Chip Cookie Dough in LA."

Mike's brow creased in a frown. "Who'd do that to us?"

"Your competition, that's who. After what you guys done—putting the fish under the cushions of their motor home."

Mike grimaced and wondered if every market within a 10-mile radius had been raided. "You heard about that, huh?"

"Everybody heard about it. So you know what? If I wasn't your true friend, you guys would be all outta luck. But I saw it coming. There was three of them two nights ago. Greasy red coveralls. Your competition. They come in laughin' and talkin' about what they gonna do to you guys to get even. So I hid it."

"You hid it?"

"I got two whole crates of Ben & Jerry's Chocolate Chip Cookie Dough back in the freezer. Saved it for you guys."

Mike laughed loudly, feeling enormously relieved. The winning tradition would be upheld! "You're the man!"

Joseph sauntered toward the door leading to the cold room. Then the clerk looked out the windows. His grin faded. "Here come trouble, Mike. That girl. You broke up with that jihad hottie, right?"

"You mean Frenchie?"

"She ain't French, but call her whatever you like. She just got outta her car in the parking lot there."

Mike followed Joseph's gaze to the tall, slim, dusky beauty wearing short shorts and a tight T-shirt with a faded American flag stretched across her bosom. She stood talking to a Hispanic-looking man at the back of her car.

Mike ducked behind the cookie section. "Oh, man, Joseph! Is she comin' in here?"

"I don't know. She's talking to some guy. Oh. There. She just leaned in and took a big brown envelope outta her front seat. She's giving the envelope to the guy now. He's looking in it. Looks real happy."

"Well, is she coming in?" Mike was on the edge of panic.

"He's leaving. The guy is leaving. And she's . . . yep, she's coming into the store."

"Oh, man! Joseph, hide me!"

The clerk held open the cooler door and motioned Mike in. Bent at the middle, Mike made a dash into the cold room. Joseph slammed the door and locked it behind him just as Frenchie entered.

Safe!

Mike watched through the glass of the refrigerator section from behind a screen of chocolate milk cartons.

Joseph, sullen and suspicious, resumed his station behind the cash register.

Frenchie tossed her dark hair and gave Joseph a look mean enough to kill as she passed him. Neither one liked the other—that was plain. But why?

Joseph crossed his arms in a posture of belligerence.

What was it the little Lebanese clerk had called her? Jihad hottie? And what did Joseph mean she wasn't French? Mike wondered. For months she had spoken French and broken English with a sexy accent meant to entice him and every male within earshot. Mike hadn't understood a word, but it was French all right. She might have been calling him the biggest fool in America for falling for her, but in French it sounded really good to him.

Mike rubbed his cheek and thought about Tracy and the boys. About what he had thrown away for long legs, a flashy smile, and a mysterious foreign accent. He had suspected Frenchie wanted to marry an American to get a permanent visa and citizenship. He wasn't the only one to suspect that was her plan. Mike really had been the biggest fool in America to fall for it.

Frenchie picked up a bag of pretzels and read the label.

Joseph called to her, "Pork rinds are good. Ever try pork rinds?"

Her bored expression instantly transformed to fury. She whirled and let loose a stream of angry gibberish aimed at Joseph. It was definitely not French.

Joseph picked up the Windex bottle and gave it a squirt, as if he was firing back. His lip curled in a smile of disdain. "What is it they call you? Frenchie? I'm Christian Lebanese; you know that, don't you? You don't fool me. You're in America now, Frenchie. Speak American. Or Arabic's okay if you're more comfortable. I understand Lebanese Arabic very well."

Again she responded with a hail of unintelligible epithets.

Joseph laughed derisively. A sort of sticks-and-stones-may-break-my-bones laugh. He replied with the same sort of gobbledygook language, which she appeared to understand fully. Throwing bags of pretzels and Cheetos and Tostitos onto the floor, she finally ripped open a large sack of pork rinds and hurled them at Joseph. Then she stormed out.

Joseph stood glaring at her until she got into her blue Toyota Camry and squealed out of the parking lot.

With a broad I-told-you-so grin, Joseph looked toward the refrigerator section, gave Mike a thumbs-up, and wiped his brow in mock relief. Then he opened the walk-in door and set Mike free.

"Thanks. Thanks."

"She's something else, that one. Probably after you for citizenship."

"I figgered that out. But she don't think much of you, buddy." Mike clapped Joseph on the back.

"I'm Christian Lebanese. She's Lebanese too. Muslim. What I said to her about the pork rinds? Just fueling the fire. Muslims don't eat pork. Probably was her relatives that run my family out of Beirut."

"What? She's what?"

"As Muslim as Usama, that one."

"But all the French talk?"

"Lebanon was once a French colony. Beirut? It was the Paris of the Middle East. French is a common language. Lebanon was invaded by Syria. Syria and Islamic terrorists occupy my homeland now. But no one in the West hears about that. She's Muslim, all right."

"You sure?"

"I seen her in here a few times. Besides her accent, and the pork-rind thing, you can tell by the way she eats the snack stuff she picks up in here. Watch her some time. Uses her right hand only. Thumb and first two fingers. That's how she picks up her food. Maybe not religious now, but that's how she was raised." Joseph wagged his head in disbelief. "You didn't know what kind of tiger you had by the tail, huh?"

"No. No, sir. I did not."

"Well, you're lucky, eh? Even without Chocolate Chip Cookie Dough ice cream."

"I reckon I am. But if I don't bring back what I came for, I'll be in big trouble. Ben & Jerry's."

"Two crates. Did you see them in the back? I saved them for you. Good to know who your true friends are, eh?"

Galbraith Fertilizer Factory
Santa Clarita, California
2135 hours, Pacific Time

ASHES TO ASHES, DUST TO DUST

Patrick Dennison wiped his nose with the back of his hand. It refused to stop running. Thick, coppery-tasting mucus clogged his head and throat as his body fought against the metallic dust. His eyes felt as if the lids had been held open and sprayed with grit. The left one was swollen nearly shut; the right watered in streams that ran down his cheek.

Beside him in the cement truck Mohammed al Krefa was more sullen than ever. He dabbed at his face with a pocket handkerchief and responded to all of Dennison's conversation with irritated grunts.

Rubbing his face again, Dennison offered, "Last time I came by to check on this place I could smell it from a mile away. Place stinks like the parking garage at Union Square after all the Friday night drunks get through with it."

Another grunt.

"'Course, I can't smell anything now."

"Shut up and drive!"

The Galbraith Fertilizer Factory was just off a deserted side road branching away from Highway 14. Its specialty was the production of ammonium nitrate in powder form. About a mile from the plant the cement truck passed a silver Dodge Ram pickup going the opposite direction.

"Just like clockwork," Dennison noted. He hacked at the phlegm jamming the back of his throat, then spat noisily out the window before continuing. "Guard goes off between 9:30 and 10:00 to get his burger or something. Takes him 45 minutes, round-trip. Plenty of time for us."

Unlike chemical fertilizers sold in bags for home use, AN powder was three times more concentrated. Lawn and garden products were also pelletized and treated with a coating to make them resistant to moisture and thus slow down the release of the active ingredients into grass and soil. AN had no such barrier to prevent it from instantly dissolving.

As al Krefa pointed out, a bomb could be made from the home variety of AN, but it would be less effective and require three times the amount. A semitruck-sized trailer load of ammonium nitrate pellets would be both difficult to handle and to keep secret.

Spotting the gravel-lane turnoff leading to the fertilizer plant, Dennison slowed the cement truck and shut off the headlights. The truck turned and rolled through the open gate.

Light gleamed from the office window behind the expanse of the 60-foot-long truck scales.

"The hopper we want is round back of the office." Dennison gestured with his right hand toward a barely lit jumble of factory structures, pole buildings. Massive black bins mounted on steel stilts resembled monsters from bad '50s sci-fi films.

Dennison jumped when al Krefa grabbed his arm and dug fingernails into his skin. "I saw a shadow move. There. In the office."

"Can't be! There's never been more than one guard here!"

"And the gate left open for 45 minutes every night? Idiot!"

"I . . . I never saw anybody else. When I timed the guy I never saw . . ."

Al Krefa already had a 9mm Beretta in his hand. "Shut up! Where is your weapon?"

"I ditched it, man!"

Al Krefa was disgusted. "Come now!"

The pair approached the office doorway, flanking it from either side. Staying in the shadows, away from the glass pane in the center, al Krefa rapped sharply on the door.

Moments later shuffling footsteps approached the entry. "Billy? How'd y'get back so fast? You forget your wallet again?" The door opened a crack, far enough for the guard to get a look at al Krefa's face.

"Hey! You ain't—"

Al Krefa thrust the Beretta forward as the watchman threw his weight against the panel, slamming it on al Krefa's hand. The 9mm cracked once, the bullet punching a hole through the truck-scale window; then the Beretta bounced on the floor.

The Bombmaker screamed, then shouted to Dennison, "Help me!"

Dennison threw his shoulder into the door, and the combined force of the two terrorists flung the guard backwards. The back of the watchman's legs collided with a desk. Reaching behind him, he snatched a three-hole punch and swung it at al Krefa's head, knocking The Bombmaker to the ground.

The security guard went for the Beretta.

Dennison leaped over his fallen comrade, colliding forehead to forehead with the guard. Their hands closed around the pistol at the same moment, and they wrestled for it.

The guard was out of shape and older than Dennison, but he was also heavier. Dennison's eyes and throat closed up again in the exertion of the struggle. The weapon was being twisted from his grasp.

Out of the corner of his vision Dennison saw a hand slide past his face. The backup piece al Krefa carried in an ankle holster, a .380-caliber AMT, went under the guard's chin.

Something exploded next to Dennison's left ear, deafening him.

Dennison flung himself backward, clutching in succession his head, his chest, and his arms, before realizing that he himself had not been shot.

The toe of al Krefa's shoe nudged Dennison in the ribs, hard. "Get up. We have work to do."

FOURTEEN

BEATING THE SYSTEM

A hot Santa Ana breeze blew over the sandy San Andreas fault line riverbed. As calmly as Tom Sawyer on a rock in the sun, Patrick Dennison hung his arm out the window of the cement truck, letting his hand sail through the wind. Heading back toward Palmdale, Mohammed al Krefa drove, while the giant cement drum tumbled, mixing the aluminum and magnesium powders into a dry slurry with the AN fertilizer. White metallic dust escaping from the hopper clouded the highway behind them.

✪ ✪ ✪

The traffic on I-5, the main West Coast artery from Mexico to Canada, moved steadily and was as light as it ever was on a weekend. This suited Officer Stuart Blake of the California Highway Patrol.

Officer Blake had been on the force for more than five years, stationed in one of the roughest neighborhoods in the States: South

Central LA. He'd worked high-speed pursuits in excess of 146 mph down the Grapevine Ridge. All those years without an accident—he wore his five-year pendant proudly above his name tag.

Currently Officer Blake enjoyed the quiet summer graveyard shift, driving from Santa Clarita on I-5 south to the 210 interchange, then west on 14 to Placerita Canyon. In the summers that was the best place to be. It was quite a drive to his home in Bakersfield, an hour and a half north, but houses were more affordable there, and the department let him take the patrol car home.

Not too much action out now, and Blake liked it that way. He still loved a good high-speed chase, *once a day,* if he could get it. But since little Abbey had been born last year, Officer Blake had settled down a bit.

Five years is a long time to spend doing one thing, he thought. It was particularly long enough to know that cement trucks don't operate on that stretch of highway. Not at 10 o'clock on a Saturday night. Long enough to know that cement mixers don't roll down the highway with the candy-striped drum churning shiny powder out of the back, polluting the environment.

If there was one absolutely true thing Officer Blake knew about the job, it was the undisputable fact that more good busts happen after minor traffic and vehicle-code violations. Felony warrant arrests and dope confiscations, even mass murderers, had been picked up in a traffic stop for the stupid little stuff like a broken taillight, or some unknown dust blowing out of a cement truck at this time of night.

Blake's tires broke traction as he rolled, black out, until he hit about 45 mph. Kicking on all his lights and sirens, he stomped the gas pedal to the floor. First stop of the night, and another chance to work on his system.

Roll up on 'em quick and out of nowhere. Let 'em wonder where you came from and worry about what you're doin'.

The cement truck eased on the brakes as it pulled off onto a wide turnout.

Don't give 'em any time to think or plan an escape.

The Mack came to a stop. A *whoosh* of air was released from the pneumatic brake system.

Pull 'em over fast; then wait it out. Run their numbers while they get nervous. See if they do something stupid.

Pulling up behind the truck, Officer Blake lifted the radio handset. "Control 3, 3-Paul-1. 10-28/29 a white cement truck, number 1, Victor 56326 to check a suspicious metallic powder spilling on the highway from the drum."

Gleaming dust still tumbled from the back as the drum continued to turn.

"3-Paul-1. Code 2?" The controller asked if he needed backup.

Backup? For a stop like this? Probably just some tweakers, loaded up on meth after a long week's work. "3-Paul-1, Code 4," he replied in code for no assistance needed.

"3-Paul-1. 10-23." The controller told him to stand by for information.

Officer Blake flipped on the spotlight, aiming it directly at the driver's mirror and into his face. *Blind him with light and sneak up on the dark side.* By that time if he had a reason to fear arrest, he'd be squirming in the rearview mirror.

Officer Blake affectionately referred to the whole process as his "lie detector test." It hadn't failed him yet.

He exited his patrol car, walking behind his vehicle in order to avoid creating a silhouette.

✪ ✪ ✪

In the cement truck Dennison was sweating it out. He squirmed around to look back. "We've got to do something. He's gonna bring the whole thing down, I'm telling you!"

Al Krefa commanded in a burst of expression, "Shut up and do what I tell you! He will come up on your side." He pressed the .380 into

Dennison's sweaty palm. "Watch the darkness in the mirror. When you see him, tap me and I will slide out."

"Okay, man. This better work."

Al Krefa rolled the dimmer switch down to disengage the dome light. He gently pulled on the latch. The door popped free. A moment later he felt the signal and slipped out, just as Dennison's face was illuminated by Officer Blake's flashlight.

"California Highway Patrol. Do you know why I stopped you tonight?"

An instant later something caught the officer's eye at the front of the rig. Shadows cast by the spot beam moved on the road ahead.

"You in front! Stop!" Blake broke leather, unholstering his stainless Smith & Wesson 4006. But before he could level his sights, Dennison hung his arm out the window and fired.

The first .380 round caught Blake in the neck. The officer dove for cover beside the polished-metal, fuel-tank step. Dennison leaned out the window and fired again, this time striking Officer Blake in the head. He slumped in the dirt.

Al Krefa scrambled back into the driver's seat, jamming the truck in gear. The transmission shuddered and moaned as he crammed on the accelerator. The cement truck rolled away into the night.

Dennison and al Krefa were free men once again.

✪ ✪ ✪

Officer Blake felt himself losing consciousness. He couldn't move. He felt cold and numb. As the blood pooled around his face, he remembered what his father, a 33-year California Highway Patrol veteran had told him: "A plan is good, a system even better. But best to have a backup. Nobody can plan for everything."

Officer Blake's radio hissed: "3-Paul-1. Be advised. Vehicle was reported missing earlier today. Use caution when approaching. 3-Paul-1, do you copy?"

✪ ✪ ✪

Shukor Gorge, Peshawar Region
Western Pakistan
Sunday, 6 September
0859 hours, Local Time

WAS IT WORTH IT?

It was morning in Pakistan. The canyon had been cleared for threats and the downed Black Hawk searched for survivors. The Pakistani government had been contacted and a deal struck.

A decision had been made at SOIC in Kabul to send in a CH-40 Chinook for an ambitious recovery effort. The powerful twin-rotor bird, capable of lifting 20,000 pounds, would hook to the downed aircraft and carry it back to base in Afghanistan.

By daybreak Delta 2 and 3 teams had scattered to lookout points across the nearby mountaintops. Delta 1 had cut up several canyons with their climbing gear in search of Agent Marcos Caracas. It hadn't been until 0821 hours, local time, that a pool of blood and some nylon rope fragments were discovered at the base of Shukor Gorge. No doubt the body had been hidden and the supplies confiscated.

With an M-16 hanging behind each of them, the seven-man team had set up several top ropes and begun descending the face. Their progress was slow but steady as they covered every inch of the rock wall that could possibly be reached by a climber. Once at the bottom the men began to climb, retracing areas that had been missed.

Things picked up speed when the Delta 1 lead climber, Michael Meanly, discovered some freshly broken rock. The focus narrowed further when he found a rock nut with a torn cable loop still wedged tightly into a crevasse.

In black BDU pants and a fully loaded tac vest, Meanly checked his watch. At 32 years of age he sported a noticeable ratio of gray to black hair, but the striated muscles in his forearms were indicative of a much younger, stronger man than the lie of his hair implied.

Meanly clipped his stitch plate safety loop into a newly placed snap link. Leaning out over the 150-plus feet beneath him, he caught his breath. Having watched his friends die in the chopper crash weighed heavily on him mentally as well as physically. Hanging from the rock face, he gazed out over the wide expanse of rugged gray mountains that dropped off into lush green valleys. What breathtaking beauty. *A shame it has to be here,* he told himself.

The familiar *whoop whoop* of the twin screws atop a Chinook caught his attention. A moment later it emerged above a craggy peak on the opposite side of the valley, coming in to get the wreckage.

Meanly unhooked his safety loop and climbed on, hooking into what he believed was the logical place. He scanned left to right in search of this cleft Marcos had spoken of. *Had died speaking of,* he reminded himself. A left pull and a right. Another snap link. Meanly reached for a wide ledge with his right hand.

A foot more and he spied it. Tucked well back into a hole was a small white package in a tangle of twigs that resembled a bird's nest. Meanly paused, breathing in deeply. Was this it? Was this what he had watched his friends die for?

And was it worth it?

Without taking his eyes off the package, Meanly placed another piece and hooked into his stitch plate loop. Slowly he reached for the object, half buried in sticks and grass. So it was a bird's nest. Grasping the package tightly, he removed it. He closed his eyes as he held the item to his ear and shook it. The sound of plastic tape spools rattled in his ear.

Meanly stared at it. *What could be on it?* he wondered. They'd done it—found the tape. But what did it say?

It would be hours before anyone listened to the tape—hours more before it could be translated—and perhaps days or longer before the material could be authenticated.

Was it worth it? He hated to think his friends' lives were given in vain. Would the good done by retrieving this tape truly be worth the loss required to possess it?

Suddenly Meanly remembered how high he was. He quickly tucked the cassette carefully into the side pocket of his BDUs and buttoned the flap.

Reality set in. Meanly was filled with excitement. His eyes widened as he yelled, "I've got it! I have the tape!"

✪ ✪ ✪

Gravel Quarry
Near Palmdale, California
Saturday, 5 September
2246 hours, Pacific Time

LIKE BEES TO HONEY

The pumping truck, also known as a "sucker truck," a "vacuum truck," and most euphemistically as a "honey wagon," was designed to empty portable toilets and septic tanks. In the plan designed by The Bombmaker it would not be used as its makers intended, yet Americans would never again see one of the homely machines without shuddering.

It was amazing what items were available for rent in America. The sucker truck had power steering and an automatic transmission, and the controls were easy to operate. A stolen credit card and a fake driver's license were all al Krefa had needed to produce to drive off in the final piece of equipment for his scheme.

All afternoon and evening the rented vehicle had sat hidden, parked beneath the spout of the derelict wooden gravel hopper. With its upper hatch cover unbolted and set aside, the suction truck was ready to receive what the cement mixer was poised to deliver.

The drive back from the AN plant had been uneventful, except for the encounter with the CHP officer. By the time al Krefa stepped down from the cab, the ammonium nitrate had been thoroughly mixed with the aluminum and magnesium powders into a dry slurry of near-lethal proportions.

Only two more ingredients were needed to convert fertilizer and metallic powder paint into the most dramatic terrorist attack since the

World Trade Center and the Pentagon. And it wouldn't be long before those ingredients were added to al Krefa's recipe too.

Patrick Dennison guided the dump ramp of the cement truck into a hole ripped through the rotting boards of the hopper and directly above the pumper's hatch. As al Krefa gunned the truck's motor, speeding up the revolutions of the mixer, he also yanked the dump lever.

A cascade of fine white powder mingled with gleaming flecks of metal before showering down the ramp and into the tank of the honey wagon. Contained within the crumbling wooden walls of the hopper, the mixture was at this stage mostly inert and no longer a threat to eyes or lungs.

But the roar of the engine and the whine of the spinning drum were loud, deafening in the confined space. So loud, in fact, that neither al Krefa nor Dennison heard the approaching car.

The first indication of the new arrival was when headlights swept across the scene, freezing al Krefa in silhouette and making Dennison crouch down in place. Al Krefa whipped out his pistol. He had come too far to give up without taking some of the infidels with him.

There were no sirens, no flashing lights, no demands for surrender. The figure that approached from out of the headlights held both hands high overhead in plain sight.

It was Mabrouk.

Al Krefa killed the engine and Dennison emerged from hiding as the last of the AN/metal powder slurry rattled down the ramp into the honey wagon.

"If you'd come sooner, you could have helped," The Bombmaker scolded Mabrouk. "But you have the detonators?"

Mabrouk explained how he had narrowly escaped being captured, what with his picture plastered all over the news and his health-club locker being raided.

"And the reserve detonators?" al Krefa demanded, his voice suddenly shrill.

Dennison backed away from the conference. He didn't want to be in the middle if a gun battle broke out between his two partners.

Mabrouk unslung a dark green backpack from his shoulders and set it gently on the ground. "I was late because I made up new ones."

Accepting the powder canister with its dangling wires, al Krefa grunted his approval. "Good. You made several of these?"

Mabrouk nodded. "Three."

"I will plant them in the top of the powder tonight and wire them together, but we will not add the final ingredient until tomorrow. Then our success will be assured."

"And our fame," Dennison put in, advancing into the circle of light once more. "Now we still have all night to set up our escape plan, right?"

In the glare of the headlights Dennison never saw the Beretta emerge from al Krefa's waistband, nor was there time to hear the concussions of the bullets that blew two holes in his chest.

✪ ✪ ✪

After Dennison's body had been dumped into the wooden hopper, Mabrouk and al Krefa drove the honey wagon away from the quarry. They would park all night, out of sight, inside the abandoned warehouse.

Al Krefa patted Mabrouk on the shoulder. "I'm glad you arrived in time, my friend. I didn't want to rely on someone whose motive is his ego . . . or his survival. This operation is too important."

FIFTEEN

California Speedway
Fontana, California
Sunday, 6 September
0515 hours, Pacific Time

ALL GOOD

Mike Roberts completed his final check of the Jericho four-speed transmission. He and his team of mechanics had been working 23 hours straight—well, other than his quick break at the 7-Eleven last night—making certain the NASCAR Cup car met every specification. The 358-cubic-inch engine's compression ratio was 12 to 1. The bottom line was 750 horsepower at about 8000 rpm, dropping to about 500 hp with the required restrictor plate in place. The "rocket" attached to a 110-inch Chevy wheelbase was ready to go the distance.

There was time enough, the crew chief thought, for a quick catnap in the motor home. "Wake me up in 30." Mike wiped his greasy hands on a rag and instructed Bill Price.

Bill, completing the final check of the power-steering gear box, gave Mike the thumbs-up. "Get some beauty sleep. Wife and boys coming today, right?"

Mike returned the gesture. "A first. First time Tracy's come to a race with the boys. I got 'em VIP ID passes. They'll be able to hang out in the restricted areas."

"Your boys'll like it."

"It's all good, man."

The air was filled with the zip of mechanic's air tools and the clank of metal as Mike made his way past other crews to the motor home that served as a crash pad and retreat for exhausted crew members. The bunks were empty. Mike was the last to take a break. He smiled at the heap of empty Chocolate Chip Cookie Dough cartons that overflowed the garbage can.

Sinking onto a sofa, he closed his eyes. He had not yet told the team this was his last season on the NASCAR circuit. He had decided it was time to settle down. Time to go home. He would tell Tracy after the race.

Yes. It was all good.

Tracy should be calling soon to let him know where she was. He would see her and his boys today. Today would mark a new beginning in their lives.

On impulse he got up and rummaged through his duffel in search of the VIP ID tags he had obtained for Tracy, Connor, and Justin. Not all that easy to get restricted entry passes. But the guy in the front office had owed Mike a favor and rushed his request through. Mike dug beneath socks and shorts, looking for the large brown envelope. It wasn't there.

"What the—?"

It had to be there. He had put it in his duffel himself. Hadn't he? Standing erect, he glared around the messy interior of the motor home. Where had the passes gone? Had he left them out on the counter? on the table? He tore through the clutter, searching for the precious passes.

"Oh, man! What'd I do with them?" Upending his bag, he pawed through the contents again. Had he taken the envelope back to the motel maybe? No. No. Not possible. He hadn't been back to the motel since he picked up the envelope.

Mike sank down on the sofa again. Head in hands, he tried to think it through. Tried to remember. It was a big brown envelope. An envelope. Big and brown. Three VIP restricted admission passes inside. He had picked it up from Morrie in the front office yesterday. What then? What?

Mike stared at the empty ice-cream cartons. Had the envelope fallen into the garbage? He dumped out the trash can, kicking through the contents. Nothing. No big brown envelope.

Had someone stolen them? It was a possibility. But who would do such a thing?

And why?

Mike frowned and looked through his belongings one last time. Something else was missing. His own ID tag. He never wore it because everybody knew him. And besides that, why would anyone steal his ID?

Bill Price stuck his head through the door. "Hey, Mike. You said wake you in 30. Did you have a good nap?"

"Hey, Bill. Have you seen . . . I mean . . . I can't find my ID. Or Tracy's and the boys'. They were all in a big brown envelope."

"Nope. Sorry. Maybe you left it at the motel."

"Couldn't have. I wasn't back there. It don't make any sense."

"Well, call Morrie or somethin'. You comin', buddy?" Bill seemed unconcerned.

"Yeah, yeah." Mike shrugged. Nothing he could do about it now.

⊙ ⊙ ⊙

Grassy Knoll Apartments
San Francisco, California
0737 hours, Pacific Time

WE DON'T KEEP JUNK

Miles was late as usual. A 7:30 appointment meant get up at 7:28, since getting ready only meant pulling on a different T-shirt. Today it was his '80s washed-out green, "Un's the One" 7-Up shirt again.

Downing was parked in the red zone, directly in front of Miles's apartment. The car was running. He held up a carton of chocolate-flavored soy milk for Miles.

Miles's face lit up as he opened the door. "Chocolate Silk! My favorite." Life was simple for Miles, who enjoyed the same small rewards that any five-year-old kid did. "Donuts too! Right on."

Downing grinned as he pulled out into traffic. "Thought that would get you going."

Miles was already digging for a donut in the bottom of the pile. "Nothin' like a little oily dough and sugar in the morning. Especially maple ones."

Somehow the same sweets seemed so much less appetizing to Downing when viewed that way. "A couple of the guys from the call center were in at six this morning, phoning more computer places. Got an answer at one about five minutes from here. Has old stuff."

Miles crammed a third of the donut in his mouth before talking. "Which one? Arknology?"

Downing eyed Miles curiously. "That's it. How'd you know?"

"That's about the only place in the city that really keeps all the good stuff around. Lots of other places can fix hardware, but they'd rather throw old junk away and sell you something new. I know one of the guys who works there. Adam."

"You do?" Downing was astounded. "Why didn't you tell us?"

"I heard Adam's out of town, and anyway, they were closed by the time we needed them."

✪ ✪ ✪

The trip along Market Street west of downtown was fast. Much better driving downtown on Sundays—the streets were virtually empty.

Downing parked beneath a broken neon sign that read, *Ark—g Computer ales and ervice.* "Hmm, looks . . . old. Hope they have what we want."

Miles hopped out to peek through the windows. He saw no one

through the water-stained glass, but spied that a coffeepot was on. He signaled to Downing. "I'll try around back."

"Fine. I'll catch up with the senator."

Miles bounced off around the side alley. Someone's car was there. Not Adam's. Miles rapped on the metal door with the flaking white paint.

A minute passed before a mangy-looking guy opened the door. His hair was matted and greasy. His belly hung out of a shirt about as worn and ancient as Miles's. Obviously the guy was someone who had fallen in love with computers and forgotten everything else in the world. "Oh, hey, dude. You're Adam's friend, huh?"

"Yeah, is . . . ?"

"He's not around," the computer geek said. "Went over to Napa to, like, see his parents about some money or something. I'm Jimmy. Come on in."

Miles followed Jimmy past piles of gutted hardware stacked from floor to ceiling. With the blank stares of unloved CRTs and the forlorn carcasses of abandoned CPUs heaped floor to ceiling on metal shelving, the room looked like something out of the wrecking yard of junked 'droids from *Star Wars*.

Miles had forgotten how much stuff this business had collected in the back. "I like this place. It reminds me of Mojave."

Jimmy snorted a laugh, as if he understood the reference to Miles's desert mobile home, and then walked behind the showroom counter.

Miles followed. The space was a little cleaner in front, though not much. It was difficult for the average customer to imagine how the place stayed in business. Perhaps it ran on house calls, since a normal person would run away, thinking they'd wandered into a computer graveyard.

"So what are you needin'?" Jimmy slipped on a pair of reading glasses.

"Actually I'm looking for a Webster's Dictionary, Beta 0.1, for Windows 95."

"Oh, yeah. I remember. Got over 300,000 entries. Beta failed 'cause it was so big. The 95 system kept crashing during searches."

Miles perked up. "Have you got one?"

Clenching his jaw as he closed one eye, Jimmy stared across the room. "See that clear plastic tub there? It's got all the old 95 software."

"Cool." Miles made his way over and slid the crate off the shelf.

"Pretty sure I saw one in there not too long ago," Jimmy said, lifting his copy of the Sunday *San Francisco Chronicle* open to the comics.

Miles dug through the piles of CD-ROMs. Some of them were scratched, others even cracked or broken. "You guys don't throw anything away."

"Not when it's still good."

Miles held up half a CD, displaying it for Jimmy's view.

"You wanna buy that too?"

"Never mind." Miles returned to his digging. "Come on, be here, be here," he hoped aloud, spilling mounds of CDs onto the floor. Somewhere in the last third of the tub he found it—in a soft plastic slipcover. "Please be okay," Miles begged as he pulled out the Webster's CD-ROM Dictionary.

The back was a little scratched, though much better even than some of the newer stuff. "Is this the only one you have?" Miles asked, holding it up.

Jimmy's face turned grumpy. "Well, how many do you need?"

"Just one, but this is a little scratched up, and I need it for helping the FBI crack some encrypted messages sent to a terror cell in LA."

Jimmy stared blankly at him before sliding off his reading glasses. "Adam said you were, like, weird." He shook his head before returning to the funnies.

"Um, so is that no?" Miles asked delicately.

"That's it! That's the one. Do you want it gold plated or something?"

Miles agreed he'd try it and paid the man $20 in cash. "The FBI is going to want a . . . can I get a—"

"A receipt?!" the man interrupted him, slamming Garfield facedown on the counter. "No receipts for old stuff!"

"But this is *all* old stuff."

"Like I said, no receipts for old stuff."

"All right, then—" Miles made a move toward the back door—"tell Adam I said hello."

No reply.

Guessing that was good-bye, Miles rushed back out to Downing with the good news.

✪ ✪ ✪

Highway 14
Santa Clarita, California
0746 hours, Pacific Time

THE CRIME SCENE WIDENS

Carter drove.

Steve rubbed his eyes. "I don't know why you never look tired."

Carter's shiny bald head and clean, ornery smile made him appear fresh as ever. "I don't need more than about four and a half hours. Slept in till six today. Nice."

"I'm exhausted." Steve reared back with his eyes closed and mouth open. A moment later he cut loose a roaring sneeze. "It smells like a chem toilet out here. Urine or something . . ."

"That's probably the urea fertilizer. The plant is just up ahead." Carter motioned with his finger.

Late Saturday night an 11-99 call had gone out when one of Officer Blake's fellow cops found him lying on the side of the road. Officer down.

Blake had been pronounced dead on the scene, after which a Crime Scene Investigation unit closed that stretch of Highway 14 for several hours.

The ground was processed for footprints and tire tracks. Even more valuable was the video recording taken from the dash of the patrol car. There hadn't been time to enhance and clarify yet, but investigators were sure of two things: It was Lonnie Bertrand's truck and it contained two suspects. One suspect was Hispanic or Middle Eastern, the other pale-skinned and thin. Both believed to be male.

The shooting appeared to be a singular and random event, until the murder at the fertilizer plant was also reported.

Tire tracks. Irrefutable evidence. Tire make and model, even the same chips and divots were present at both scenes. The same CSI photographer who shot the roadside murder ended up photographing the fertilizer plant 45 minutes later.

It was a rural area. Murders were uncommon occurrences there. Sure, bodies from LA crimes were dumped there frequently, but this time the clues were obvious even to the naked eye. Hemoglobin dating later suggested what investigators believed: The guys in the truck killed Officer Blake not more than a few minutes after they killed the AN plant guard. When the tire tracks from the cement truck were later discovered under the powdered fertilizer hopper, investigators knew they had a match, and a much more serious problem than a pair of psychopaths murdering at random.

Word of the murders and evidence of the ammonium nitrate theft filtered up to Special Operations Director Davis, who of course knew at once they were looking at a possible ANFO scenario.

Davis had immediately phoned Morrison, who woke Steve and Carter.

Arriving at the fertilizer plant, Steve and Carter made their way under the bright yellow crime-scene tape and into the office.

One look inside the office was enough for Steve. "Glad I didn't eat breakfast."

Carter ducked in to take a peek before following Steve around to a group of men near the hopper-loader.

"Gentlemen." Steve let his badge wallet fall open. Carter did the same. The men nodded.

Steve put his wallet away. "Whose scene is this?"

An older white-haired man in a wool suit coat that was about 10 years out of style and at least three months out of season introduced himself. "Commander Fred Peltier. You boys from the FBI?" His tanned, loose facial skin moved when he talked.

Steve nodded. "Special Agent Alstead, FBI Chapter 16, counter-terrorism."

Carter shook Peltier's hand as well, introducing himself. "Special Agent Thomas."

Peltier slowly pulled them aside. "You fellas here to take over the scene?"

"Actually, we're working to crack a terror cell operating out of LA. We think this may be related and are hoping you can tell us what you've found out in the last hour or so."

"Sure." Commander Peltier didn't miss a beat. He'd probably seen everything in the years he'd been working for the LA Sheriff's Office. "The guy over there is the owner. He says these hoppers are loaded up every night, last thing before closing, so they're ready for early deliveries. He checked and said this hopper is short about six cubic yards of ammonium nitrate powder."

Steve stood with his arms crossed, one hand on his chin. "What grade is it? How strong?"

Peltier glanced over at the owner again. He pressed Steve on the arm to move a little farther out of earshot. "He's pretty upset, already. Said this is the really pure stuff. In this batch, nitrate runs about 70 percent plus. It's not like the kind you throw on your lawn. They make that too, which has a chemical sealant to make it time release. But this stuff here, it's pure."

Steve closed his eyes at the grim thought. Whoever they were up against had it figured out. Get the good stuff—that way it'll dissolve better. More volatile. More reactive. He looked at Carter.

Carter stuck his finger in the air. "And what was it about a metallic powder?"

Peltier suddenly remembered. "Yeah. Under the hopper was a small pile of some kind of metal. We aren't really sure what it is."

Steve nudged Carter. "Material from Neilson's Metal Finishing Factory. Just like by the CHP shooting."

"I'll bet you're right," Carter agreed.

"Heard about that." Peltier nodded. "So far no sign of the suspects from the officer's video. We got the road shut down all the way past the other crime scene. How easy can you hide a cement truck? Strangest getaway vehicle I ever heard of."

"Pretty big crime scene," Carter interjected. He bumped Steve on the arm. "While you were sleeping on the way, back a couple miles, we got stopped."

Peltier shook his head doubtfully. "Got 'em on tape, but I can't imagine they're still in the area."

Steve had another thought as he sneezed again. "I heard CHP say that Officer Blake pulled these guys over 'cause of the powder coming out the back. Do we have any K-9 bomb dogs on the highway yet?"

"They're all working pretty close in right now, but not a bad idea. I'll see if I can get a couple dogs freed up. See if we can find out how far this trail goes. Excuse me a minute." Peltier walked over to the group of men.

Steve rolled his eyes. "Six yards of AN! Can you believe that?"

"And the pure kind, not the 10-percent stuff," Carter added. "And we're in the deep stuff here, partner."

Steve thought about Oklahoma City. He estimated the amount of material now in the terrorist's possession to be about twice the amount used in that blast. "We knew they had homemade detonators. Now we know they have the metallic powder and the AN. All that's left is the fuel . . . and that they can just buy! The timer could be counting down toward zero right now! We've gotta stop these guys." A chill ran through his whole body.

Peltier made his way back over. "In about 10, 15 minutes we can get a couple dogs out on the road. Also, it made me think of getting some sensitive metal-detection equipment out there as well."

"Good thinking," Steve praised. "Even if the scent is lost, traces of the metallic powder will still be left in the dirt."

Peltier began to walk off again. "About 10 minutes, out on the highway."

Steve agreed. He and Carter returned to the Caprice to make calls to Morrison and Cindy while they waited for the sniffers, canine and mechanical, to arrive.

SIXTEEN

California Speedway
Fontana, California
Sunday, 6 September
0758 hours, Pacific Time

DOWN THE TOILET

The mechanics affectionately called her Frenchie. That was not her name, of course, but she had become accustomed to answering with a wave and a smile when she heard it.

At the very beginning stages of The Plan, when she first infiltrated the ranks of those who followed the NASCAR circuit, she had introduced herself using the stolen identity of a French tourist. But who among the crews remembered that name now?

Frenchie. That was good enough for them. She spoke French. Was as pretty as they imagined French girls to be. They all knew her. Accepted her.

They had been surprised when she lavished her affection on Mike Roberts, the soft-spoken crew chief of the Hank Rebo team. He was not particularly good-looking, so he had been easily impressed that any woman other than his ever-absent wife would be interested in him. He had floated within Frenchie's grasp like a big fish stunned by dynamite. He had been an easy target and, in the end, an unwitting accomplice.

Then Mike's conscience had awakened, and he had broken off their romance. But that no longer mattered. Frenchie was already a long-established presence at the track. She no longer needed Mike Roberts.

A few felt sorry for her. Others, the moral sort, were relieved Mike had broken it off. But after the race today no one she had known would remain alive to ask Frenchie what her real name was.

For now no one remembered how or why Frenchie had hooked up with the crews who spent months on end on the road. At every NASCAR race across America Frenchie was there, behind the scenes, pitching in, speaking the NASCAR lingo, fetching coffee and donuts all night for the guys preparing for the race. She was a sort of permanent fixture. A groupie. A helpful mascot. Frenchie had her own official NASCAR team ID card, which she wore proudly around her neck on a blue lanyard.

That was how she had managed to easily steal the envelope of ID cards that Mike Roberts had stuffed into his duffel in the motor home.

Tracy Roberts. Now there was a name. What gate guard would suspect the truth? Who could tell if Tracy was a male or female name? It worked equally well as identity for a male terrorist as it did for Mike Roberts's pathetic little wife.

And then there was the tag for Connor Roberts. What security guard would guess that the real Connor was only four years old? Or that the real Justin Roberts was only seven? Stolen VIP passes, as well as entry papers for the pump truck, assured The Plan's triumph. All of Frenchie's pretense was about to come to a successful and permanent conclusion.

She would be long gone before the explosion ripped through the stands and decimated everyone. There would not be anyone left alive to remember that "French" woman who had been an official part of the vaporized NASCAR teams.

The roar of engines, the collective rumble of thousands of NASCAR fans—all would soon be drowned out by a bigger roar.

There was only one thing left for Frenchie to do to fulfill her part of The Plan.

Shouldering a large backpack crammed full of Huggies disposable diapers, she made her way to each of the deserted lavatories on the track level. Entering each stall, Frenchie locked the door behind her, removed a diaper from her pack, and flushed it down the toilet.

Simple.

Today when the gates of the California Speedway swung open, there would be approximately 100,000 bathroom pit stops by NASCAR fans and crews within the first two hours. That would finish the damage the diapers had begun on the sewage system.

What Americans witnessed on television the day the twin Trade Center Towers collapsed was a minor disaster compared to what they were about to see at California Speedway.

NASCAR, America's favorite spectator sport, was about to be flushed down the toilet. And tens of thousands of human lives would go down with it.

ELFS Room
FBI, Chapter 16 Offices
San Francisco, California
0805 hours, Pacific Time

SHARING THE BURDEN

"What is it, Miles?" Morrison burst through the ELFS door with Downing. "What's happened?"

"I can't read it. The disk is too scratched up!" Miles yelled in a tantrum. The pressure of preventing a major terrorist attack that might happen within hours—or even minutes—and knowing that at any moment some piece of America might explode, killing thousands, was overwhelming. Miles broke down. "I don't want to be responsible if this . . . thing . . . goes off! I can't . . . help it." He let his face fall into his hands.

Morrison felt it too. The immense weight that the men and women of Homeland Security held every day was at times unbearable. Especially when it was so unevenly spread over those at the edge of the mission. Those who risked their lives physically, mentally, and financially every day while doing their jobs. Expectations were so high, and there was no room for failure.

Morrison comforted him. "Miles, Miles. You aren't alone here. We're with you on this."

"But it won't work," Miles argued. Logic had left him blind to reason. "Just having the dictionary isn't going to translate the code for us."

"But it's a start," Morrison consoled, trying to keep Miles focused on one task at a time. "Didn't I hear of some filler, a kind of liquid, that will repair those scratches?"

Miles sighed, leaning his head back, eyes closed. "I just don't—"

"One step at a time, Miles. One step at a time." Morrison patted him on the back. "Do you have a scratch-repair kit?"

Miles paused before answering. "Yeah."

Gently Morrison pressed him. "Can you try it? See if it'll work?"

"Okay," Miles answered without enthusiasm. He lifted his head. "It's right behind you, in that drawer."

Downing stepped aside and opened the filing cabinet. "And there it is." He handed the tube and a soft cloth to Miles.

Miles put a few drops on the bottom of the CD-ROM and began to rub.

Morrison pulled up a chair beside him. "Now tell me. What else are we missing in order for this thing to work?"

"An encryption key." Miles blinked rapidly as he spoke the impossible.

"And where would we find that?" Morrison coached him.

"It has to be in the e-mail somewhere. A set of numbers or letters that could be translated into instructions to tell us where to look."

Downing lifted the stacks of printed e-mails. "Numbers . . ." He handed a stack to Senator Morrison. The pair of them began to scan each line of the printed e-mails. Downing scanned another sheet and said, "The encryption key *has* to be original to each message, hidden in each one."

"Why's that?" Morrison asked.

Miles answered for Downing. "Because many of the words use the same first letters, but we've never seen the same code word repeated in any of the e-mails."

Downing furthered the point. "If these e-mails are plans, as we believe they are, logic would suggest that the messages must have a few of the same words—at least a few. But there are no repeats."

"So the code must be different in each of them," Miles added. He began to pull himself together.

The three men fell silent as they reviewed the numbers and letters for clues.

Morrison paused. "Now I see these numbers on e-mails—coded pathways, I suppose—when I print them out. I'm just a layman, but can any of that be forged? Could it be under our noses all this time?"

Miles's answer was as casual as if someone had asked him what he'd had for breakfast. "Sure, stuff like the return IP. Spammers fake that stuff all the time. They don't want people knowing where the e-mail actually came from." Miles realized what he had said.

All three searched the return Internet Provider line of the page Morrison held. Downing began to compare the return IP of several other e-mails. "They're all different."

"Mine too," replied Miles.

"Same here," Morrison agreed.

As if someone had fired a booster rocket attached to his office chair, Miles jetted over to the Encryption Translator. With a stack of e-mails in hand, he began typing in the long strings of numbers inhabiting the return IP line.

"What are you doing?" Downing asked, while staring at Morrison with confusion.

Miles's fingers flew over the keys. "I'm programming the parameters of the search. ET has to have an order of operations for each decoded message."

Morrison slapped his legs as he stood up. "Did we just get a taste of the old Miles?"

"I guess so," Downing joked. "I wish I was that easily energized."

"It'll be a little while," Miles noted abruptly. "I'll call you when I get something."

✪ ✪ ✪

Westbound I-10
Moreno Valley, California
0816 hours, Pacific Time

WHEELS OF OUR LIVES

Tracy heard the rumble of engines in the background when Mike called from the garage. She knew he hadn't had much sleep in preparation for today's NASCAR race. He sounded tired, irritable. Tracy knew his team was eleventh in points and had not come in first in 32 outings. This was an important race for them.

Mike shouted into the receiver. "Look, hon, I wanted this to be so special for y'all today. I would've met you at the gate with flowers and a brass band if I could. About the best I figgered I could do is have your passes waiting at the gate when you came in."

Tracy shouted back in an attempt to be heard over the background noise. "So we should just go to the VIP gate? And they'll have our passes into the infield?"

He sounded desperate. "That's what I'm trying to say. Trace, your passes have disappeared. Don't know what happened to them. Stolen maybe. You know how it is around here. A regular soap opera. *As the Wheel Turns.* I think I know who might've stole 'em, but I don't know why."

Tracy considered the news. Maybe it was best if they not be in the center of the action while the race was going on. Best not to distract Mike. "What should we do? Buy tickets? Sit in the stands?"

"No. No. I just talked to the guy in the front office. Told him how your passes were stolen. He said he'd put your names on a special list. So go straight to security at gate 3. Tell 'em who you are and that I said y'all were on the list. They'll let you and the boys in. Escort you out to the garage. I'll be there. Now you know I won't have time for anything until after the race is over."

"Sure. The boys are lookin' forward to it. You know Connor never misses a race on TV. He's always lookin' to see your face along pit row. Now to get to see it all up close! Thanks, Mike."

Pondering who would be mean enough to steal the boys' VIP passes, Tracy signed off with a loud sigh.

"What is it, Mom?" Justin asked.

"Nothin', son. Just . . . we're gonna have to let your daddy do his thing while the race is on. Don't expect much more than a howdy, a hug, and then him runnin' off to do what he's gotta do."

Connor was indignant. "Sure, Mom. I know that. How you think we'll win if Daddy isn't out there?"

Tracy nodded and switched on the radio. The LA station came through loud and clear. All news all the time. A train derailment. Riots in a prison. The explosion of a factory. A stolen cement mixer. The murder of a highway patrolman. All the local news seemed bad, even if it wasn't earthshaking.

Tracy scanned the stations and turned up the radio when the announcer began to talk about the record crowds expected at the Nextel Cup race at California Speedway.

NASCAR news seemed to be the only news worth listening to.

✪ ✪ ✪

SOIC Center
Kabul, Afghanistan
1941 hours, Local Time

PACK YOUR STUFF!
"Colonel Borland here." It pained him to answer the phone.

"Colonel Borland, this is General Crown." The voice was gruff and roughly smoky.

This was it. The bad news—an order to shut all missions into Pakistani territory. "Yes, sir, General. What can I do for you?"

"I just finished a conference call with the Joint Chiefs and the CIA's Authentication Department."

Colonel Borland hung on the edge of his seat, staring wide-eyed. His mouth hung wide open too. Borland's entire future career hung in the balance, as he well knew. Operation Rock Audio had turned into a pile of slag as quickly as the terrorist animals in head rags had made it. Ten U.S. soldiers killed and a 30-million-dollar helicopter trashed. It was a catastrophic tragedy for which he'd carry the blame for the rest of his life.

Colonel Borland had rushed things. He knew it. But at the time, Rock Audio seemed to be the appropriate action. Moreover, the Joint Chiefs had approved the plan before a single magazine was loaded.

Borland also knew why his behind was on the line . . . because when an op goes cataclysmically wrong, somebody always gets his face rubbed in it. Colonel Borland knew it was easier for the Joint Chiefs to blame him for the result than take the heat themselves. He could end up on the ash heap just for trying to do his job.

Colonel Borland hesitated. "Yes, sir?"

General Crown cleared his throat like he was getting ready to yell. "Pack your stuff."

Borland's heart sank. He feared the worst. "I'm being sacked, sir?"

"Is that what you think you deserve?" General Crown inquired.

"I . . . uh . . . I don't know, sir. But I do know things went pretty badly out there this morning."

"Well, that goes without saying." Crown's voice softened. "We lost some fine men today . . . doing their jobs. And we created such a whirlwind for diplomatic relations with Pakistan that the Secretary of State will have to pay a bunch of baksheesh to smooth it over."

"Going to be hard to deny we're operating on their side of the border now," Borland admitted.

"True," Crown agreed. "So pack your stuff."

Borland was speechless. They'd done it . . . deciphered it. And obviously thought the tape was a phony. Something some old tribal warlord had cooked up for the money. And Borland had fallen for it, like a Ranger dropping 20,000 feet with a faulty chute.

Borland chastised himself. He shouldn't have been so convincing to the Joint Chiefs. Still, it hadn't been a tough sale. They believed al Qaeda was still hiding out in the Peshawar region. Borland's voice was glum when he answered again, "Yes, sir."

"Stop sounding like a thousand bricks just fell on you! You're not getting pounded. You're getting promoted!"

Borland's face came alive. "I am?"

Crown burst into laughter. "CIA says they're 99 percent certain the tape is authentic."

"What?" Borland was floored.

"But that isn't all of it. The tape talked about a terrorist hit on LA. Guess they wanted the tape to be timely, but this just tipped their hand. Homeland Security is unraveling the cell right now!"

"No kidding?!"

"No kidding. How we find the poor soul who coughed it up to pay him the reward is the *only* thing left to worry about. So pack your stuff. You're moving up."

"Thank you, sir," Colonel Borland added quietly. He was flooded with relief that was mingled with the impossible-to-suppress sense of the loss of his men.

"Remember," General Crown said, "Rock Audio is still under hush. We've got several birds watching the area. Already getting good visual intel of the small military encampment too. But until we get a deal worked out with Islamabad, can't say a word. Can't make another move either."

With everything under control, Colonel Borland wondered how he was going to fit in. "So what's my role from here?"

"If they take my recommendation, you'll be a one star. In charge of Task Force 121, Central Eastern Afghan Operations. How's that sound?"

"Perfect." Borland grinned as if he'd just been kissed for the first time.

"We'll start shifting resources south tomorrow, planning our next move."

"Very good, General Crown! Thank you, sir!"

SEVENTEEN

ZERO HOUR

It felt like zero hour to Steve. *Zero,* as in "nothing's happening." He couldn't help but think he was wasting his time. Chasing hounds along a deserted stretch of highway. It was a fine idea. A bloodhound's sense of smell is 10,000 times more powerful than a human's—a fine idea that Steve really didn't need to be present for.

Peltier's K-9s had come and gone. One of the greatest breeds of working dogs ever, German shepherds were smart and obedient. A great animal assistant, they could be taught to check for drugs or money, and were capable of finding much smaller amounts than the 10 grams' worth they were trained on. Shepherds were also employed to search for bodies, even bombs.

Nitrogen, commonly found in some form in most types of explosives, was the reason Commander Peltier thought K-9s would be able to follow the fertilizer-spillage trail. But while shepherds were a good breed for doing many tasks, they were not first choice for tracking. They weren't bloodhounds, who could actually be given a specific odor to follow.

German shepherds were normally good for three or four hours of steady work. Unfortunately, by the time they arrived at the highway location, they'd already burned their noses out on the raw chemicals in the air at the fertilizer plant. So a dusty trail proved impossible to follow.

Steve and Carter had waited still longer for the bloodhounds to arrive. Steve felt as bored and useless as he could possibly be. Sitting in the car, knowing that terrorists had everything they needed to do some real damage, drove him crazy. He felt like he should be driving 100 mph somewhere, just so he was doing something—anything—to take his mind off Anton and the likely impending doom facing LA.

Steve and Carter had driven to the edge of the crime scene, about a mile from where Officer Blake had been killed. The road was still blocked.

The bloodhounds finally arrived at 8:45. They'd come the long way around to avoid catching wind of the fertilizer plant and picking up a false trail. The three hounds were prepped on a sample of the fertilizer and metallic powders that Peltier's men had picked up from under the hopper.

The dogs were quiet at first. Not that they were calm. A hound is one of the rowdiest breeds known. And no wonder. With a sense of smell like they possessed, Steve imagined they must be continually tortured by all the odors in the air.

The fact that the dogs didn't pick up anything that far out meant one of two things. Either the killers left the ammonium nitrate plant, killed the officer, and then turned around; or they had cut up one of the dozens of roads that peeled off Highway14, between Officer Blake and Interstate 5.

To compensate and speed things up, the handler, Les, drove his silver Civic slowly along the side of the highway, stirring up dust as he headed toward the crime scene. About half a mile out, the dogs caught a whiff of their target from the backseat. They went nuts. It sounded as though the hounds were being skinned alive the way they howled and bayed to be cut loose.

Les, a skinny country boy in red flannel shirt and blue jeans, grinned big when his dogs caught the scent. He took pride in them like a mother would her new baby. And why wouldn't he? For $1,250, Orville, Harold, and Blanche promised to tree a bear. "They got it now."

Les's wife scooted over into the driver's seat as he leashed the dogs and freed them from the backseat. She followed at the back of the convoy that included three other police units, all moving at about 3 mph.

It tortured Steve to even watch. "I don't know how they can ride with all that racket! My two boys are bad enough."

It was one thing for Steve to drive at the speed of a turtle, but many times worse to ride in a car while someone else did the driving. He'd had it. "Carter, roll up the window, would you?" Steve stuck his teeth over his lower lip. "The sound of those dogs is drivin' me crazy!"

Not even a sniff of a laugh. Carter blinked as though he had a headache too. "Sound to me like they need to be *shot*."

Just then Steve's B-com rang. He checked the ID. "It's Morrison."

Carter ran his window up.

Steve answered, "Any news?"

Senator Morrison sounded urgent. "Steve, I'm in the middle of a videoconference call with the Director of Homeland Security and several others. Some big news just hit, and I need you and Agent Thomas to head south—fast."

"What's going on?" Steve signaled Carter to pull out of the pack and flip around. Lowering the phone, he told Carter, "Back to LA," before resuming with Morrison. "Don't we need to find out where this scent leads us? Got the hounds on it now."

"I'd be willing to bet they're gone. CIA made contact with Homeland Security a few minutes ago. Said they just intercepted an al Qaeda audio tape that talked about hitting a sporting event in LA—*today*!"

"Al Qaeda and a sporting event? Which one? What kind?"

"Don't know. They're still working on the translation. What they do have is a sporting event, or something bigger even, sometime before noon today."

Steve swirled his finger at Carter. "Stomp on it, man."

The jolt of acceleration even from the Caprice threw Steve back in the seat. "Did Miles come through yet?"

"Still working on it. Won't know until—" Senator Morrison paused—"I don't know. I don't know if he'll get it in time. Just pray. That's all we can do. Listen, I need to get back in there. I'll call you soon."

"Thanks, Senator." Steve disconnected.

Carter could hardly contain himself. "All right, man. It's killin' me. What's this about al Qaeda?"

"Watch the road!" Steve pointed through the dusty glass as Carter drifted toward the shoulder. "We may really be headed into zero hour," Steve urged as he began to explain.

✪ ✪ ✪

ELFS Room
FBI, Chapter 16 Offices
San Francisco, California
0916 hours, Pacific Time

CRACKER JACKED

ET, the supercomputing Encryption Translator, beeped long and loud, like a microwave informing the operator that the popcorn is done. Miles rolled his chair over to check. An image of the little alien waved from the window of a spaceship before it flew away. "Oh, good job, ET. Let's see what you've got."

Miles selected the print command. A few seconds later a laser-printed list shot out into the tray. "What are you doing, ET?" Miles exclaimed in a worried tone.

Downing, who was bent over an adjacent desk, tore himself away from a page of text strings. "What's wrong?"

"This is no good." Miles glided back over to Downing. "It spit out a list of only fifteen possibilities."

"Let me look at that." Downing took the sheet that displayed each combination and the formula used to reach each conclusion. He scratched his head as he compared it with the list of return IP digits. Suddenly an idea came to him. "Miles, get your printout of the dictionary."

Miles grabbed a massive stack of paper—one half of the entire contents of the 300,000-entry electronic dictionary, freshly printed on the FBI's high-speed press. "What are we looking for?"

Downing pulled out the *A* tab section. "Ammonium. We managed to figure out the first four or five words in that one translation. I don't know why I didn't think of this before."

"What?" Miles hounded him.

"All we have to do is take the first code word and count the number of entries forward or backward to the word *ammonium.*"

Miles caught on. "Then use that same differential to decipher all the rest of the encoded words."

"Exactly!" Downing exclaimed as he began to count forward from *ammonium* to *amice*: ". . . 21, 22, 23—" he looked up—"if I counted right, *ammonium* should be a positive 23. Give me ET's list again."

Miles yanked the sheet out from under the stack of dictionary pages. "I'll see if 23 is one of the possible answers. And it is!"

"Perfect!" exclaimed Downing. "Get that other stack and start counting forward 23 entries from *sirup.* I'll work on *quotation.*"

The pair were silent for two or three minutes.

Miles finished first. "*Sirup* comes out to six. I'll bet that means September six."

Downing nodded, pausing with his finger in place. "Ah! Lost count!" He handed Miles the encrypted e-mail. "See if you can find 23 on the list of numbers on the return IP line," he instructed before starting again.

Miles scanned the long string of numbers for the double digit *23.*

93209403284009324035323329832473280932983081230138906956

"Got it!" he yelled, again interrupting Downing's count. "The digits 2 and 3 are paired at 22 and 23 places from the left."

Downing's eyes flicked back and forth as he thought about the answer. "How simple is that?" He set down the *Q* section and grabbed a pencil. Above the string of numbers, he began to write consecutive digits, starting with 1 above the very left of the code, then placing a decimal point as a marker in front of the *23*. When he finished, the paper, with Downing's count above and the numerical string below, read:

123456789012345678901.23456789012345678901234567890123456

932094032840093240353.233298324732809329830812301389006956

"How juvenile. How Cracker Jack is that?! They've simply hidden the key in a list of numbers. The correct code number is the same count from the left, or possibly from the right if the code says 'negative.'" Downing stared at Miles with amazement before dropping the sheet and resuming with the *Q* section. "See if you can find the key in the other e-mails."

Miles grabbed his pencil.

Downing counted to eight before he came to the end of the *Q* section. "There must be something wrong; there are no more *Q* words. But this has to be it. I can't imagine we're . . . is there another sheet or something? Maybe I'm missing the last page."

Miles lifted the alphabetically ordered stacks. "Nope. Just the *R*s."

"Let me have those." Downing began to count at 9 from the first entry: "22 . . . 23 . . ." he stopped counting as he looked up at Miles. "*Race*. The twenty-third word is *race*."

"What kind of race?" Miles scratched his head.

"I don't know, but if our translation is correct, it says ANFO September Six Race. I'm not sure what they have in LA. A marathon? Horse races?" Downing reached out his arm. "Quick, Miles. Get Morrison on the phone."

EIGHTEEN

WHO'S THE BIGGER FOOL?

Mabrouk argued in favor of taking the back way from Palmdale down to Fontana—out to Highway 395 and then south—through the desert sagebrush country. There would be less attention paid to them there than on an interstate.

Al Krefa countered that if The Plan had involved moving the cement truck, he would have agreed. The mixer's part in the scheme was finished. There were no murders connected with an innocent suction rig, nor an open hopper to spill incriminating dust onto the roadway. Hide in plain sight was always a good idea. In this instance, that strategy meant driving the speed limit amidst other weekend traffic out toward the racetrack.

A cell-phone call to Frenchie had confirmed two things: There were no traffic tie-ups on the selected route, and no one would be surprised to see a sucker truck arrive trackside.

Between Mabrouk, who was driving, and al Krefa rested the wires running to the detonators buried in the cargo. One wire was already connected to a battery terminal. The other wire was attached to a simple push button screwed into a block of wood. The remaining connection between button and battery was not yet in place, preventing any chance of a premature explosion.

Not that the explosion was quite ready to happen.

One ingredient remained to be added.

Exiting the I-5 at al Krefa's command just south of Burbank, Mabrouk directed the honey wagon into the driveway of a Gas 'n' Go station that offered a pump for diesel fuel. Mabrouk parked next to it.

The timing of the last addition had also been the source of discussion. Mabrouk thought they should fill up early in the morning, when no other customers were around to see.

Al Krefa had urged the opposite: Add the diesel at the last possible moment. Then, even if their actions were noticed and reported, they would already be so close to their target as to be unstoppable.

As in all matters of plotting, al Krefa's view prevailed.

The station was deserted, except for the clerk inside. "I'll distract him while you fill up," al Krefa ordered.

Adding diesel to the mixture of AN and powdered metal was the final step required to change the separately benign materials into a devastating combination capable of leveling several city-block-sized buildings and the surrounding area. Diesel would be the Fuel Oil part of the ANFO bomb.

Mabrouk swiped a stolen credit card and waited for the diesel pump to cycle to On. The screen requested he furnish a zip code to match the billing address on the card and, when he could not give a correct response, the machine refused to cooperate.

Mabrouk wiped his brow and glanced around nervously. This could not be happening! Yanking a different card from his wallet, he slashed it viciously through the reader.

No dice!

Fumbling with his wallet, Mabrouk sized up the amount of cash on hand. Not enough to even wet the load with fuel. What use did a man about to die have for cash?

A third card slipped from his sweaty fingers. Mabrouk retrieved it and swiped it at high speed. Maybe he could fool the machine into accepting it.

It worked. Probably that brand of card had not yet connected with the new security requirements.

Whatever!

A look into the tiny convenience store window. Al Krefa was keeping the lone clerk occupied, bent over the counter. Pretending to ask directions?

Mabrouk, diesel-pump nozzle in hand, hopped up on the running board and thrust the spout into the loosened hatch. Smelly diesel spurted over the ammonium nitrate. Mabrouk kept his head turned away while using a piece of metal rain gutter to spread the fuel to each end of the tank. The combined odors, bad enough separately, could now knock you down.

✪ ✪ ✪

Al Krefa's finger rested on the plate-glass pane covering the LA regional map on the checkout counter. He clicked his fingernail against Highway 134. "And when we get to the 405, we go south, yes? Then what exit for Long Beach? The *Queen Mary*?"

The gas-station attendant didn't answer. He stared over al Krefa's shoulder and out the window. The Bombmaker didn't need to turn around to know what the clerk was studying so intently. Soon enough the man's words confirmed it. "What the—? What in blazes is that guy doin'? Pumpin' diesel into that sewage truck for?"

Al Krefa's hand dropped to the butt of the Beretta, but his tone sounded bored. "Yes. Crazy, isn't it? This is what I say to our boss when he tells us to do this. But we just follow instructions."

"Yeah? But if he needed that much diesel he coulda had it delivered. Why rent a truck and pay retail for it besides? What a fool!"

Al Krefa nodded his complete agreement, and his hand moved away from the weapon.

The clerk looked at his readout of the diesel pump. The gallon counter whirled around and around, on and on. He and al Krefa stood together in silence broken only by the electronic ticking of the meter. "Does your boss know the rules about where and how he can pump that out?"

"Eh?" Al Krefa feigned being hard of hearing.

"*Queen Mary*," the attendant emphasized. "Best not let any of that get into the ocean. Harbor Patrol and Coast Guard really crackin' down. Sheesh! Spill a cup of gas in the water, and you gotta squirt some kinda solvent on it."

"Yes. Thank you for the advice. I will warn him when we fill up the boat."

As the counter reached 100 gallons the pump automatically shut off. Al Krefa's head snapped up; through the window he saw Mabrouk's do the same. "What has happened?"

"Gotta get new authorization to go over 100 gallons," the clerk explained. "You know, the way prices are and all."

"You can restart it, yes?"

The clerk rubbed the stubble on his chin. "Guess I better call my boss about that," he mused. "Never happened before."

"Please," Al Krefa urged, "we are in a hurry."

It was the wrong thing to say.

"Nope, guess I better not . . . not without getting approval. Otherwise it comes outta my own pocket."

Al Krefa's fingers twitched. Could he force the man to comply? What if more customers showed up . . . or a cop? Was 100 gallons of diesel enough to do the job? Had it adequately soaked the AN? Probably not.

Glancing at his watch, al Krefa decided it would have to be sufficient. There was no more time. "Thank you," he said to the clerk. Then he waved to Mabrouk to get down from the tank.

Minutes later, eastbound on Interstate 10 and heading directly away from the *Queen Mary*, a CHP patrol car tore up behind the sucker truck with lights and sirens going full tilt.

His eyes glued to the mirror, Mabrouk couldn't help tapping the brake pedal.

"No!" al Krefa scolded. "You do nothing wrong! Keep going!"

The Beretta was in his hand.

The CHP car blew past them doing at least 85mph, the Doppler effect changing the siren from a high scream to a lower-pitched shriek.

The officer didn't even slow to look them over.

"After a speeder, eh?" al Krefa commented. "More fool, he."

✪ ✪ ✪

I-5/I-10 Interchange
Los Angeles, California
0934 hours, Pacific Time

IF WE LIVE . . .

Steve and Carter blasted down Interstate 5, the siren on their Chevy Caprice blaring. Steve held on to the handle above his window as the entire car shuddered. "Slow down, Carter. I think this piece of junk is about to throw a shoe!"

Carter eased off the gas pedal, dropping it below 104 mph, to where the speed vibration went away.

"We won't be any good to this operation if you kill us."

"Look at this idiot!" Carter slammed on the brakes as he hit the horn, narrowly missing the back of a bright yellow VW Beetle by a couple feet. "People see a red light and hear sirens, so they slow down right in front of you." Carter lifted the PA microphone. "Get out of the way!" he yelled. The Beetle swerved, narrowly missing a maroon Dodge pickup in the middle lane. "Is that the phone?"

"I don't know." Steve lifted his B-com, seeing by the display that it had already rung several times. "Shoot!" The sound had been undetected due to the road noise. He answered, "Alstead."

"Agent Alstead, this is Special Operations Director Davis."

"Yes, sir."

"Since we went to Orange Alert status, LA and San Bernadino

sheriff deputies are all tied up at the prisons, rail yards, and airports. But the new intel specifies a *race*. The SWAT team is headed to Santa Anita Racetrack. We need you to roll out to Fontana. We've only got a handful of PD out there directing traffic right now and could use all the bodies we can get. Can you make it?"

"Can we make it to Fontana?" Steve asked Carter.

"We can if I make this exit!" Carter clenched his jaw in concentration as he swerved, cutting hard across four lanes of traffic at 100 mph plus. They banked left, crossing over onto the 10 interchange.

"If we live, sir."

"All right. Need you boys to exit about 40 miles out on Cherry Avenue. May be a wild-goose chase—in fact, we hope it is—but we need somebody out at California Speedway who knows what this is all about."

Still moving at nearly top speed, Carter drove down the emergency lane in order to merge ahead of traffic. "Tell him we'll be there in 22 minutes."

NINETEEN

California Speedway
Fontana, California
Sunday, 6 September
0942 hours, Pacific Time

GENTLEMEN, START YOUR ENGINES!

The line of traffic leading to the California Speedway was over a mile long. Tracy remembered now why she had not wanted to leave Arkansas. She had never seen anything like this. Bumper to bumper, the SUV crept forward at a snail's pace.

And the boys seemed to have received an extra dose of energy. "Mom! Mom! Isn't there another way to get there?"

"Mom! You think we'll make it in time for the beginning?"

That set off a string of imitations of every sight and sound Connor had ever witnessed during a NASCAR afternoon in front of the television.

Perhaps Connor would never be part of a crew on the NASCAR circuit like his daddy, but he had learned all the words to the national anthem and each inflection and intonation from every celebrity who had ever called out that rousing American battle cry:

"Gentlemen, START your engines!"

"GENTLEMEN, start . . . your engines!"

"GENTLEMEN, start YOUR . . . ENGINES!"

Problem was, the engines of the spectators inching toward the speedway were practically idling. Tracy figured she and the boys could walk to the track quicker than they could drive and park.

To add insult to injury, a beat-up sewage-pumping truck zipped past, led to the head of the line by a NASCAR gate security officer riding a quad runner!

✪ ✪ ✪

The guard at the gated entry to the infield tunnel glanced at the ID tags Mabrouk handed him.

"Tracy Roberts?" he said doubtfully, looking at Mabrouk's dark brown hair and eyes.

"I changed my name to be more American." Mabrouk laughed. "It's not exactly pleasant to be on the street nowadays and have a friend yell, 'Hey, Mohammed,' at you. Everyone turns and stares."

The guard looked embarrassed. "Yeah, I s'pose so. Anyway, maintenance is fit to be tied, so we heard to expect you guys. VIP passes . . . it must be real bad!"

"Our work always is," al Krefa put in.

"Don't envy you what you're facin' today, then," the sentry added.

"We all have our jobs to do," al Krefa concluded.

The guard waved them through.

Mabrouk wiped his forehead with the back of his hand.

✪ ✪ ✪

0958 hours, Pacific Time

GOD'S WILL

Earl Plumber pulled a trash bag up to his shoulder as he stood over the last unchecked toilet bowl in the pit area. The others, all of them plugged, had long since been condemned. All of them. "Every last stinkin' one!" as Plumber told CS Maintenance Chief Brimmage.

Plumber managed to run off several of the pit-crew members before he'd found the trash bag. Things were so bad someone had better do something quick. The mechanics were having to run all the way back to their RVs. And with the infield nearly three-quarters of a mile across, that made for a long run.

Plumber leaned over the toilet bowl, flexing his wrist so it passed the U-bend. "What is this?" He felt something soft and swollen trapped there. Muttering, he observed, "I think someone has sabotaged these here heads with a whole roll of toilet paper." Earl dug deeper, stretching for a good hold. When he finally dragged the culprit out, he was amazed. "A baby diaper!"

With a name like Plumber, Earl was born for the job. Fixing toilets and ice machines. "No drainpipe ever scared me, and neither will no diaper," he vowed.

Earl opened the sodden diaper as if looking for evidence, as if someone might have left a name tag there. "This diaper ain't even been used." He held it up curiously, just as he heard one of the drivers walking in.

"Hey, Earl! Hear you got one last clean—" The man in the shiny red fire suit held up his hands as if Earl was threatening him with the white swollen mass. "No thanks, man. I got enough good luck." The driver backed away slowly before hightailing it out of there.

"Bet it was one of them drivers! Lousy pranksters! Gettin' millions to drive a car round in a circle. Don't even go nowhere!" Plumber ranted, throwing the dripping mess into a trash can.

He lifted his radio. "Earl ta base."

A few seconds passed before the honey-dripping, Southern voice of a woman answered him. *"This is base, Earl. Whatcha doin'?"*

"Hey, Eva. Found out why all these here toilets is clogged in the infield and the pits."

"Well, aren't you Mister Sherlock today."

"Yes, ma'am. Someone has done put diapers in all the holes, thinkin' it'd be funny, I expect. But I'll get 'em fixed. You can go ahead and cancel the pumper-truck guys." He knew saving a few bucks for the track might mean job security for himself.

"Pumper guys are already here. Headed up toward the back stretch now. You know they're gonna charge for the call anyway. Might as well let 'em work." Eva had a loose cough. "One of the breakers is down over in pit 25. Why don't you go check it out instead?"

"Good enough, then. Tell 'em I'm on my way."

✪ ✪ ✪

The maintenance office at the California Speedway shared a room with security. Lowering the phone from his ear, Lee Carson, Track Security director, had overheard the conversation between Eva and Earl. "Please hang on, Lieutenant Dixon. I need to check up on the tracks."

Lee made his way over to Eva. "Did Earl say someone stuffed diapers in the toilets?"

Eva raised her hand like she was about to say something, then coughed. After clearing her throat, she blew off his concerns. "Just pranksters. You remember the fish in the motor-home cushions? Always up to something. It's a wonder they don't kill each other on purpose before they ever head out on the track."

Lee gazed out through the wide window overlooking the vast panorama of the stands and the two-mile racetrack below. He lifted his binoculars, searching the distant corners of the infield. Seeing nothing, he returned to his call with Dixon. "No, sir, nothing suspicious so far. . . . Yes, I appreciate all your concerns and we understand your resources are tied up elsewhere today. . . . Thank you."

Lee hung up as a call came in regarding a fistfight at the west-side concession stand. The toilet-plugging pranksters moved way down on Lee's list, and he gave them no further thought.

✪ ✪ ✪

With lights and sirens all blazing, Carter rolled the left tires up onto the curbing in order to charge past the half-mile length of cars ahead of them.

Over the phone, Senator Morrison delivered the news via B-com. "Going to Red immediately! And you're at what we believe will be ground zero!"

Steve's head banged against the window as Carter drove over a parking block. "A tape of UBL from Afghanistan?!"

Morrison replied, "Pentagon just called me! Said it was authentic! Said he was talking about the blessings of Allah in the destruction at the racetrack. Miles cracked another e-mail that used the word *fontanel*."

"Fontanel. That's the soft spot on the baby's head." Steve argued, hoping everyone else was wrong.

"Fontanel . . . so . . . Fontana?" Morrison guessed.

"But isn't the target a little obscure?" Steve asked.

Morrison defended his answer. "It's a target of opportunity. One with several hundred thousand people."

As Steve looked at the miles of cars, all backed up to get in to the track, the immense gravity of the situation sank in. "What am I supposed to do—jump on a five-ton bomb?!!! Which part of the track? How? More importantly, when?!!"

"Haven't gotten that far yet." Even the usually calm Morrison sounded frantic. "I'll call as soon as I know."

Carter rolled right past the officers busy inspecting all the vehicles prior to entry.

"We're here." Steve hung up as soon as Carter slammed the car into Park at the gate.

They jumped out and simultaneously headed for the security guard on duty at the check-in. Steve whipped out his badge. "FBI. Large vehicles come through these gates!"

The guard acted confused. "All day. What's—?

Carter interrupted him. "Anything strange! Out of the ordinary?"

The startled man shook his head. "A sump-pump truck, but they had passes and everything. We were told to expect them."

"Anything else?" Carter demanded. "A cement truck!"

The guard looked like he thought Carter was crazy. "Nope, that's it." The man scanned his list of names. "See, they're right here: Tracy Roberts and—"

"Tracy Roberts!!" a woman waiting her turn at the guard post exclaimed. "*I'm* Tracy Roberts! You said my name wasn't on the list!"

At that point the guard was really confused. "Uh . . . you . . ."

"How long ago did this truck enter?" Steve grabbed the sentry by the arm to get his attention. "We need to get in there right now."

"Five minutes . . . okay."

"Radio your boss to locate and stop that truck!" Steve and Carter ran for the Caprice. A pair of young guys in black Windbreakers swung the gates wide.

Carter gunned the car through the gates, down the ramp, and into the tunnel. Steve tried to call Morrison, but the phone wouldn't connect. He cringed as he visualized the bomb going off while they were in the tunnel. The pressure would blast the car out like a cannonball.

Carter honked at an electric golf cart in front of them, then yelled, "Move it!"

A very angry cart driver swerved out of the way as Carter spun the tires again.

When the tunnel sloped upward, the sun temporarily blinded them. As Steve's eyesight came back to him, he was stunned by the endless sea of RVs and trailers parked in the infield. Finding a truck would be more difficult than he imagined. "Go right!" Steve pointed.

The engine rpm's rose and fell as Carter gassed it, then locked them up. The prerace traffic in the infield was insane.

Steve scanned all the way across to the pits. Between gaps in the shop buildings he could see the Cup cars lining up for the green flag. "The race is getting ready to start."

"Look at the stands." Carter, stunned, pointed in midsearch. "Must be a hundred thousand here, at least."

"Oh, dear God . . ." Steve moaned. "This can't be. Lord, let it be a mistake." As he swung his head back to center, he spotted the pumping truck. "There it is!" Two men in blue coveralls had climbed out and begun to pull hoses from the racks.

Carter instinctively flicked on the sirens as he punched the gas pedal. Again Steve's head was thrown back.

They witnessed the men drop the hoses and scramble for the truck's cab.

Carter fumed. "They've seen us now."

Carter bolted through the infield parking lot, sometimes clearing other vehicles by only inches. Steve cringed as they bounced over a concrete drainage gutter. Tires left the ground momentarily. Steve's head hit the ceiling, and when they landed his seat belt was so tight, he couldn't breathe.

The pumper truck began to roll faster. Just as Steve thought they were closing the gap, a black Dodge duallie crossed their path.

Bang!

Air bags exploded. Steve and Carter were slammed backward. An instant later they had freed themselves from the belts and were out, but at a loss as to their next move.

There was no doubt in either man's mind that a disaster of monumental size was only moments from happening, if it wasn't already too late to prevent.

The owner of the Dodge truck shook his fist and glared at them as he rattled the jammed driver's-side door.

Steve searched the parked vehicles for an answer as to their next move. He spotted a race-team crew pushing a red Chevrolet. The thin young guy geared up as the driver pacing beside the Chevy's open window asked, "What're you boys in such a hurry for?"

Steve flung out his badge. There was no time for explanations yet no time to hold back either. "We're FBI!" Steve shouted. "And that sewer truck is loaded with explosives!"

At first the driver must have thought it was a joke. But a second glance at the badge and the serious look on Steve's face made the driver's eyeballs bulge. "It is?"

"We think he's going to set it off by the stands, and we need to stop him!"

"Good night!" the man exclaimed. "Take my rig if you need it."

Steve and Carter hurried to the race car. Steve was confused as he looked for the door handles. "How do you . . . ?"

"Shoot!" the driver yelled. "Climb in the other window. You prob'ly couldn't drive it anyway." He jumped through the opening into the driver's seat.

Inside the vehicle Steve found himself sitting on large black bars and sheet metal, not on a seat like he had expected.

Carter threw his hands up. "What am I supposed to do?"

Steve's driver had just started the engine when another driver called out to Carter. "Come on, man! I'll help you too."

"Go, go, go!" Steve shouted as they burned out.

By then the pumper truck had turned onto the track. It tried to make a right turn as the closest route to the front of the grandstand, but the embankment was too high, so it backed up and went left.

Steve pulled out his Glock and checked its chamber. Thirteen rounds of .40. He hoped that'd be enough.

The driver looked a little frightened when he glanced over at the weapon. "Boy! You aren't kiddin' around."

Steve stared, wondering if the driver even realized what he'd gotten himself into. "No, I'm not." He hoped the guy wouldn't back out now. "This is deadly serious."

"All right, man. If you're willing, so am I. Name's Kevin," the driver threw in before he whipped the car out onto the tracks.

By then the pumper was a good quarter mile along the back stretch, but the distance was made up in no time.

Steve turned backward to see where Carter was. Sure enough, the bright red Budweiser Chevy was tearing up the track behind them.

"Ease off here; I gotta think," Steve pondered aloud. After a moment, he said, "Okay. When your friend catches up with us, we'll take the left side and he can take the right. Both of us shooting!"

"I'll radio my crew chief to tell Dale!"

A few seconds later Kevin eased off the gas. Carter's ride edged up alongside as they headed toward turn 3.

The crowd, packed out for the start of the race, began gesturing toward the strange spectacle. They were completely unaware of the stupendous danger, Steve knew.

Steve had to stop the truck before it made it around to the finish line. Instinctively he knew more would be lost than a race if he did not.

They were running out of time.

The only reason the bomb hadn't gone off yet, he figured, was because the terrorists were waiting to get closer to the grandstand.

✪ ✪ ✪

Pursued!

How was it possible? Race cars roared up behind the pumper truck, aiming to intercept it. There was no time to complete the circuit of the track.

It had been al Krefa's fondest wish that the explosion that would vaporize thousands of spectators would take place in clear view of the television cameras watching pit row.

A global audience for terror triumphant!

But the situation they had now would have to do.

"Here, take this." Al Krefa thrust his Beretta into Mabrouk's hands.

"What?" Mabrouk already struggled with the steering of the lumbering honey wagon. The high-banked track pressed him heavily against the door, made the truck wallow as if he were driving through deep sand, made him fight to keep it from rolling down into the infield.

Now I'm supposed to manage a pistol too? Mabrouk wondered.

The Beretta slipped from his lap and dropped under the accelerator pedal. Automatically Mabrouk bent to retrieve it. His elbow collided with al Krefa's hands, where he fumbled with the final battery connection.

The truck lurched, tossing al Krefa toward the downhill side.

The sudden heave of al Krefa's anxious fingers tore a wire loose from the battery terminal instead of attaching the other. He cursed in Arabic as Mabrouk raised the Beretta by the barrel.

Shoving the muzzle of the pistol out of his face, al Krefa ignored the snarl of the approaching race cars and concentrated on bringing the electric current to the detonator circuit.

✪ ✪ ✪

With his left hand raised and a Glock 23 in his right, Steve gave the signal. The engine roared as Kevin muscled up beside the driver of the pumper truck.

Steve could see it was Mabrouk. Clean-shaven and waving a gun out the window.

The speed of time dimmed.

Seconds passed like slow breaths. Steve's intense focus dulled the deafening screams of the engines.

Steve took aim . . . finger in the trigger . . . front sight . . . press. . . .

Fire tore from the muzzle as Mabrouk's head jerked from view.

There was another more distant pop, and Steve was sure that Carter had also fired no later than a second after his own shot.

And the bomb still hadn't gone off.

There was still a chance.

The drivers must be dead, Steve reasoned, or at least incapacitated, or surely they'd set off the charge.

But why wasn't the truck slowing?

The next step came to him in a flash—before there was time to think it through, before he had time to be afraid.

"Get as close as you can!" Steve shouted before climbing out the window of the Chevy.

Kevin edged up alongside the truck. Steve's body was halfway out. He managed to grab the windowsill and the mirror of the truck, just as it grazed the wall of turn 3. The whole pumper unit bounced, slamming into Kevin's car and shaking Steve loose. He dangled above the road, holding onto the mirror by one arm and the window with the other, as the diesel rumbled along.

Kevin, fearful of crushing Steve between the car and the truck, peeled away to give Steve some room.

Steve struggled as the truck jolted against the wall, but it still wasn't slowing. Then, just as his hands began to slip, Steve found the step with his left foot. He quickly switched his right grip from the window to the handle.

As he pulled himself up, the door swung open.

Steve's body swung out over the high-banked track. His feet bounced off the pavement, which almost dragged him down. Kicking like a gymnast, he managed to get his toes on the running board again. He pulled himself into the cab of the pumper truck.

Mabrouk's body was slumped over, lying in the way, his booted foot wedged on the gas pedal. A button connected to a set of wires lay on the seat, inches from his hand. Another man, someone Steve had never seen before, lay folded downward across his seat belt, bleeding from his head.

The truck slowed, the engine protesting in a loud whine.

Wasting no more time, Steve grasped the steering wheel with both hands, yanking Mabrouk's body from the seat. It rolled out the door, almost taking Steve with it, but once more he managed to hang on.

An instant later Steve was back in the cab with both feet on the brake. Out the windshield he could see the roof and crumpled tail of Kevin's car. The Chevy driver had planted his car directly in front of the pumper truck and heroically locked up his brakes to help slow it.

The truck came to a stop.

Steve looked out at the stands. Some scrambled for higher ground or trampled each other on the way toward the exits. Others just stared, as if they were watching a movie.

Steve turned off the ignition, afraid to even look at the wired switch.

The world became a blur. Emergency crews racing with lights and sirens pounced on the scene. Steve climbed from the cab, stumbling. Carter yelled at him to go. Steve tried to hurry, but it was like a dream, where nothing moved fast enough.

He staggered down the steep hill toward the infield.

Something Kevin yelled snapped Steve out of his trance. "Come on, buddy. Let's get outta here!"

Steve came to his senses. He ran for Kevin's car, diving in through the window. Ahead of them, the vehicle roasted its tires to get away. Kevin followed, the exhaust howling as they drove for safety.

As Steve maneuvered himself inside, crumpling onto the thin aluminum floor, he realized they had done it. Even with the bomb still intact—and enough ANFO to blow the racetrack clear to Hawaii—somehow Steve knew it was over.

After the longest day of Steve's life, they had made it just in time.

Allah's Will had been foiled. Rejected and shot down. Stopped by the heroic actions of a few small men and the will of the very big one true God.

EPILOGUE

Rooftop of FBI Building, Chapter 16 Offices
San Francisco, California
Friday, 11 September
1407 hours, Pacific Time

UNDERSTANDING SACRIFICE

Near the large white cross of the helipad, Steve held tightly to the ornate wooden box containing the urn of Anton's ashes. Steve's right arm was wrapped around his son Matthew's shoulder. They stood next to Janae Brown, Anton's estranged wife, and Travelle, the Browns' 12-year-old son.

No one said a word while the four of them waited for the U.S. Coast Guard chopper to arrive.

The chorus from the song "I Can Only Imagine" looped through Steve's mind on an endless track. It had been programmed into his brain earlier that day when he heard it at Anton's memorial service.

Not since Ronald Reagan's funeral had Steve seen such an elaborate procession and ceremony, though he could recall nothing more of them than Senator Morrison speaking about how a bittersweet victory had been possible through Anton's death.

The air was cool. The sky, gray. Overcast. Like the shadows over Steve's heart.

A soft breeze stole his breath away. His chest felt tight as he inhaled deeply, fighting back the urge to let go.

I have to be strong, he thought. *Can't lose it in front of these guys. Gotta be here for them.* Suddenly remembering his sunglasses, Steve slipped them on to hide his eyes.

Janae, a pretty and well-kept 35-ish black woman, was quiet, expressionless. She acted disinterested, almost as if she'd rather be somewhere else.

Of course she would.

Janae had been angry at Anton for his dedication to the FBI and his great commitment to keeping the country safe. She blamed him for the death of their daughter. Blamed him for her unhappiness. She blamed him for everything.

When Anton had been transferred to the West Coast HRT division, Janae had decided he was too selfish to ever be a good husband and father. So she had won custody of Travelle and stayed behind in Virginia.

Selfish. How ironic, Steve thought. Anton was the most selfless guy he'd ever met.

It was sad though, after all her garbage about self-empowerment, Janae was even angrier now, to the point of blaming Anton for his own death.

Travelle, on the other hand, seemed numb—still in shock. He had lived the past two and half years without his father, anticipating the day when Anton would return home . . . then experiencing the icy plunge of losing his father a week before that was finally to happen. Travelle's face appeared stone-cold, tired, all cried out. Lost.

The sight wrenched Steve as he thought of life without his best friend . . . of what Travelle must be feeling . . . and of the terrible image of his own two boys having to go through the same loss.

Steve's chest shook and he pulled Matthew closer.

Matthew looked up with a kind, understanding smile that was well beyond his years and whispered, "I love you, Dad."

A single sob sounded from deep within Steve's throat as he realized how much Matthew comforted *him*. He whispered back, "I love you too, Son."

In the distance the bright orange-and-white HH-65A Dolphin, U.S.C.G. chopper suddenly became visible from behind the tall buildings of San Francisco. Steve was grateful for the distraction. Now he would have something to do. Back to directing . . . keeping his mind busy by keeping everyone else moving. "Here it comes." His voice cracked as he motioned to the horizon.

The group was silent.

Normally a helicopter ride out over the Bay would be the opportunity of a lifetime for any 12-year-old—something a child would never forget. Unfortunately, *this* moment would never be forgotten, as it would be their last with Anton—friend, father, blood brother.

Once the Dolphin landed, Crew Chief Cooper rolled back the side door. Steve remembered the name and face of the man from the last time he and Anton had been out to the Bridge, inspecting it for vulnerabilities. The memory caused the tears to well up again. Steve motioned for the others to board as he stepped back.

This time he couldn't fight it. It was hard to breathe. Steve rubbed his eyes, trying to wipe the moisture away, but the tears wouldn't stop.

Matthew leaned out. "Are you okay, Dad?"

Steve cleared his throat, sniffing. He tried to answer with words, but when nothing came out, he quickly nodded and boarded. *How odd,* Steve thought, that his own son would be there to care for *him*. "Thank you, Son," he replied softly.

Moments later they soared out over the water.

Steve found himself silently questioning. *Why, Lord? Why did he have to die?*

Confusion and doubt chased the music around and around in his head. Steve was searching the tiny sailboats for answers when he heard the answer.

In a powerful voice that only he could hear, Steve recognized it unmistakably as God's. The simple reply: *"Servare Vitas."*

Steve blinked as he considered his argument, but before he could even think the words, he heard it again . . . the HRT's motto: To Save Lives.

The events surrounding Anton's death flashed through his mind. Anton had shielded Steve from the blast, saving Steve's life. Even if he'd made it out alive but dropped the check and lost the lead generated by the fingerprints, Steve would never have been able to locate the suspects in time to stop the avalanching disaster.

Steve recognized that Anton really *had* made the ultimate sacrifice—laid down his life for the lives of others—even for the wicked, who had ultimately killed him. Just as Christ had so many years ago.

Coincidence . . . or divine intervention?

Tracy Roberts would never have come to see her husband if Mike hadn't called her to patch things up.

All things work together for good, Steve reflected, *for those who love God and are called according to his purpose.*

It was true.

Tracy had arrived just in time to hear her name on the security roster, tipping Steve into action.

Awe filled Steve's spirit.

Most would never know. Many might not believe it, even if they were told, but that could never change the truth. Anton Brown was a hero—a savior for thousands, providing a second chance at life for the many who may not yet know Christ. And because of Anton's death they would have an extended opportunity to know Him and be saved eternally.

Travelle pulled his father's badge from his pocket. He smiled with pride as he gazed upon the gleaming gold emblem. Then he broke the silence. "My father is a hero."

Steve gathered his voice. "Yeah." He nodded in breathless astonishment. "He is. . . . Your father *is* a hero."

Travelle looked up, clutching the badge with determination. "Someday—" he nodded with strong resolve—"I'm gonna be just like him."

"He *is* a role model to live by," Steve found himself answering as he thought of Father God.

Suddenly, it all made sense.

A warmth spread through Steve's body, chasing the shiver down his spine, replacing the cold with complete understanding and acceptance.

Peace washed over him.

At that very moment sun broke through the clouds, casting a beam of light out over the Bridge, illuminating a place on the water beyond the Golden Gate.

As they neared their destination, Steve knew Anton was *there,* basking in that warm glory, beyond the Golden Gates with *his* Father.

God is Truth.

Other than God, there may be no topic more important for discussion in this day and age than the lengths we are willing to go in order to stop terrorism.

You see, what terrorism really boils down to is Good vs. Evil. And what the discussion really revolves around is how we recognize and react to evil.

There is a very real, very dangerous blurring of the lines these days, where black is becoming white, and white is becoming black. In Matthew 24:10-11, Christ talks about the deception that will occur in the final days before his return: "Many will turn away from me and betray and hate each other. And many false prophets will appear and will lead many people astray" (NLT).

Unfortunately, politics play much too powerful a role in our world's leadership for political leaders to be truly honest. One party stands for truth (on most issues) while the other is *left* in a position to disagree in order to be *right* (at least in the minds of their constituents). After all, how can any candidate be better and worthy of electing if he or she agrees with everything that comes from the mouths of opponents? This desperate need to be different results in a bending of the truth until it points 180 degrees in the opposite direction . . . and leads us down the path to destruction.

But in the face of such confusion, Christ encourages us to be persistent. In Matthew 24:13, he goes on to say, "Those who endure to the end will be saved." It is up to each of us to have a memory like an elephant. To be discerning like a dog. And to remain eternally vocal about the truths we witness every day. To choose wisely and hold our leaders accountable.

We must recognize that, like a firearm or a knife, new legislation like the Patriot Act is a tool. All have the potential to do harm, while they were designed to do so much good. I pray that I—and each of you—will be vigilant in understanding the difference.

We must arm ourselves with knowledge and live righteously, so as not to give the enemy any ammunition to use against us in an attempt to discredit the truths that we strongly support. Then we must live transparently, for what should we fear if we have nothing to hide?

May we one day meet beyond the Golden Gates. Until then, I wish you the best of blessings in all your pursuits of the truth.

Jake Thoene
jake@jakethoene.com

AFB Air Force Base
AFSOC Air Force Special Operations Command
AFSOIC Air Force Strategic Operations Information Command
AIF 17 Alpha Indigo Frank (a unit of Task Force 121)
ANFO Ammonium Nitrate Fuel Oil; or **AN** Ammonium Nitrate
AP Associated Press
APB All Points Bulletin
AR Assault Rifle

B-com Bureau Communications Device
BDU Battle Dress Uniform

Caltrans California Department of Transportation
Charlie Field team's name for Command and Control
CHP California Highway Patrol
CIA Central Intelligence Agency
CO Corrections Officer
Com-Data Communications Data
Com-op Communications Operative
CPU Central Processing Unit (of a computer)
CRT Cathode Ray Tube (computer monitor)
CS California Speedway
CSI Crime Scene Investigations
CT Team Counterterrorism Team

DEA Drug Enforcement Administration
DECOM Decontamination
Delta A Special Operations Force (SOF) of the U. S. Army Special
    Operations Command, utilized for counterattack terrorism
DHS Department of Homeland Security

ELFS Room Electronic Lab of Forensic Surveillance
EMS Emergency Medical Service

EMT Emergency Medical Technician
EOD Explosive Ordnance Disposal
ET Encryption Translator
ETS Emergency Tracking System

FAA Federal Aviation Administration
FBI Federal Bureau of Investivation
FFAR Folding-Fin Aerial Rocket
FOB Forward Operating Base

Gen 3 Generation 3 night optics/night-vision equipment
GLOSAT Global Satellite phone
GPS Global Positioning System

HAZMAT Hazardous Materials
HRT Hostage Rescue Team

IED Improvised Explosive Device
INS Immigration and Naturalization Service
IP Internet Provider

JTTF FBI's elite, urban-based Joint Terrorism Task Force

K-9 Canine unit

LASO Los Angeles Sheriff's Office
LACJ Los Angeles County Jail
LAPD Los Angeles Police Department
LZ Landing Zone

MOB Mobile Operation Bag
MSA Mass Spectrum Analyzer
MSGT Master Sergeant

NCIC National Crime Investigation Center
NRA National Rifle Association
NSA National Security Agency
NVS Night Vision System; **NVGs** Night-vision goggles

OD Overdose
op operation
OS Teams Observer-Sniper Teams; **OS 1, OS 2** in narrative/**Oz 1, Oz 2** in
    dialogue

Ped team Pedestrian team
PNVS Pilot Night Vision Sensor system

SatCom Satellite Communications System
SoCal Southern California
SOD Special Operations Director
SOIC Strategic Operations Information Command—national FBI headquar-
    ters
Spec Ops Special Operations
SWAT Special Weapons and Tactics

tac vest tactical assault vests
Tango An enemy target
TF 121 Task Force 121

UBL Usama bin Laden

suspense with a mission

TITLES BY

Jake Thoene

"The Christian Tom Clancy"
Dale Hurd, *CBN Newswatch*

Shaiton's Fire

In this first book in the techno-thriller series by Jake Thoene, the bombing of a subway train is only the beginning of a master plan that Steve Alstead and Chapter 16 have to stop . . . before it's too late.

ISBN-10: 1-4143-0890-6 SOFTCOVER

ISBN-13: 978-1-4143-0890-6

US $12.99

Firefly Blue

In this action-packed sequel to Shaiton's Fire, Chapter 16 is called in when barrels of cyanide are stolen during a truckjacking. Experience heart-stopping action as you read this gripping story that could have been ripped from today's headlines.

ISBN-10: 1-4143-0891-4 SOFTCOVER

ISBN-13: 978-1-4143-0891-3

US $12.99

Fuel the Fire

In this third book in the series, Special Agent Steve Alstead and Chapter 16, the FBI's counterterrorism unit, must stop the scheme of an al Qaeda splinter cell . . . while America's future hangs in the balance.

ISBN-10: 1-4143-0892-2 SOFTCOVER

ISBN-13: 978-1-4143-0892-0

US $12.99

for more information on other great Tyndale fiction,
visit www.tyndalefiction.com

THOENE FAMILY CLASSICS™

✪ ✪ ✪

THOENE FAMILY CLASSIC HISTORICALS
by Bodie and Brock Thoene
Gold Medallion Winners*

THE ZION COVENANT
Vienna Prelude*
Prague Counterpoint
Munich Signature
Jerusalem Interlude
Danzig Passage
Warsaw Requiem*
London Refrain
Paris Encore
Dunkirk Crescendo

THE ZION CHRONICLES
The Gates of Zion*
A Daughter of Zion
The Return to Zion
A Light in Zion
The Key to Zion*

THE SHILOH LEGACY
In My Father's House*
A Thousand Shall Fall
Say to This Mountain

SHILOH AUTUMN

THE GALWAY CHRONICLES
Only the River Runs Free*
Of Men and of Angels
Ashes of Remembrance*
All Rivers to the Sea

THE ZION LEGACY
Jerusalem Vigil
Thunder from Jerusalem
Jerusalem's Heart
Jerusalem Scrolls
Stones of Jerusalem
Jerusalem's Hope

A.D. CHRONICLES
First Light
Second Touch
Third Watch
Fourth Dawn
Fifth Seal
and more to come!

THOENE FAMILY CLASSICS™

✪ ✪ ✪

THOENE FAMILY CLASSIC AMERICAN LEGENDS

LEGENDS OF THE WEST
by Bodie and Brock Thoene

The Man from Shadow Ridge
Riders of the Silver Rim
Gold Rush Prodigal
Sequoia Scout
Cannons of the Comstock
Year of the Grizzly
Shooting Star
Legend of Storey County
Hope Valley War
Delta Passage
Hangtown Lawman
Cumberland Crossing

LEGENDS OF VALOR
by Luke Thoene

Sons of Valor
Brothers of Valor
Fathers of Valor

✪ ✪ ✪

THOENE CLASSIC NONFICTION
by Bodie and Brock Thoene

Writer-to-Writer

THOENE FAMILY CLASSIC SUSPENSE
by Jake Thoene

CHAPTER 16 SERIES

Shaiton's Fire
Firefly Blue
Fuel the Fire

✪ ✪ ✪

THOENE FAMILY CLASSICS FOR KIDS
by Jake and Luke Thoene

BAKER STREET DETECTIVES
The Mystery of the Yellow Hands
The Giant Rat of Sumatra
The Jeweled Peacock of Persia
The Thundering Underground

LAST CHANCE DETECTIVES
Mystery Lights of Navajo Mesa
Legend of the Desert Bigfoot

✪ ✪ ✪

THOENE FAMILY CLASSIC AUDIOBOOKS

Available from
www.thoenebooks.com or
www.TheOneaudio.com